Ross Macdonald

THE DOOMSTERS

Ross Macdonald's real name was Kenneth Millar. Born near San Francisco in 1915 and raised in Ontario, Millar returned to the U.S. as a young man and published his first novel in 1944. He served as the president of the Mystery Writers of America and was awarded their Grand Master Award as well as the Mystery Writers of Great Britain's Gold Dagger Award. He died in 1983.

ALSO BY ROSS MACDONALD

The Dark Tunnel
Trouble Follows Me
Blue City
The Three Roads
The Moving Target
The Drowning Pool
The Way Some People Die
The Ivory Grin
Meet Me at the Morgue
Find a Victim
The Name Is Archer
The Barbarous Coast
The Galton Case
The Ferguson Affair
The Wycherly Woman
The Zebra-Striped Hearse
The Chill
Black Money
The Far Side of the Dollar
The Goodbye Look
The Underground Man
Sleeping Beauty
The Blue Hammer

THE DOOMSTERS

Ross Macdonald

VINTAGE CRIME/BLACK LIZARD
Vintage Books
A Division of Random House, Inc.
New York

For John and Dick, Hill-climbers

FIRST VINTAGE CRIME/BLACK LIZARD EDITION, DECEMBER 2007

The Library of Congress has cataloged
the Knopf edition as follows:
Macdonald, Ross.
The Doomsters [by] Ross Macdonald
[1st ed.]
New York, Knopf, 1958.
1. Archer, Lew (Fictitious Character)—Fiction.
2. Private Investigators—California—Fiction.
3. Detectives and mystery stories.
p. cm.
PZ3. M59943
PS3525.I486
58005829

Vintage ISBN: 978-0-307-27904-0

www.vintagebooks.com

146028962

THE DOOMSTERS

chapter 1

I WAS dreaming about a hairless ape who lived in a cage by himself. His trouble was that people were always trying to get in. It kept the ape in a state of nervous tension. I came out of sleep sweating, aware that somebody was at the door. Not the front door, but the side door that opened into the garage. Crossing the cold kitchen linoleum in my bare feet, I saw first dawn at the window over the sink. Whoever it was on the other side of the door was tapping now, quietly and persistently. I turned on the outside light, unlocked the door, and opened it.

A very large young man in dungarees stepped awkwardly backward under the naked garage bulb. There was dirt in his stubble of light hair. His unblinking pale blue eyes looked up at the light in an oddly pathetic way.

"Turn it off, will you?"

"I like to be able to see."

"That's just it." He glanced through the open garage door, out to the quiet gray street. "I don't want to be seen."

"You could always go away again." Then I took another look at him, and regretted my surliness. There was a kind of oily yellowish glaze on his skin which was more than a trick of the light. He could be in a bad way.

He looked again at the hostile street. "May I come in? You're Mr. Archer, aren't you?"

"It's kind of early for visiting. I don't know your name."

"Carl Hallman. I know it's early. I've been up all night."

He swayed, and steadied himself against the doorpost. His hand was black with grime, and there were bleeding scratches on the back of it.

"Been in an accident, Hallman?"

"No." He hesitated, and spoke more slowly: "There was an accident. It didn't happen to me. Not the way you mean."

"Who did it happen to?"

"My father. My father was killed."

"Last night?"

"Six months ago. It's one of the things I want to ask you—speak to you about. Can't you give me a few moments?"

A pre-breakfast client was the last thing I needed that morning. But it was one of those times when you have to decide between your own convenience and the unknown quantity of another man's trouble. Besides, the other man and his way of talking didn't go with his rag-bag clothes, his mud-stained work shoes. It made me curious.

"Come in then."

He didn't seem to hear me. His glazed eyes stayed on my face too long.

"Come in, Hallman. It's cold in these pajamas."

"Oh. Sorry." He stepped up into the kitchen, almost as broad as the door. "It's hellish of me to bother you like this."

"No bother if it's urgent."

I shut the door and plugged in the coffee-maker. Carl Hallman remained standing in the middle of the kitchen floor. I pulled out a chair for him. He smelled of country.

"Sit down and tell me about it."

"That's just it. I don't *know* anything. I don't even know if it is urgent."

5

"Well, what's all the excitement about?

"I'm sorry. I don't make much sense, do I? I've been running half the night."

"Where from?"

"A certain place. It doesn't matter where." His face closed up in blankness, almost stuporous. He was remembering that certain place.

A thought I'd been suppressing forced its way through. Carl Hallman's clothes were the kind of clothes they give you to wear in prison. He had the awkward humility men acquire there. And there was a strangeness in him, stranger than fear, which might be one of guilt's chameleon forms. I changed my approach:

"Did somebody send you to me?"

"Yes. A friend gave me your name. You *are* a private detective?"

I nodded. "Your friend has a name?"

"I don't know if you'd remember him." Carl Hallman was embarrassed. He popped his dirty knuckles and looked at the floor. "I don't know if my friend would want me to use his name."

"He used mine."

"That's a little different, isn't it? You hold a—sort of a public job."

"So I'm a public servant, eh? Well, we won't play guessing games, Carl."

The water in the coffee-maker boiled. It reminded me how cold I was. I went to my bedroom for a bathrobe and slippers. Looked at the gun in my closet, decided against it. When I came back to the kitchen, Carl Hallman was sitting in the same position.

"What are you going to do?" he asked me dully.

"Have a cup of coffee. How about you?"

"No, thanks. I don't care for anything."

I poured him a cup, anyway, and he drank it greedily.

"Hungry?"

"You're very kind, but I couldn't possibly accept—"

"I'll fry a couple of eggs."

"No! I don't want you to." His voice was suddenly high, out of control. It came queerly out of his broad barrel chest, like the voice of a little boy calling from hiding. "You're angry with me."

I spoke to the little boy: "I don't burn so easy. I asked for a name, you wouldn't give it. You have your reasons. All right. What's the matter, Carl?"

"I don't know. When you brushed me off, just now, all I could think of was Father. He was always getting angry. That last night—"

I waited, but that was all. He made a noise in his throat which might have been a sob, or a growl of pain. Turned away from me and gazed at the coffee-maker on the breakfast bar. The grounds in its upper half were like black sand in a static hourglass that wouldn't let time pass. I fried six eggs in butter, and made some toast. Carl gobbled his. I gobbled mine, and poured the rest of the coffee.

"You're treating me very well," he said over his cup. "Better than I deserve."

"It's a little service we provide for clients. Feeling better?"

"Physically, yes. Mentally—" He caught himself on the downbeat, and held steady. "That's good coffee you make. The coffee on the ward was terrible, loaded with chicory."

"You've been in a hospital?"

"Yes. The State Hospital." He added, with some defiance: "I'm not ashamed of it." But he was watching closely for my reaction.

"What was the trouble?"

"The diagnosis was manic-depressive. I don't think I *am* manic-depressive. I know I was disturbed. But that's all past."

7

"They released you?"

He hung his head over his coffee cup and looked at me from underneath, on the slant.

"Are you on the run from the hospital?"

"Yes. I am." The words came hard to him. "But it's not the way you imagine. I was virtually cured, ready to be discharged, but my brother wouldn't let them. He wants to keep me locked up." His voice fell into a singsong rhythm: "As far as Jerry is concerned, I could stay there until I rotted."

The melody was familiar: incarcerated people always had to be blaming someone, preferably a close relative. I said:

"Do you know for a fact your brother was keeping you there?"

"I'm certain of it. He had me put away. He and Dr. Grantland made Mildred sign the commitment papers. Once I was there, he cut me off entirely. He wouldn't visit me. He made them censor my mail so I couldn't even write letters." The words had been rushing faster and faster, tumbling out of his mouth. He paused and gulped. His Adam's apple bobbed like a ball valve under the skin of his throat.

"You don't know what it's like being cut off like that, not knowing what goes on. Of course, Mildred came to see me, every chance she got, but she didn't know what it was all about, either. And we couldn't talk freely about family matters. They made her visit me on the ward, and they always kept a nurse there, within hearing. As if I couldn't be trusted with my own wife."

"Why, Carl? Were you violent?"

Suddenly and heavily, as if I'd rabbit-punched him, his head sank low between his shoulders. I looked him over, thinking that he could be formidable in a violent mood. His shoulders were overlaid with laminated muscle, and wide enough to yoke a pair of oxen. He was saying:

"I made a fool of myself the first few days—tore up a couple of mattresses, things like that. They put me in wet packs. But I never hurt anyone. At least I don't remember, if I did." His voice had sunk almost out of hearing. He raised it, and lifted his head. "Anyway, I never stepped out of line after that, not once. I wasn't going to give them any excuse to keep me locked up. But they did. And they had no right to."

"So you came over the wall."

He looked at me in surprise, his pale eyes wide. "How did you know we came over the wall?"

I didn't bother explaining that it was only an expression, which seemed to have hit the literal truth. "More than one of you broke out, eh?"

He didn't answer. His eyes narrowed suspiciously, still watching my face.

"Where are the others, Carl?"

"There's only the one other," he said haltingly. "Who he is doesn't matter. You'll read about it in the papers, anyway."

"Not necessarily. They don't publicize these things unless the escapees are dangerous."

chapter 2

I LET that last word hang in the silence, turning this way and that, a question and a threat and a request. Carl Hallman looked at the window over the sink, where morning shone unhampered. Sounds of sporadic traffic came from the street. He turned to look at the door he had come in by. His body was taut, and the cords in his neck stood out. His face was thoughtful.

He got up suddenly, in a brusque movement which sent his chair over backwards, crossed in two strides to the door. I said sharply:

"Pick up the chair."

He paused with his hand on the knob, tension vibrating through him. "Don't give me orders. I don't take orders from you."

"It's a suggestion, boy."

"I'm not a boy."

"To me you are. I'm forty. How old are you?"

"It's none of your—" He paused, in conflict with himself. "I'm twenty-four."

"Act your age, then. Pick up the chair and sit down and we'll talk this over. You don't want to go on running."

"I don't intend to. I never wanted to. It's just—I have to get home and clean up the mess. Then I don't care what happens to me."

"You should. You're young. You have a wife, and a future."

"Mildred deserves someone better than me—than I. My future is in the past."

But he turned from the door, from the bright and fearful morning on the other side of it, and picked up the chair and sat in it. I sat on the kitchen table, looking down at him. His tension had wrung sweat out of his body. It stood in droplets on his face, and darkened the front of his shirt. He said very youngly:

"You think I'm crazy, don't you?"

"What I think doesn't matter, I'm not your headshrinker. But if you are, you need the hospital. If you're not, this is a hell of a way to prove you're not. You should go back and get yourself checked out."

"Go back? You must be cr—" He caught himself.

I laughed in his face, partly because I thought he was funny and partly because I thought he needed it. "I must be crazy? Go ahead and say it. I'm not proud. I've got a friend in psychiatry who says they should build mental hospitals with hinged corners. Every now and then they should turn them inside out, so the people on the outside are in, and the people on the inside are out. I think he's got something."

"You're making fun of me."

"What if I am? It's a free country."

"Yes, it is a free country. And you can't make me go back there."

"I think you should. This way, you're headed for more trouble."

"I can't go back. They'd never let me out, now."

"They will when you're ready. If you turn yourself in voluntarily, it shouldn't go against you very hard. When did you break out?"

"Last night—early last evening, after supper. We didn't exactly break out. We piled the benches against the wall of the courtyard. I hoisted the other fellow up to the top and he helped me up after him, with a knotted sheet. We got away without being seen, I think. Tom—the other fellow—had a car waiting. They gave me a ride part of the way. I walked the rest."

"Do you have a special doctor you can see, if you go back?"

"Doctor!" It was a dirty word in his vocabulary. "I've seen too many doctors. They're all a bunch of shysters, and Dr. Grantland is the worst of them. He shouldn't even be allowed to practice."

"Okay, we'll take away his license."

He looked up, startled. He was easy to startle. Then anger rose in him. "You don't take me seriously. I came to you for help in a serious matter, and all I get is cheap wisecracks. It makes me mad."

"All right. It's a free country."

"God damn you."

I let that pass. He sat with his head down for several minutes, holding himself still. Finally he said: "My father was Senator Hallman of Purissima. Does the name mean anything to you?"

"I read in the papers that he died last spring."

He nodded jerkily. "They locked me up the next day, and wouldn't even let me go to his funeral. I know I blew my top, but they had no right to do that. They did it because they didn't want me snooping."

"Who are 'they'?"

"Jerry and Zinnie. Zinnie is my sister-in-law. She's always hated me, and Jerry's under her thumb. They want to keep me shut up for the rest of their lives, so that they can have the property to themselves."

"How do you know that?"

"I've had a lot of time to think. I've been putting things together for six months. When I got the word on Dr. Grantland— Well, it's obvious they paid him to have me committed. They may even have paid him to kill Father."

"I thought your father's death was accidental."

"It was, according to Dr. Grantland." Carl's eyes were hot and sly, and I didn't like the look of them. "It's possible it really was an accident. But I happen to know that Dr. Grantland has a bad record. I just found that out last week."

It was hard to tell if he was fantasying. Like any other private detective, I'd had to do with my share of mental cases, but I was no expert. Sometimes even the experts had a hard time distinguishing between justified suspicion and paranoid symptoms. I tried to stay neutral:

"How did you get the word on Dr. Grantland?"

"I promised never to divulge that fact. There's a—there are other people involved."

"Have you talked to anybody else about these suspicions of yours?"

"I talked to Mildred, last time she visited me. Last Sunday. I couldn't say very much, with those hospital eavesdroppers around. I don't *know* very much. It's why I had to *do* something." He was getting tense again.

"Take it easy, Carl. Do you mind if I talk to your wife?"

"What about?"

"Things in general. Your family. You."

"I don't object if she doesn't."

"Where does she live?"

"On the ranch, outside Purissima— No, she doesn't live there now. After I went to the hospital, Mildred couldn't go on sharing the house with Jerry and Zinnie. So she moved back into Purissima, with her mother. They live at 220 Grant—but I'll show you, I'll come along."

"I don't think so."

"But I must. There are so many things to be cleared up. I can't wait any longer."

"You're going to have to wait, if you want my help. I'll make you a proposition, Carl. Let me take you back to the hospital. It's more or less on the way to Purissima. Then I'll talk to your wife, see what she thinks about these suspicions of yours—"

"She doesn't take me seriously, either."

"Well, I do. Up to a point. I'll circulate and find out what I can. If there's any real indication that your brother's trying to cheat you, or that Dr. Grantland pitched any low curves, I'll do something about it. Incidentally, I charge fifty a day and expenses."

"I have no money now. I'll have plenty when I get what's coming to me."

"Is it a deal then? You go back to the hospital, let me do the legwork?"

He gave me a reluctant yes. It was clear that he didn't like the plan, but he was too tired and confused to argue about it.

chapter 3

THE morning turned hot and bright. The brown September hills on the horizon looked like broken adobe walls you could almost reach out and touch. My car went miles before the hills changed position.

As we drove through the valley, Carl Hallman talked to me about his family. His father had come west before the first war, with enough inherited money to buy a small orange grove outside of Purissima. The old man was a frugal Pennsylvania German, and by the time of his death he'd expanded his holdings to several thousand acres. The main single addition to the original grove had come from his wife, Alicia, who was the descendant of an old land-grant family.

I asked Carl if his mother was still alive.

"No. Mother died, a long time ago."

He didn't want to talk about his mother. Perhaps he had loved her too much, or not enough. He went on talking about his father instead, with a kind of rebellious passion, as though he was still living in his father's shadow. Jeremiah Hallman had been a power in the county, to some extent in the state: founding head of the water association, secretary of the growers' co-operative, head of his party's county central committee, state senator for a decade, and local political boss to the end of his life.

A successful man who had failed to transmit the genes of success to his two sons.

Carl's older brother Jerry was a non-practicing lawyer. For a few months after he graduated from law school, Jerry had had his shingle out in Purissima. He'd lost several cases, made several enemies and no friends, and retired to the family ranch. There he consoled himself with a greenhouseful of cymbidium orchids and dreams of eventual greatness in some unnamed field of activity. Prematurely old in his middle thirties, Jerry was dominated by his wife, Zinnie, a blonde divorcee of uncertain origin who had married him five years ago.

Carl was bitter on the subject of his brother and sister-in-law, and almost equally bitter about himself. He believed that he'd failed his father all the way down the line. When Jerry petered out, the Senator planned to turn over the ranch to Carl, and sent Carl to Davis to study agriculture. Not being interested in agriculture, Carl flunked out. His real interest was philosophy, he said.

Carl managed to talk his father into letting him go to Berkeley. There he met his present wife, a girl he'd known in high school, and shortly after his twenty-first birthday he married her, in spite of the family's objections. It was a dirty trick to play on Mildred. Mildred was another of the people he had failed. She thought that she was getting a whole man, but right at the start of their marriage, within a couple of months, he had his first big breakdown.

Carl spoke in bitter self-contempt. I took my eyes from the road and looked at him. He wouldn't meet my look:

"I didn't mean to tell you about my other—that other breakdown. Anyway, it doesn't prove I'm crazy. Mildred never thought I was, and she knows me better than anybody. It was the strain I was under—working all day and studying half the night. I wanted to be something great, someone even Father would respect—a medical missionary or something like that. I was trying to get together enough credits for admission to medical school, and studying theology at the same time, and— Well, it was too much for me. I cracked up, and had to be taken home. So there we were."

I glanced at him again. We'd passed through the last of the long string of suburbs, and were in the open country. To the right of the highway, the valley lay wide and peaceful under the bright sky, and the hills had stepped backwards into blueness. Carl was paying no attention to the external world. He had a queer air of being confined, almost as though he were trapped in the past, or in himself. He said:

"It was a rough two years, for all of us. Especially for Mildred. She did her best to put a good face on it, but it wasn't what she had planned to do with her life, keeping house for in-laws in a dead country hole. And I was no use to her. For months I was so depressed that I could hardly bear to get up and face the daylight. What there was of it. I know it can't be true, but the way I remember those months, it was cloudy and dark every day. So dark that I could hardly see to shave when I got up at noon.

"The other people in the house were like gray ghosts around me, even Mildred, and I was the grayest ghost of all. Even the house was rotting away. I used to wish for an earthquake, to knock it down and bury us all at once—Father and me and Mildred and Jerry and Zinnie. I thought a good deal about killing myself, but I didn't have the gumption.

"If I'd had any gumption, or any sense, I'd have gone for treatment then. Mildred wanted me to, but I was too ashamed to admit I needed it. Father wouldn't have stood for it, anyway. It would have disgraced the family. He thought psychiatry was a confidence game, that all I really needed was hard work. He kept telling me that I was pampering myself, just as Mother had, and that I'd come to the same bad end if I didn't get out in the open air and make a man of myself."

He snickered dolefully, and paused. I wanted to ask him how his mother had died. I hesitated to. The boy was digging pretty deep as it was, and I didn't want him to break through into something he couldn't handle. Since he'd told me of his earlier breakdown and the suicidal depression that followed it, my main idea was to get him back to the hospital in one mental piece. It was only a few miles more to the turnoff, and I could hardly wait.

"Eventually," Carl was saying, "I did go to work on the ranch. Father had been slowing down, with some sort of heart condition, and I took over some of his supervisory duties. I didn't mind the work itself, out in the groves with the pickers, and I suppose it did me some good at that. But in the long run it only led to more trouble.

"Father and I could never see eye to eye on anything. He was in orange-growing to make money, the more money the better. He never thought in terms of the human cost. I couldn't stand to see the way the orange-pickers were treated. Whole families, men and women and kids, herded into open trucks and hauled around like cattle. Paid by the box, hired by the day, then shunted on their way. A lot of them were wetbacks, without any legal rights. Which suited Father fine. It didn't suit me at all. I told Father what I thought of his lousy labor policy. I told him that this was a civilized country in the middle of the twentieth century and he had no right to push people around like peons, cut them off from employment if they asked for a living wage. I told him he was a spoiled old man, and I wasn't going to sit idly by and let him oppress the Mexican people, and defraud the Japanese!"

"The Japanese?" I said.

Carl's speech had been coming in a faster rhythm, so fast that I could hardly follow it. There was an evangelical light in his eye. His face was flushed and hot.

"Yes. I'm ashamed to say it, but my father cheated some of his own best friends, Japanese people. When I was a kid, before the War, there used to be quite a few of them in our county. They had hundreds of acres of truck gardens between our ranch and town. They're nearly all gone now. They were driven out during the war, and never came back. Father bought up their land at a few cents on the dollar.

"I told him when I got my share of the ranch, I'd give those people their property back. I'd hire detectives to trace them and bring them back and give them what was theirs. I intended to do it, too. That's why I'm not going to let Jerry cheat me out of the property. It doesn't *belong* to us, you see. We've got to give it back. We've got to set things right, between us and the land, between us and other people.

"Father said that was nonsense, that he'd bought the land perfectly honestly. In fact, he thought that my ideas were crazy. They all did, even Mildred. We had a big scene about it that last night. It was terrible, with Jerry and Zinnie trying to turn him against me, and Mildred in the middle, trying to make peace. Poor Mildred, she was always in the middle. And I guess she was right, I *wasn't* making too much sense. If I had been, I'd have realized that Father was a sick man. Whether I was right or wrong —and of course I *was* right—Father couldn't stand that kind of a family ruction."

I turned off the highway to the right, onto a road which

curved back through an underpass, across flat fields, past a giant hedge of eucalyptus trees. The trees looked ancient and sorrowful; the fields were empty.

chapter 4

CARL sat tense and quiet in the seat beside me. After a while he said:

"Did you know that words can kill, Mr. Archer? You can kill an old man by arguing with him. I did it to my father. At least," he added on a different note, "I've thought for the last six months that I was responsible. Father died in his bath that night. When Dr. Grantland examined him, he said he'd had a heart attack, brought on by overexcitement. I blamed myself for his death. Jerry and Zinnie blamed me, too. Is it any wonder I blew my top? I thought I was a parricide.

"But now I don't know," he said. "When I found out about Dr. Grantland, it started me thinking back all over again. Why should I go by the word of a man like that? He hasn't even the right to call himself a doctor. It's the strain of not knowing that I can't stand. You see, if Father died of a heart attack, then I'm responsible."

"Not necessarily. Old men die every day."

"Don't try to confuse me," he said peremptorily. "I can see the issue quite clearly. If Father died of a heart attack, I killed him with my words, and I'm a murderer. But if he died of something else, then someone else is the murderer. And Dr. Grantland is covering up for them."

19

I was pretty certain by now that I was listening to paranoid delusions. I handled them with kid gloves:

"That doesn't sound too likely, Carl. Why don't you give it a rest for now? Think about something else."

"I can't!" he cried. "You've got to help me get at the truth. You promised to help me."

"I will—" I started to say.

Carl grabbed my right elbow. The car veered onto the shoulder, churning gravel. I braked, wrestling the wheel and Carl's clutching hands. The car came to a stop at a tilt, one side in the shallow ditch. I shook him off.

"That was a smart thing to do."

He was careless or unaware of what had happened. "You've got to believe me," he said. "Somebody's got to believe me."

"You don't believe yourself. You've told me two stories already. How many others are there?"

"You're calling me a liar."

"No. But your thinking needs some shaking out. You're the only one who can do that. And the hospital is the place to do it in."

The buildings of the great hospital were visible ahead, in the gap between two hills. We noticed them at the same time. Carl said:

"No. I'm not going back there. You promised to help me, but you don't intend to. You're just like all the others. So I'll have to do it myself."

"Do what?"

"Find out the truth. Find out who killed my father, and bring him to justice."

I said as gently as possible: "You're talking a little wild, kid. Now you keep your half of the bargain, and I'll keep mine. You go back in and get well, I'll see what I can find out."

"You're only trying to humor me. You don't intend to do anything."

"Don't I?"

He was silent. By way of proving that I was on his side, I said:

"It will probably help if you'd tell me what you know about this Grantland. This morning you mentioned a record."

"Yes, and I wasn't lying. I got it from a good source—a man who knows him."

"Another patient?"

"He's a patient, yes. That doesn't prove anything. He's perfectly sane, there's nothing the matter with his mind."

"Is that what he says?"

"The doctors say it, too. He's in for narcotic addiction."

"That hardly recommends him as a witness."

"He was telling me the *truth*," Carl said. "He's known Dr. Grantland for years, and all about him. Grantland used to supply him with narcotics."

"Bad enough, if true. But it's still a long way to murder."

"I see." His tone was disconsolate. "You want me to think I did it. You give me no hope."

"Listen to me," I said.

But he was deep in himself, examining a secret horror. He sobbed once in dry pain. Without any other warning, he turned on me. Dull sorrow filmed his eyes. His hooked hands swung together reaching for my throat. Immobilized behind the steering wheel, I reached for the doorhandle to gain some freedom of action. Carl was too quick for me. His large hands closed on my neck. I struck at his face with my right hand, but he was almost oblivious.

His close-up face was immense and bland, spotted with clear drops of sweat. He shook me. Daylight began to wane.

"Lay off," I said. "Damn fool." But the words were a rusty cawing.

I hit at him again, ineffectually, without leverage. One of his hands left my neck and came up hard against the point of my jaw. I went out.

I came to in the dry ditch, beside the tiremarks where my car had stood. As I got up the checkerboard fields fell into place around me, teetering slightly. I felt remarkably small, like a pin on a map.

chapter 5

I TOOK off my jacket and slapped the dust out of it and started to walk toward the hospital. It lay, like a city state, in the middle of its own fields. It had no walls. Perhaps their place was taken by the hills which stood around it, jagged and naked, on three sides. Broad avenues divided the concrete buildings which gave no outward indication of their use. The people walking on the sidewalks looked not much different from people anywhere, except that there was no hurry, nowhere to hurry to. The sun-stopped place with its massive, inscrutable buildings had an unreal quality; perhaps it was only hurry that was missing.

A fat man in blue jeans appeared from behind a parked car and approached me confidentially. In a low genteel voice he asked me if I wanted to buy a leather case for my car keys. "It's very good hand-carved leather, sir, hand-crafted in the hospital." He displayed it.

"Sorry, I don't have any use for it. Where do I go to get some information, about a patient?"

"Depends what ward he's on."

"I don't know the ward."

"You'd better ask at Administration." He pointed toward a new-looking off-white building at the intersection of two streets. But he was unwilling to let me go. "Did you come by bus?"

"I walked."

"From Los Angeles?"

"Part of the way."

"No car, eh?"

"My car was stolen."

"That's too bad. I live in Los Angeles, you know. I have a Buick station wagon, pretty good car. My wife keeps it up on blocks in the garage. They say that keeps the tires from deteriorating."

"Good idea."

"Yes," he said. "I want that car to be in good condition."

Broad concrete steps led up to the entrance of the administration building. I put on my jacket over my wet shirt, and went in through the glass doors. The highly groomed brunette at the information desk gave me a bright professional smile. "Can I help you, sir?"

"I'd like to see the superintendent."

Her smile hardened a little. "His schedule is very full today. May I have your name, please?"

"Archer."

"And what do you wish to see him about, Mr. Archer?"

"A confidential matter."

"One of our patients?"

"Yes, as a matter of fact."

"Are you a relative?"

"No."

23

"Which patient are you interested in, and what exactly is your interest? Sir."

"I'd better save that for the superintendent."

"You might have to wait all morning to see him. He has a series of conferences. I couldn't promise even then that he could find time for you."

It was gently administered, but it was the brush-off. There was no way to get around her quiet watchdog poise, so I gave it a frontal push:

"One of your patients escaped last night. He's violent."

She was unruffled. "You wish to lodge a complaint?"

"Not necessarily. I need some advice."

"Perhaps I can help you to it, if you'll give me the patient's name. Otherwise, I have no way of knowing which doctor is responsible for him."

"Carl Hallman."

Her thin eyebrows twitched upward: she recognized the name. "If you'll sit down, sir, I'll try to get the information for you."

She picked up one of her telephones. I sat down and lit a cigarette. It was still early in the morning, and I was the only one in the waiting-room. Its colored furniture and shiny waxed tile floors were insistently cheerful. I cheered up slightly myself when a covey of bright young nurses came in, and went twittering down a corridor.

The woman behind the desk put down her telephone and crooked a finger at me. "Dr. Brockley will see you. He's in his office now. You'll find it in the building behind this one, in the main corridor."

The second building was enormous. Its central corridor looked long enough to stage a hundred-yard-dash in. I contemplated making one. Ever since the Army, big institutions depressed me: channels, red tape, protocol, buck-passing, hurry up and wait. Only now and then you met a man with enough gumption to keep the big machine from bogging down of its own weight.

The door with Dr. Brockley's name above it was standing open. He came around from behind his desk, a middle-sized, middle-aged man in a gray herringbone suit, and gave me a quick hard hand.

"Mr. Archer? I happened to come in early this morning, so I can give you fifteen minutes. Then I'm due on the ward."

He placed me in a straight chair against the wall, brought me an ashtray, sat at his desk with his back to the window. He was quick in movement, very still in repose. His bald scalp and watchful eyes made him resemble a lizard waiting for a fly to expose itself.

"I understand you have a complaint against Carl Hallman. Perhaps you should understand that the hospital is not responsible for his actions. We're interested, but not responsible. He left here without permission."

"I know that. He told me."

"You're a friend of Hallman's?"

"I don't know him at all. He came to my house early this morning to try and get my help."

"What sort of help did he want?"

"It's a pretty involved story, having to do with his family. I think a lot of it was pure delusion. The main thing seems to be, he feels responsible for his father's death. He wants to get rid of the feeling. So he came to me. I happen to be a private detective. A friend of his recommended me to him."

When I named my profession, or sub-profession, the temperature went down. The doctor said frostily:

"If you're looking for family information, I can't give it to you."

"I'm not. I thought the best thing I could do for Hallman was bring him back here. I talked him into it, and we almost made it. Then he got excited and started throwing his weight around. As a matter of fact—" I'd been holding it back, because I was ashamed of it—"he took me by surprise and stole my car."

"It doesn't sound like him."

"Maybe I shouldn't say he stole it. He was upset, and I don't think he knew what he was doing. But he took it, and I want it back."

"Are you sure he took it?"

Another bureaucrat, I thought, with a noose of red tape up his sleeve. Another one of those. I said:

"I confess, Doctor. I never had a car. It was all a dream. The car was a sex symbol, see, and when it disappeared, it meant I'm entering the change of life."

He answered without a flicker of expression, smile or frown: "I mean, are you sure it wasn't the other one who stole your car? Another patient was with him when he took off last night. Didn't they stick together?"

"I only saw the one. Who was the other?"

Dr. Brockley lifted a manila folder out of his in-basket and studied its contents, or pretended to. "Normally," he said after a while, "we don't discuss our patients with outsiders. On the other hand, I'd like—" He closed the folder and slapped it down. "Let me put it this way. What do you intend to do about this alleged car theft? You want to see Hallman punished, naturally."

"Do I?"

"Don't you?"

"No."

"Why not?"

"I think he belongs in the hospital."

"What makes you think so?"

"He's flying, and he could be dangerous. He's a powerful boy. I don't want to be an alarmist, but he tried to throttle me."

"Really? You're not exaggerating?"

I showed him the marks on my neck. Dr. Brockley forgot himself for a second, and let his humanity show through, like a light behind a door. "Damn it, I'm sorry." But it was his patient he was sorry for. "Carl was doing so well these last few months—no acting out at all. What happened to set him off, do you know?"

"It may have been the idea of coming back here—this happened just up the road. The situation was sort of complicated. I let him talk too much, about his family, and then I made the mistake of arguing with him."

"Do you remember what about?"

"A fellow patient of his. Carl said he was a narcotics addict. He claimed the man gave him some suspicious information about a doctor he knew, a Dr. Grantland."

"I've met him. He's the Hallman family doctor. Incidentally, Grantland was instrumental in having Carl committed. It's natural that Carl would have feelings against him."

"He made some accusations. I don't think I'll repeat them, at least to another doctor."

"As you please." Brockley had resumed his poker face. "You say the source of the accusation was another patient, a narcotics addict?"

"That's right. I told Carl he should consider the source. He thought I was calling *him* a liar."

"What was the addict's name?"

"He wouldn't tell me."

Brockley said thoughtfully: "The man who escaped with him last night was a heroin addict. He's just another patient, of course—we treat them all alike—but he's quite a different kettle of fish from Carl Hallman. In spite of his disturbance, Carl's essentially a naïve and idealistic young man. Potentially a valuable man." The doctor was talking more to himself than to me. "I'd hate to think he's under Tom Rica's influence."

"Did you say Tom Rica?"

But the doctor had reached for his phone: "Miss Parish. This is Dr. Brockley. Tom Rica's folder, please— No, bring it to my office."

"I used to know a Tom Rica," I said when he put down the phone. "Let's see, he was eighteen about ten years ago, when he left Compton High. That would make him twenty-eight or -nine now. How old is Carl Hallman's friend?"

"Twenty-eight or -nine," Brockley said drily. "He looks a good deal older. Heroin has that effect, and the things that heroin leads to."

"This Rica has a record, eh?"

"Yes, he has. I didn't think he belonged here, but the authorities thought he could be rehabilitated. Maybe he can, at that. Maybe he can. We've had a few heroin cures. But he won't get cured wandering around the countryside."

There was a tap at the door. A young woman carrying a folder came in and handed it to Brockley. She was tall and generously made, with a fine sweep of bosom and the shoulders to support it. Her black hair was drawn back severely in a chignon. She had on a rather severely tailored dress which seemed intended to play down her femininity, without too much success.

"Miss Parish, this is Mr. Archer," Brockley said. "Mr. Archer ran into Carl Hallman this morning."

Her dark eyes lit with concern. "Where did you see him?"

"He came to my house."

"Is he all right?"

"It's hard to say."

"There's been a little trouble," Brockley put in. "Nothing too serious. I'll fill you in later if you like. I'm a bit rushed right now."

She took it as a reproof. "I'm sorry, Doctor."

"Nothing to be sorry about. I know you're interested in the case."

He opened the folder and began to scan it. Miss Parish went out rather hastily, bumping one hip on the doorframe. She had the kind of hips that are meant for childbearing and associated activities. Brockley cleared his throat, and brought my attention back to him:

"Compton High School. Rica's your boy all right."

chapter 6

I WASN'T surprised, just disappointed. Tom had played his part in the postwar rebellion that turned so many boys against authority. But he had been one of the salvageable ones, I thought. I'd helped to get him probation after his first major conviction—car theft, as usual—taught him a little boxing and shooting, tried to teach him some of the other things a man should know. Well, at least he remembered my name.

"What happened to Tom?" I said.

"Who can say? He was only in a short time, and we hadn't got to him yet. Frankly, we don't spend much time on personal work with addicts. It's mostly up to them. Some of them make it, some don't." He looked down into the folder on his desk. "Rica has a history of trouble. We'll have to notify the police of his escape."

"What about Carl Hallman?"

"I've been in touch with his family. They're contacting Ostervelt, the sheriff in Purissima—he knows Carl. I'd rather handle it unofficially, if it's all right with you. Keep this car trouble off the books until Carl has a chance to think twice about it."

"You think he'll come to his senses and bring it back?"

"It wouldn't surprise me. We could at least give him a chance."

"He's not dangerous, in your opinion?"

"Everybody's dangerous, given the wrong circumstances. I can't predict individual behavior. I know that Carl got rough with you. Still, I'd be willing to take a chance on him. His hospital record is good. And there are other considerations. You know what happens when a patient goes out of here, with or without leave, and gets into any kind of trouble. The newspapers play it up, and then there's public pressure on us to go back to the snake-pit days—lock the loonies up and forget about them." Brockley's voice was bitter. He passed his hand over his mouth, pulling it to one side. "Are you willing to wait a bit, Mr. Archer? I can get you transportation back to town."

"I'd like a few questions answered first."

"I'm overdue on the ward now." He glanced at the watch on his wrist, then shrugged. "All right. Shoot away."

"Was Carl being kept here by his brother Jerry, after he needed it?"

"No. It was a staff matter, essentially my decision."

"Did he tell you he blamed himself for his father's death?"

"Many times. I'd say that guilt feeling was central in his illness. He also attached it to his mother's death. Her suicide was a great shock to him."

"She killed herself?"

"Yes, some years ago. Carl thought she did it because be

broke her heart. It's typical of psychotic patients to blame themselves for everything that happens. Guilt is our main commodity here." He smiled. "We give it away."

"Hallman has a lot on his mind."

"He's been getting rid of it, gradually. And shock therapy helped. Some of my patients tell me that shock treatment satisfies their need for punishment. Maybe it does. We don't know for certain how it works."

"How crazy is he, can you tell me that?"

"He was manic-depressive, manic phase, when he came in. He isn't now, unless he's starting to go into a windup. Which I doubt."

"Is he likely to?"

"It depends on what happens to him." Brockley stood up, and came around the desk. He added, in a casual voice, but glancing sharply down at me: "You needn't feel that it's any responsibility of yours."

"I get your message. Lay off."

"For a while, anyway. Leave your telephone number with Miss Parish down the hall. If your car turns up, I'll get in touch with you."

Brockley let me out, and walked rapidly away. A few steps down the hall, I found a door lettered with Miss Parish's name and her title, Psychiatric Social Worker. She opened it when I knocked.

"I've been hoping you'd come by, Mr. Archer, is it? Please sit down."

Miss Parish indicated a straight chair by her desk. Apart from the filing cabinets the chair and desk were about all the furniture the small office contained. It was barer than a nun's cell.

"Thanks, I won't take the time to sit down. The doctor asked me to leave my telephone number with you, in case our friend changes his mind and comes back."

I recited the number. She sat down at her desk and

wrote it on a memo pad. Then she gave me a bright and piercing look which made me self-conscious. Tall women behind desks had always bothered me, anyway. It probably went back to the vice-principal of Wilson Junior High, who disapproved of the live bait I used to carry in the thermos bottle in my lunch pail, and other ingenious devices. Vice-Principal Trauma with Archer's Syndrome. The hospital atmosphere had me thinking that way.

"You're not a member of Mr. Hallman's immediate family, or a close friend." The statement lifted at the end into a question.

"I never saw him until today. I'm mainly interested in getting my car back."

"I don't understand. You mean he has your car?"

"He took it away from me." Since she seemed interested, I outlined the circumstances.

Her eyes darkened like thunderclouds. "I can't believe it."

"Brockley did."

"I'm sorry, I don't mean I doubt your word. It's simply—this eruption doesn't fit in with Carl's development. He's been making such wonderful strides with us—helping us look after the less competent ones— But of course you're not interested. You're naturally resentful about the loss of your car."

"Not so very. He's had a good deal of trouble. I can afford a little, if he had to pass it on."

She looked more friendly. "You sound as though you talked to him."

"He talked to me, quite a lot. I almost got him back here."

"Did he seem disturbed? Apart from the outburst of violence, I mean?"

"I've seen worse, but I'm no judge. He was pretty bitter about his family."

"Yes, I know. It was his father's death that set him off in the first place. The first few weeks he talked of nothing else. But the trouble had died down, at least I thought it had. Of course I'm not a psychiatrist. On the other hand, I've had a lot more to do with Carl than any of the psychiatrists." She added softly: "He's a sweet person, you know."

Under the circumstances, the sentiment seemed slightly sticky. I said: "He picked a funny way to show it."

Miss Parish had emotional equipment to match her splendid physical equipment. The thunderclouds came into her eyes again, with lightning. "He's not responsible!" she cried. "Can't you see that? You mustn't judge him."

"All right. I'll go along with that."

This seemed to calm her, though her brow stayed dark. "I can't imagine what happened to stir him up. Considering the distance he'd had to come back, he was the most promising patient on the ward. He was due for a P-card in a very few weeks. He'd probably have gone home in two or three months. Carl didn't have to run away, and he knew it."

"Remember he had another man with him. Tom Rica may have done some pretty good needling."

"Is Tom Rica with him now?"

"He wasn't when I saw Carl."

"That's good. I shouldn't say it about a patient, but Tom Rica is a poor risk. He's a heroin addict, and this isn't his first cure. Or his last, I'm afraid."

"I'm sorry to hear it. I knew him when he was a boy. He had his troubles even then, but he was a bright kid."

"It's queer that you should know Rica," she said with some suspicion. "Isn't that quite a coincidence?"

"No. Tom Rica sent Carl Hallman to me."

"They are together, then?"

"They left here together. Afterwards, they seem to have gone separate ways."

"Oh, I hope so. An addict looking for dope, and a vulnerable boy like Carl—they could make an explosive combination."

"Not a very likely combination," I said. "How did they happen to be buddies?"

"I wouldn't say they were buddies, exactly. They were committed from the same place, and Carl's been looking after Rica on the ward. We never have enough nurses and technicians to go around, so our better patients help to take care of the worse ones. Rica was in a bad way when he came in."

"How long ago was that?"

"A couple of weeks. He had severe withdrawal symptoms—couldn't eat, couldn't sleep. Carl was a positive saint with him: I watched them together. If I'd known how it was going to turn out, I'd have—" She broke off, clamping her teeth down on her lower lip.

"You like Carl," I said in a neutral tone.

The young woman colored, and answered rather sharply: "You would, too, if you knew him when he's himself."

Maybe I would, I thought, but not the way Miss Parish did. Carl Hallman was a handsome boy, and a handsome boy in trouble was a double threat to women, a triple threat if he needed mothering.

Not needing it, and none being offered, I left.

chapter 7

THE address which Carl had given me for his wife was near the highway in an older section of Purissima. The highway traffic thrummed invisibly like a damaged artery under the noon silence in the street. Most of the houses were frame cottages or stucco boxes built in the style of thirty years ago. A few were older, three-story mansions surviving from an era of elegance into an era of necessity.

220 was one of these. Its long closed face seemed abashed by the present. Its white wooden walls needed paint. The grass in the front yard had grown and withered, untouched by the human hand.

I asked the cab-driver to wait and knocked on the front door, which was surmounted by a fanlight of ruby-colored glass. I had to knock several times before I got an answer. Then the door was unlocked and opened, reluctantly and partially.

The woman who showed herself in the aperture had unlikely purplish red hair cut in bangs on her forehead and recently permanented. Blue eyes burned like gas-flames in her rather inert face. Her mouth was crudely outlined in fresh lipstick, which I guessed she had just dabbed on as a concession to the outside world. The only other concession was a pink nylon robe from which her breasts threatened to overflow. I placed her age in the late forties. She couldn't be Mrs. Carl Hallman. At least I hoped she couldn't.

"Is Mrs. Hallman home?"

"No, she isn't here. I'm Mrs. Gley, her mother." She

smiled meaninglessly. There was lipstick on her teeth, too, gleaming like new blood. "Is it something?"

"I'd like very much to see her."

"Is it about—him?"

"Mr. Hallman, you mean?"

She nodded.

"Well, I would like to talk to him."

"Talk to him! It needs more than talk to him. You might as well talk to a stone wall—beat your head bloody against it trying to change his ways." Though she seemed angry and afraid, she spoke in a low monotone. Her voice was borne on a heavy breath in which Sen-Sen struggled for dominance. You inhaled it as much as heard it.

"Is Mr. Hallman here?"

"No, thank God for small mercies. He hasn't been here. But I've been expecting him ever since she got that call from the hospital." Her gaze, which had swiveled past me to the street, returned to my face. "Is that your taxi?"

"Yes."

"Well, that's a relief. Are you from the hospital?"

"I just came from there."

I'd intended some misrepresentation, which she made me regret immediately:

"Why don't you keep them locked up better? You can't let crazy-men run around loose. If you knew what my girl has suffered from that man—it's a terrible thing." She took the short easy step from motherly concern to self-concern: "Sometimes I think I'm the one who suffered most. The things I hoped and planned for that girl, and then she had to bring *that* one into the family. I begged and pleaded with her to stay home today. But no, she has to go to work, you'd think the office couldn't go on without her. She leaves me here by myself, to cope."

She spread out her hands and pressed them into her

bosom, the white flesh rising like dough between her fingers.

"It isn't fair. The world is cruel. You work and hope and plan, then everything goes to pieces. I didn't deserve it." A few easy tears ran down her cheeks. She found a ball of Kleenex in her sleeve and wiped her eyes. They shone, undimmed by her grief, with a remarkable intensity. I wondered what fuel fed them.

"I'm sorry, Mrs. Gley. I'm new on this case. My name is Archer. May I come in and talk to you?"

"Come in if you like. I don't know what *I* can tell you. Mildred ought to be home over the noon-hour, she promised she would."

She moved along the dim hallway, a middle-aged woman going to seed, but not entirely gone. There was something about the way she carried herself: old beauty and grace controlling her flesh, like an unforgotten discipline. She turned at a curtained archway behind which voices murmured.

"Please go in and sit down. I was just changing for lunch. I'll put something on."

She started up a flight of stairs which rose from the rear of the hallway. I went in through the curtains, and found myself in a twilit sitting-room with a lighted television screen. At first the people on the screen were unreal shadows. After I sat and watched them for a few minutes, they became realer than the room. The screen became a window into a brightly lighted place where life was being lived, where a beautiful actress couldn't decide between career and children and had to settle for both. The actual windows of the sitting-room were heavily blinded.

In the shifting light from the screen, I noticed an empty glass on the coffeetable beside me. It smelled of gin. Just to keep my hand in, I made a search for the bottle. It was stuffed behind the cushion of my chair, a half-empty Gordon's bottle, its contents transparent as tears. Feeling a little embarrassed, I returned it to its hiding place. The woman on the screen had had her baby, and held it up to her husband for his approval.

The front door opened and closed. Quick heels clicked down the hallway, and paused at the archway. I started to get up. A woman's voice said:

"Who—Carl? Is that you, Carl?"

Her voice was high. She looked very pale and dark-eyed in the light from the screen, almost like a projection from it. She fumbled behind the curtains for a lightswitch. A dim ceiling light came on over my head.

"Oh. Excuse me. I thought you were someone else."

She was young and small, with a fine small head, its modeling emphasized by a short boyish haircut. She had on a dark business suit which her body filled the way grapes fill their skins. She held a shiny black plastic bag, like a shield, in front of it.

"Mrs. Hallman?"

"Yes." Her look said: who are you, and what are you doing here?

I told her my name. "Your mother asked me to sit down for a minute."

"Where is Mother?" She tried to speak in an ordinary tone, but she looked at me suspiciously, as if I had Mother's body hidden in a closet.

"Upstairs."

"Are you a policeman?"

"No."

"I just wondered. She phoned me at the office about half an hour ago and said she was going to ask for police protection. I couldn't get away immediately."

She stopped abruptly, and looked around the room. Its furnishings would have been antiques if they'd ever possessed distinction. The carpet was threadbare, the wallpaper faded and stained brown in patches. The mohair sofa that matched the chair I'd sat in was ripped and spilling its guts. The mahogany veneer was peeling off the coffeetable which held the empty glass. It was no wonder Mrs. Gley preferred darkness and gin and television to the light of morning.

The girl went past me in a birdlike rush, snatched up the glass, and sniffed at it. "I thought so."

On the screen behind her a male announcer, not so very male, was telling women how to be odorless and beloved. The girl turned with the glass in her hand. For a second I thought she'd throw it at the screen. Instead she stooped and switched the television off. Its light faded slowly like a dream.

"Did Mother pour you a drink?"

"Not yet."

"Has anyone else been here?"

"Not that I know of. But your mother may have the right idea. I mean, about police protection."

She looked at me in silence for a minute. Her eyes were the same color as her mother's, and had the same intensity, almost tangible on my face. Her gaze dropped to the glass in her hand. Setting it down, she said under cover of the movement: "You know about Carl? Did Mother tell you?"

"I talked to Dr. Brockley at the hospital this morning. I had a run-in with your husband earlier. As a matter of fact he took my car." I told her about that.

She listened with her head bowed, biting one knuckle like a doleful child. But there was nothing childish about the look she gave me. It held a startled awareness, as if she'd had to grow up in a hurry, painfully. I had a feeling that she was the one who had suffered most in the family trouble. There was resignation in her posture, and in the undertones of her voice:

"I'm sorry. He never did anything like that before."

"I'm sorry, too."

"Why did you come here?"

I had several motives, some more obscure than others. I picked the easiest: "I want my car back. If I can handle it myself, without reporting it as a theft—"

"But you said yourself that we should call the police."

"For protection, yes. Your mother's frightened."

"Mother's very easily frightened. I'm not. Anyway, there's no basis for it. Carl's never hurt anyone, let alone Mother and me. He talks a lot sometimes—that's all it amounts to. I'm not afraid of him." She gave me a shrewd and very female glance. "Are you?"

Under the circumstances, I had to say I wasn't. I couldn't be sure, though. Perhaps that was my reason for coming there—the obscurest motive that underlay the others.

"I've always been able to handle Carl," she said. "I'd never have let them take him to the hospital, if I could have kept him here and looked after him myself. But somebody had to go to work." She frowned. "What can be keeping Mother? Excuse me for a minute."

She left the room and started up the stairs. The ringing of a telephone brought her down into the hallway again. From somewhere upstairs her mother called:

"Is that you, Mildred? The phone's ringing."

"Yes. I'll get it." I heard her lift the receiver. "This is Mildred. Zinnie? What do you want? . . . Are you sure? . . . No, I can't. I can't possibly. . . . I don't believe it. . . ." Then, on a rising note: "All *right.* I'll come."

The receiver dropped in its cradle. I went to the door and looked into the hallway. Mildred was leaning against the wall beside the telephone table. Her face was wan, her eyes shock-bright. Her gaze shifted to me, but it was so inward I don't think it took me in.

"Trouble?"

She nodded mutely and drew in a shuddering breath. It came out as a sigh:

"Carl's at the ranch now. One of the hands saw him. Jerry isn't there, and Zinnie's terrified."

"Where's Jerry?"

"I don't know. In town, probably. He follows the stock market every day until two, at least he used to."

"What's she so scared about?"

"Carl has a gun with him." Her voice was low and wretched.

"You're sure?"

"The man who saw him said so."

"Is he likely to use it?"

"No. I don't think so. It's the others I'm worried about—what they might do to Carl if there's any shooting."

"What others?"

"Jerry, and the sheriff and his deputies. They've always taken orders from the Hallmans. I've got to go and find Carl—talk to him, before Jerry gets back to the ranch."

But she was having a hard time getting under way. She stood stiff against the wall, hands knotted at the ends of their straight arms, immobilized by tension. When I touched her elbow, she shied:

"Yes?"

"I have a taxi waiting. I'll take you out there."

"No. Taxis cost money. We'll go in my car." She scooped up her bag and pressed it under her arm.

"Go where?" her mother cried from the top of the stairs. "Where are you going? You're not going to leave me alone."

Mrs. Gley came down in a rush. She had on a kind of tea gown whose draperies flew out behind her, like the tail of a blowzy comet. Her body swayed softly and heavily against the newel post at the foot of the stairs. "You can't leave me alone," she repeated.

"I'm sorry, Mother. I have to go to the ranch. Carl's out there now, so there's nothing for you to worry about."

"Nothing to worry about, that's a good one. I've got my life to worry about, that's all. And your place is with your mother at this time."

"You're talking nonsense."

"Am I? When all I ask is a little love and sympathy from my own daughter?"

"You've had all I've got."

The younger woman turned and started for the door. Her mother followed her, a clumsy ghost trailing yellowing draperies and the powerful odor of Sen-Sen. Either her earlier drinks were catching up with her, or she had another bottle upstairs. She made her final plea, or threat:

"I'm drinking, Mildred."

"I know, Mother."

Mildred opened the door and went out.

"Don't you care?" her mother screamed after her.

Mrs. Gley turned to me as I passed her in the doorway. The light from the window over the door lent her face a rosy youthfulness. She looked like a naughty girl who was trying to decide whether or not to have a tantrum. I didn't wait to find out if she did.

chapter 8

MILDRED HALLMAN'S car was an old black Buick convertible. It was parked behind my cab, wide of the curb. I paid off the cab-driver and got in.

Mildred was sitting on the righthand side of the front seat.

"You drive, will you?" She said as we started: "Between Carl and Mother, I'm completely squeezed out. They both need a keeper, and in the end it always turns out to be me. No, don't think I'm feeling sorry for myself, because I'm not. It's nice to be needed."

She spoke with a kind of wilted gallantry. I looked at her. She'd leaned her head against the cracked leather seat, and closed her eyes. Without their light and depth in her face, she looked about thirteen. I caught myself up short, recognizing a feeling I'd had before. It started out as paternal sympathy but rapidly degenerated, if I let it. And Mildred had a husband.

"You're fond of your husband," I said.

She answered dreamily: "I'm crazy about him. I had a crush on him in high school, the first and only crush I ever had. Carl was a big wheel in those days. He barely knew I existed. I kept hoping, though." She paused, and added softly: "I'm still hoping."

I stopped for a red light, and turned right onto the highway which paralleled the waterfront. Gas fumes mixed with the odors of fish and underwater oil wells. To my left, beyond a row of motels and seafood restaurants, the sea lay low and flat and solid like blue tiling, swept clean and polished. Some white triangular sails stood upright on it.

We passed a small-boat harbor, gleaming white on blue, and a long pier draped with fishermen. Everything was as pretty as a postcard. The trouble with you, I said to myself: you're always turning over the postcards and reading the messages on the underside. Written in invisible ink, in blood, in tears, with a black border around them, with postage due, unsigned, or signed with a thumbprint.

Turning right again at the foot of the main street, we passed through an area of third-rate hotels, bars, pool halls. Stunned by sun and sherry, unemployed field hands and rumdums paraded like zombies on the noon pavements. A Mexican movie house marked the upper limits of the lower depths. Above it were stores and banks and office buildings, sidewalks bright with tourists, or natives who dressed like tourists.

The residential belt had widened since I'd been in Purissima last, and it was still spreading. New streets and housing tracts were climbing the coastal ridge and pushing up the canyons. The main street became a country blacktop which wound up over the ridge. On its far side a valley opened, broad and floored with rich irrigation green. A dozen miles across it, the green made inlets between the foothills and lapped at the bases of the mountains.

The girl beside me stirred. "You can see the house from here. It's off the road to the right, in the middle of the valley."

I made out a sprawling tile-roofed building floating low like a heavy red raft in the ridged green. As we went downhill, the house sank out of sight.

"I used to live in that house," Mildred said. "I promised myself I'd never go back to it. A building can soak up emotions, you know, so that after a while it has the same emotions as the people who live in it. They're in the cracks in the walls, the smokestains on the ceiling, the smells in the kitchen."

I suspected that she was dramatizing a little: there was some of her mother in her after all: but I kept still, hoping she'd go on talking.

"Greed and hate and snobbery," she said. "Everyone who lived in that house became greedy and hateful and snobbish. Except Carl. It's no wonder he couldn't take it.

He's so completely different from the others." She turned toward me, the leather creaking under her. "I know what you're thinking—that Carl is crazy, or he was, and I'm twisting the facts around to suit myself. I'm not, though. Carl is good. It's often the very best people who crack up. And when he cracked, it was family pressure that did it to him."

"I gathered that, from what he said to me."

"Did he tell you about Jerry—constantly taunting him, trying to make him mad, then running to his father with tales of the trouble Carl made?"

"Why did he do that?"

"Greed," she said. "The well-known Hallman greed. Jerry wanted control of the ranch. Carl was due to inherit half of it. Jerry did everything he could to ruin Carl with his father, and Zinnie did, too. They were the ones who were really responsible for that last big quarrel, before the Senator died. Did Carl tell you about that?"

"Not very much."

"Well, Jerry and Zinnie started it. They got Carl talking about the Japanese, how much the family owed them for their land— I admit that Carl was hipped on the subject, but Jerry encouraged him to go on and on until he was really raving. I tried to stop it, but nobody listened to me. When Carl was completely wound up, Jerry went to the Senator and asked him to reason with Carl. You can imagine how much reasoning they did, when they got together. We could hear them shouting all over the house.

"The Senator had a heart attack that night. It's a terrible thing to say about a man, but Jerry was responsible for his father's death. He may even have planned it that way: he knew his father wasn't to be excited. I heard Dr. Grantland warn the family myself, more than once."

"What about Dr. Grantland?"

"In what way do you mean?"

"Carl thinks he's crooked," I hesitated, then decided she could hold it: "In fact, he made some pretty broad accusations."

"I think I've heard them. But go on."

"Conspiracy was one of them. Carl thought Grantland and his brother conspired to have him committed. But the doctor at the hospital says there's nothing to it."

"No," she said. "Carl needed hospital treatment. I signed the necessary papers. That was all aboveboard. Only, Jerry made me and Carl sign other papers at the same time, making him Carl's legal guardian. I didn't know what it meant. I thought it was just a part of the commitment. But it means that as long as Carl is ill, Jerry controls every penny of the estate."

Her voice had risen. She brought it under control and said more quietly: "I don't care about myself. I'd never go back there anyway. But Carl needs the money. He could get better treatment—the best psychiatrists in the country. It's the last thing Jerry wants, to see his brother cured. That would end the guardianship, you see."

"Does Carl know all this?"

"No, at least he's never heard it from me. He's mad enough at Jerry as it is."

"Your brother-in-law sounds charming."

"Yes indeed he is." Her voice was thin. "If it was just a question of saving Jerry, I wouldn't move a step in his direction. Not a step. But you know what will happen to Carl if he gets into any kind of trouble. He's already got more guilt than he can bear. It could set him back years, or make him permanent— No! I won't think about it. Nothing is going to happen."

She twisted in the seat away from me, as though I represented the things she feared. The road had become a green trench running through miles of orange trees. The individual rows of trees, slanting diagonally from the road, whirled and jumped backward in staccato movement. Mildred peered down the long empty vistas between them, looking for a man with straw-colored hair.

A large wooden sign, painted black on white, appeared at the roadside ahead: Hallman Citrus Ranch. I braked for the turn, made it on whining tires, and almost ran down a big old man in a sheriff's blouse. He moved away nimbly, then came heavily back to the side of the car. Under a wide-brimmed white hat, his face was flushed. Veins squirmed like broken purple worms under the skin of his nose. His eyes held the confident vacancy that comes from the exercise of other people's power.

"Watch where you're going, bud. Not that you're going anywhere, on this road. What do you think I'm here for, to get myself a tan?"

Mildred leaned across me, her breast live against my arm:

"Sheriff! Have you seen Carl?"

The old man leaned to peer in. His sun-wrinkles deepened and his mouth widened in a smile which left his eyes as vacant as before. "Why hello, Mrs. Hallman, I didn't see you at first. I must be going blind in my old age."

"Have you seen Carl?" she repeated.

He made a production out of answering her, marching around to her side of the car, carrying his belly in front of him like a gift. "Not personally, I haven't. We know he's on the ranch, though. Sam Yogan saw him to talk to, not much more than an hour ago."

"Was he rational?"

"Sam didn't say. Anyway, what would a Jap gardener know about it?"

"A gun was mentioned," I said.

The sheriff's mouth drooped at the corners. "Yeah, he's

carrying a gun. I don't know where in hell he got hold of it."

"How heavy a gun?"

"Sam said not so heavy. But any gun is too big when a man is off his rocker."

Mildred let out a small cry.

"Don't worry, Mrs. Hallman. We got the place staked out. We'll pick him up." Tipping his hat back, he pushed his face in at her window. "You better get rid of your boyfriend before we do pick him up. Carl won't like it if you got a boyfriend, driving his car and all."

She looked from him to me, her mouth a thin line. "This is Sheriff Ostervelt, Mr. Archer. I'm sorry I forgot my manners. Sheriff Ostervelt never had any to remember."

Ostervelt smirked. "Take a joke, eh?"

"Not from you," she said without looking at him.

"Still mad, eh? Give it time. Give it time."

He laid a thick hand on her shoulder. She took it in both of hers and flung it away from her. I started to get out of the car.

"Don't," she said. "He only wants trouble."

"Trouble? Not me," Ostervelt said. "I try to make a little joke. You don't think it's funny. Is that trouble, between friends?"

I said: "Mrs. Hallman's expected at the house. I said I'd drive her there. Much as I'd love to go on talking to you all afternoon."

"I'll take her to the house." Ostervelt gestured toward the black Mercury Special parked on the shoulder, and patted his holster. "The husband's lurking around in the groves, and I don't have the men to comb them for him. She might need protection."

"Protection is my business."

"What the hell does that mean?"

"I'm a private detective."

"What do you know? You got a license, maybe?"

"Yes. It's good statewide. Now do we go, or do we stay here and have some more repartee?"

"Sure," he said, "I'm stupid—just a stupid fool, and my jokes ain't funny. Only I got an official responsibility. So you better let me see that license you say you got."

Moving very slowly, the sheriff came around to my side of the car again. I slapped my photostat into his hand. He read it aloud, in an elocutionary voice, pausing to check the physical description against my appearance.

"Six-foot-two, one-ninety," he repeated. "A hunk of man. Love those beautiful blue eyes. Or are they gray, Mrs. Hallman? You'd know."

"Leave me alone." Her voice was barely audible.

"Sure. But I better drive you up to the house in person. Hollywood here has those beautiful powder-blue eyes, but it don't say here"—he flicked my photostat with his forefinger—"what his score is on a moving target."

I picked the black-and-white card out of his hand, released the emergency brake, stepped on the gas. It wasn't politic. But enough was enough.

chapter 9

THE private road ran ruler-straight through the geometric maze of the orange trees. Midway between the highway and the house, it widened in front of several barnlike packing-sheds. The fruit on the trees was unripe, and the red-painted sheds were empty and deserted-looking. In a clearing behind them, a row of tumble-down hutches, equally empty, provided shelter of a sort for migrant pickers.

Nearly a mile further on, the main house stood back from the road, half-shadowed by overarching oaks. Its brown adobe walls looked as indigenous as the oaks. The red Ford station wagon and the sheriff's patrol car on the curving gravel driveway seemed out of place, or rather out of time. The thing that struck me most as I parked in the driveway was a child's swing suspended by new rope from a branch of one of the trees. No one had mentioned a child.

When I switched off the Buick's engine, the silence was almost absolute. The house and its grounds were tranquil. Shadows lay soft as peace in the deep veranda. It was hard to believe the other side of the postcard.

The silence was broken by a screen door's percussion. A blonde woman wearing black satin slacks and a white shirt came out on the front veranda. She folded her arms over her breasts and stood as still as a cat, watching us come up the walk.

"Zinnie," Mildred said under her breath. She raised her voice: "Zinnie? Is everything all right?"

"Oh fine. Just lovely. I'm still waiting for Jerry to come home. You didn't see him in town, did you?"

"I never see Jerry. You know that."

Mildred halted at the foot of the steps. There was a barrier of hostility, like a charged fence, between the two women. Zinnie, who was at least ten years older, held her body in a compact defensive posture against the pressure of Mildred's eyes. Then she dropped her arms in a rather dramatic gesture which may have been meant for me.

"I hardly ever see him myself."

She laughed nervously. Her laugh was harsh and unpleasant, like her voice. It was easy for me to overlook the unpleasantness. She was a beautiful woman, and her green eyes were interested in me. The waist above her snug hips was the kind you can span with your two hands, and would probably like to.

"Who's your friend?" she purred.

Mildred introduced me.

"A private detective yet," Zinnie said. "The place is crawling with policemen already. But come on in. That sun is misery."

She held the door for us. Her other hand went to her face where the sun had parched the skin, then to her sleek hair. Her right breast rose elastically under the white silk shirt. A nice machine, I thought: pseudo-Hollywood, probably empty, certainly expensive, and not new; but a nice machine. She caught my look and didn't seem to mind. She switch-hipped along the hallway, to a large, cool living-room.

"I've been waiting for an excuse to have a drink. Mildred, you'll have ginger ale, I know. How's your mother, by the way?"

"Mother is fine. Thank you." Mildred's formality broke down suddenly. "Zinnie? Where is Carl now?"

Zinnie lifted her shoulders. "I wish I knew. He hasn't been heard from since Sam Yogan saw him. Ostervelt has several deputies out looking for him. The trouble is, Carl knows the ranch better than any of them."

"You said they promised not to shoot."

"Don't worry about that. They'll take him without any fireworks. That's where you come in, if and when he shows up."

"Yes." Mildred stood like a stranger in the middle of the floor. "Is there anything I can do now?"

"Not a thing. Relax. I need a drink if you don't. What about you, Mr. Archer?"

"Gibson, if it's available."

"That's handy, I'm a Gibson girl myself." She smiled brilliantly, too brilliantly for the circumstances. Zinnie seemed to be a trier, though, whatever else she was.

Her living-room bore the earmarks of a trier with a restless urge to be up to the minute in everything. Its bright new furniture was sectional, scattered around in cubes and oblongs and arcs. It sorted oddly with the dark oak floor and the heavily beamed ceiling. The adobe walls were hung with modern reproductions in limed oak frames. A row of book-club books occupied the mantel above the ancient stone fireplace. A free-form marble coffee-table held *Harper's Bazaar* and *Vogue* and a beautiful old silver handbell. It was a room in which an uneasy present struggled to overcome the persistent past.

Zinnie picked up the bell and shook it. Mildred jumped at the sound. She was sitting very tense on the edge of a sectional sofa. I sat down beside her, but she paid no attention to my presence. She turned to look out the window, toward the groves.

A tiny girl came into the room, pausing near the door at the sight of strangers. With light blond hair and delicate porcelain features, she was obviously Zinnie's daughter. The child was fussily dressed in a pale blue frock with a sash, and a matching blue ribbon in her hair. Her hand crept toward her mouth. The tiny fingernails were painted red.

"I was ringing for Juan, dear," Zinnie said.

"I want to ring for him, Mummy. Let me ring for Juan."

Though the child wasn't much more than three, she spoke very clearly and purely. She darted forward, reaching for the handbell. Zinnie let her ring it. Above its din, a white-jacketed Filipino said from the doorway:

"Missus?"

"A shaker of Gibsons, Juan. Oh, and ginger ale for Mildred."

"I want a Gibson, too," the little girl said.

"All right, darling." Zinnie turned to the houseboy: "A special cocktail for Martha."

He smiled comprehendingly, and disappeared.

"Say hello to your Aunt Mildred, Martha."

"Hello, Aunt Mildred."

"Hello, Martha. How are you?"

"I'm fine. How is Uncle Carl?"

"Uncle Carl is ill," Mildred said in a monotone.

"Isn't Uncle Carl coming? Mummy said he was coming. She said so on the telephone."

"No," her mother cut in. "You didn't understand what I said, dear. I was talking about somebody else. Uncle Carl is far away. He's living far away."

"Who is coming, Mummy?"

"Lots of people are coming. Daddy will be here soon. And Dr. Grantland. And Aunt Mildred is here."

The child looked up at her, her eyes clear and untroubled. She said: "I don't want Daddy to come. I don't like Daddy. I want Dr. Grantland to come. He will come and take us to a nice place."

"Not *us*, dear. You and Mrs. Hutchinson. Dr. Grantland will take you for a ride in his car, and you'll spend the day with Mrs. Hutchinson. Maybe all night, too. Won't that be fun?"

"Yes," the child answered gravely. "That will be fun."

"Now go and ask Mrs. Hutchinson to give you your lunch."

"I ate my lunch. I ate it all up. You said I could have a special cocktail."

"In the kitchen, dear. Juan will give you your cocktail in the kitchen."

"I don't want to go in the kitchen. I want to stay here, with people."

"No, you can't." Zinnie was getting edgy. "Now be a nice

girl and do what you're told, or I'll tell Daddy about you. He won't like it."

"I don't care. I want to stay here and talk to the people."

"Some other time, Martha." She rose and hustled the little girl out of the room. A long wail ended with the closing of a door.

"She's a beautiful child."

Mildred turned to me. "Which one of them do you mean? Yes, Martha is pretty. And she's bright. But the way Zinnie is handling her—she treats her as if she were a doll."

Mildred was going to say more, but Zinnie returned, closely followed by the houseboy with the drinks. I drank mine in a hurry, and ate the onion by way of lunch.

"Have another, Mr. Archer." One drink had converted Zinnie's tension into vivacity, of a sort. "We've got the rest of the shaker to knock back between us. Unless we can persuade Mildred to climb down off her high wagon."

"You know where I stand on the subject." Mildred gripped her glass of ginger ale defensively. "I see you've had the room redone."

I said: "One's enough for me, thanks. What I'd like to do, if you don't object, is talk to the man who saw your brother-in-law. Sam something?"

"Sam Yogan. Of course, talk to Sam if you like."

"Is he around now?"

"I think so. Come on, I'll help you find him. Coming, Mildred?"

"I'd better stay here," Mildred said. "If Carl comes to the house, I want to be here to meet him."

"Aren't you afraid of him?"

"No, I'm not afraid of him. I love my husband. No doubt it's hard for you to understand that."

The hostility between the two women kept showing its sharp edges. Zinnie said:

"Well, I'm afraid of him. Why do you think I'm sending Martha to town? And I've got half a mind to go myself."

"With Dr. Grantland?"

Zinnie didn't answer. She rose abruptly, with a glance at me. I followed her through a dining-room furnished in massive old mahogany, into a sunlit kitchen gleaming with formica and chrome and tile. The houseboy turned from the sink, where he was washing dishes:

"Yes, Missus?"

"Is Sam around?"

"Before, he was talking to policeman."

"I know that. Where is he now?"

"Bunkhouse, greenhouse, I dunno." The houseboy shrugged. "I pay no attention to Sam Yogan."

"I know that, too."

Zinnie moved impatiently through a utility room to the back door. As soon as we stepped outside, a young man in a western hat raised his head from behind a pile of oak logs. He came around the woodpile, replacing his gun in its holster, swaggering slightly in his deputy's suntans.

"I'd stay inside if I was you, Mrs. Hallman. That way we can look after you better." He looked inquiringly at me.

"Mr. Archer is a private detective."

A peevish look crossed the young deputy's face, as though my presence threatened to spoil the game. I hoped it would. There were too many guns around.

"Any sign of Carl Hallman?" I asked him.

"You check in with the sheriff?"

"I checked in." Ostensibly to Zinnie, I said: "Didn't you say there wouldn't be any shooting? That the sheriff's men would take your brother-in-law without hurting him?"

"Yes. Sheriff Ostervelt promised to do his best."

"We can't guarantee nothing," the young deputy said. Even as he spoke, he was scanning the tree-shaded recesses of the back yard, and the dense green of the trees that stretched beyond. "We got a dangerous man to deal with. He bust out of a security ward last night, stole a car for his getaway, probably stole the gun he's carrying."

"How do you know he stole a car?"

"We found it, stashed in a tractor turnaround between here and the main road. Right near where the old Jap ran into him."

"Green Ford convertible?"

"Yeah. You seen it?"

"It's my car."

"No kidding? How'd he happen to steal your car?"

"He didn't exactly steal it. I'm laying no charges. Take it easy with him if you see him."

The deputy's face hardened obtusely. "I got my orders."

"What are they?"

"Fire if fired upon. And that's leaning way over backwards. You don't play footsie with a homicidal psycho, Mister."

He had a point: I'd tried to, and got my lumps. But you didn't shoot him, either.

"He isn't considered homicidal."

I glanced at Zinnie for confirmation. She didn't speak, or look in my direction. Her pretty head was cocked sideways in a strained listening attitude. The deputy said:

"You should talk to the sheriff about that."

"He didn't threaten Yogan, did he?"

"Maybe not. The Jap and him are old pals. Or maybe he did, and the Jap ain't telling us. We do know he's carrying a gun, and he knows how to use it."

"I'd like to talk to Yogan."

"If you think it'll do you any good. Last I saw of him he was in the bunkhouse."

He pointed between the oaks to an old adobe which stood on the edge of the groves. Behind us, the sound of an approaching car floated over the housetop.

"Excuse me, Mr. Carmichael," Zinnie said. "That must be my husband."

Walking quickly, she disappeared around the side of the house. Carmichael pulled his gun and trotted after her. I followed along, around the attached greenhouse which flanked the side of the house.

A silver-gray Jaguar stopped behind the Buick convertible in the driveway. Running across the lawn toward the sports car, under the towering sky, Zinnie looked like a little puppet, black and white and gold, jerked across green baize. The big man who got out of the car slowed her with a gesture of his hand. She looked back at me and the deputy, stumbling a little on her heels, and assumed an awkward noncommittal pose.

chapter 10

THE driver of the Jaguar had dressed himself to match it. He had on gray flannels, gray suede shoes, a gray silk shirt, a gray tie with a metallic sheen. In striking contrast, his face had the polished brown finish of hand-rubbed wood. Even at a distance, I could see he used it as an actor might. He was conscious of planes and angles, and the way his white teeth flashed when he smiled. He turned his full smile on Zinnie.

I said to the deputy: "That wouldn't be Jerry Hallman."

"Naw. It's some doctor from town."

"Grantland?"

"I guess that's his name." He squinted at me sideways. "What kind of detective work do you do? Divorce?"

"I have."

"Which one in the family hired you, anyway?"

I didn't want to go into that, so I gave him a wise look and drifted away. Dr. Grantland and Zinnie were climbing the front steps. As she passed him in the doorway, Zinnie looked up into his face. She inclined her body so that her breast touched his arm. He put the same arm around her shoulders, turned her away from him, and propelled her into the house.

Without going out of my way to make a lot of noise, I mounted the veranda and approached the screen door. A carefully modulated male voice was saying:

"You're acting like a wild woman. You don't have to be so conspicuous."

"I want to be. I want everyone to know."

"Including Jerry?"

"Especially him." Zinnie added illogically: "Anyway, he isn't here."

"He soon will be. I passed him on the way out. You should have seen the look he gave me."

"He hates anybody to pass him."

"No, there was more to it than that. Are you sure you haven't told him about us?"

"I wouldn't tell him the time of day."

"What's this about wanting everybody to know then?"

"I didn't mean anything. Except that I love you."

"Be quiet. Don't even say it. You could throw everything away, just when I've got it practically made."

"Tell me."

"I'll tell you afterwards. Or perhaps I won't tell you at all. It's working out, and that's all you need to know. Anyway, it will work out, if you can act like a sensible human being."

"Just tell me what to do, and I'll do it."

"Then remember who you are, and who I am. I'm thinking about Martha. You should be, too."

"Yes. I forget her sometimes, when I'm with you. Thank you for reminding me, Charlie."

"Not Charlie. Doctor. Call me doctor."

"Yes, Doctor." She made the word sound erotic. "Kiss me once, Doctor. It's been a long time."

Having won his point, he became bland. "If you insist, Mrs. Hallman."

She moaned. I walked to the end of the veranda, feeling a little let down because Zinnie's vivacity hadn't been for me. I lit a consolatory cigarette.

At the side of the house, childish laughter bubbled. I leaned on the railing and looked around the corner. Mildred and her niece were playing a game of catch with a tennisball. At least it was catch for Mildred, when Martha threw the ball anywhere near her. Mildred rolled the ball to the child, who scampered after it like a small utility infielder in fairy blue. For the first time since I'd met her, Mildred looked relaxed.

A gray-haired woman in a flowered dress was watching them from a chaise longue in the shade. She called out:

"Martha! You mustn't get overtired. And keep your dress clean."

Mildred turned on the older woman: "Let her get dirty if she likes."

But the spell of the game was broken. Smiling a perverse little smile, the child picked up the ball and threw it over the picket fence that surrounded the lawn. It bounced out of sight among the orange trees.

The woman on the chaise longue raised her voice again:

"Now look what you've done, you naughty girl—you've gone and lost the ball."

"Naughty girl," the child repeated shrilly, and began to chant: "Martha's a naughty girl, Martha's a naughty girl."

"You're not, you're a nice girl," Mildred said. "The ball isn't lost. I'll find it."

She started for the gate in the picket fence. I opened my mouth to warn her not to go into the trees. But something was going on in the driveway behind me. Car wheels crunched in the ground, and slid to a stop. I turned and saw that it was a new lavender Cadillac with gold trim.

The man who got out of the driver's seat was wearing fuzzy tweeds. His hair and eyes had the same coloring as Carl, but he was older, fatter, shorter. Instead of hospital pallor, his face was full of angry blood.

Zinnie came out on the veranda to meet him. Unfortunately her lipstick was smeared. Her eyes looked feverish.

"Jerry, thank God you're here!" The dramatic note sounded wrong, and she lowered her voice: "I've been worried sick. Where on earth have you been all day?"

He stumped up the steps and faced her, not quite as tall as she was on her heels. "I haven't been gone all day. I drove down to see Brockley at the hospital. Somebody had to give him the bawling-out he had coming to him. I told him what I thought of the loose way they run that place."

"Was that wise, dear?"

"It was some satisfaction, anyway. These bloody doctors! They take the public's money and—" He jerked a thumb toward Grantland's car: "Speaking of doctors, what's he doing here? Is somebody sick?"

"I thought you knew, about Carl. Didn't Ostie stop you at the road?"

"I saw his car there, he wasn't in it. What about Carl?"

"He's on the ranch, carrying a gun." Zinnie saw the shock on her husband's face, and repeated: "I thought you knew. I thought that's why you were staying away, because you're afraid of Carl."

"I'm not afraid of him," he said, on a rising note.

"You were, the day he left here. And you should be, after the things he said to you." She added, with unconscious cruelty, perhaps not entirely unconscious: "I believe he wants to kill you, Jerry."

His hands clutched his stomach, as though she'd struck him a physical blow there. They doubled into fists.

"You'd like that, wouldn't you? You and Charlie Grantland?"

The screen door rattled. Grantland came out on cue. He said with false joviality: "I *thought* I heard someone taking my name in vain. How are you, Mr. Hallman?"

Jerry Hallman ignored him. He said to his wife: "I asked you a simple question. What's he doing here?"

"I'll give you a simple answer. I had no man around I could trust to take Martha into town. So I called Dr. Grantland to chauffeur her. Martha is used to him."

Grantland had come up beside her. She turned and gave him a little smile, her smudged mouth doubling its meaning. Of the three, she and Grantland formed the paired unit. Her husband was the one who stood alone. As if he couldn't bear that loneliness, he turned on his heel, walked stiffly down the veranda steps, and disappeared through the front door of the greenhouse.

Grantland took a gray handkerchief out of his breast pocket and wiped Zinnie's mouth. The center of her body swayed toward him.

"Don't," he said urgently. "He knows already. You must have told him."

"I asked him for a divorce—you know that—and he's not a complete fool. Anyway, what does it matter?" She had the false assurance, or abandon, of a woman who has made a sexual commitment and swung her whole life from it like a trapeze. "Maybe Carl will kill him."

"Be quiet, Zin! Don't even think it—!"

His voice broke off. Her gaze had moved across me as he spoke, and telegraphed my presence to him. He turned on his toes like a dancer. The blood seeped out from underneath his tan. He might have been a beady-eyed old man with jaundice. Then he pulled himself together and smiled—a downward-turning smile but a confident one. It was unsettling to see a man's face change so rapidly and radically.

I threw away the butt of my cigarette, which seemed to have lasted for a long time, and smiled back at him. Felt from inside, like a rubber Halloween mask, my smile was a stiff grimace. Jerry Hallman relieved my embarrassment, if that is what I was feeling. He came hustling out of the greenhouse with a pair of shears in his hand, a dull blotched look on his face.

Zinnie saw him, and backed against the wall. "Charlie! Look out!"

Grantland turned to face Jerry as he came up the steps, a dumpy middle-aging man who couldn't stand loneliness. His eyes had a very solitary expression. The shears projected outward from the grip of his two hands, gleaming in the sun, like a double dagger.

"Yah, Charlie!" he said. "Look out! You think you can get away with my wife and my daughter both. You're taking nothing of mine."

"I had no such intention." Grantland stuttered over the words. "Mrs. Hallman telephoned—"

"Don't 'Mrs. Hallman' me. You don't call her that in town. Do you?" Standing at the top of the steps with his legs planted wide apart, Jerry Hallman opened and closed the shears. "Get out of here, you lousy cod. If you want to go on being a man, get off my property and stay off my property. That includes my wife."

Grantland had put on his old-man face. He backed away from the threatening edges and looked for support to Zinnie. Green-faced in the shadow, she stood still as a bas-relief against the wall. Her mouth worked, and managed to say:

"Stop it, Jerry. You're not making sense."

Jerry Hallman was at that trembling balance point in human rage where he might have alarmed himself into doing murder. It was time for someone to stop it. Shouldering Grantland out of my way, I walked up to Hallman and told him to put the shears down.

"Who do you think you're talking to?" he sputtered.

"You're Mr. Jerry Hallman, aren't you? I heard you were a smart man, Mr. Hallman."

He looked at me stubbornly. The whites of his eyes were yellowish from some internal complaint, bad digestion or bad conscience. Something deep in his head looked out through his eyes at me, gradually coming forward into light. Fear and shame, perhaps. His eyes seemed to be puzzled by dry pain. He turned and went down the steps and into the greenhouse, slamming the door behind him. Nobody followed him.

chapter 11

VOICES rose on the far side of the house, as if another door had opened there. Female and excited, they sounded like chickens after a hawk has swooped. I ran down the steps and around the end of the veranda. Mildred came across the lawn toward me, holding the little girl's hand. Mrs. Hutchinson trailed behind them, her head turned at an angle toward the groves, her face as gray as her hair. The gate in the picket fence was open, but there was no one else in sight.

The child's voice rose high and penetrating. "Why did Uncle Carl run away?"

Mildred turned and bent over her. "It doesn't matter why. He likes to run."

"Is he mad at you, Aunt Mildred?"

"Not really, darling. He's just playing a game."

Mildred looked up and saw me. She shook her head curtly: I wasn't to say anything to frighten the child. Zinnie swept past me and lifted Martha in her arms. The deputy Carmichael was close behind her, unhitching his gun.

"What happened, Mrs. Hallman? Did you see him?"

She nodded, but waited to speak till Zinnie had carried the little girl out of hearing. Mildred's forehead was bright with sweat, and she was breathing rapidly. I noticed that she had the ball in her hand.

The gray-haired woman elbowed her way into the group. "I saw him, sneaking under the trees. Martha saw him, too."

Mildred turned on her. "He wasn't sneaking, Mrs. Hutchinson. He picked up the ball and brought it to me. He came right up to me." She displayed the ball, as if it was important evidence of her husband's gentleness.

Mrs. Hutchinson said: "I was never so terrified in my born days. I couldn't even open my mouth to let out a scream."

The deputy was getting impatient. "Hold it, ladies. I want a straight story, and fast. Did he threaten you, Mrs. Hallman—attack you in any way?"

"No."

"Did he say anything?"

"I did most of the talking. I tried to persuade Carl to come in and give himself up. When he wouldn't, I put my arms around him, to try and hold him. He was too strong for me. He broke away, and I ran after him. He wouldn't come back."

"Did he show his gun?"

"No." She looked down at Carmichael's gun. "Please, don't use your gun if you see my husband. I don't believe he's armed."

"Maybe not," Carmichael said noncommittally. "Where did all this happen?"

"I'll show you."

She turned and started toward the open gate, moving with a kind of dogged gallantry. It wasn't quite enough to hold her up. Suddenly she went to her knees and crumped sideways on the lawn, a small dark-suited figure with spilled brown hair. The ball rolled out of her hand. Carmichael knelt beside her, shouting as if mere loudness could make her answer:

"Which way did he go?"

Mrs. Hutchinson waved her arm toward the groves. "Right through there, in the direction of town."

The young deputy got up and ran through the gateway in the picket fence. I ran after him, with some idea of trying to head off violence. The ground under the trees was adobe, soft and moist with cultivation. I never had gone well on a heavy track. The deputy was out of sight. After a while he was out of hearing, too. I slowed down and stopped, cursing my obsolescent legs.

It was purely a personal matter between me and my legs, because running couldn't accomplish anything, anyway. When I thought about it, I realized that a man who knew the country could hide for days on the great ranch. It would take hundreds of searchers to beat him out of the groves and canyons and creekbeds.

I went back the way I had come, following my own footmarks. Five of my walking steps, if I stretched my legs, equaled three of my running steps. I crossed other people's tracks, but had no way to identify them. Tracking wasn't my forte, except on asphalt.

65

After a long morning crowded with people under pressure, it was pleasant to be walking by myself in the green shade. Over my head, between the tops of the trees, a trickle of blue sky meandered. I let myself believe that there was no need to hurry, that trouble had been averted for the present. Carl had done no harm to anybody, after all.

Back-tracking on the morning, I walked slower and slower. Brockley would probably say that it was unconscious drag, that I didn't want to get back to the house. There seemed to be some truth in Mildred's idea that a house could make people hate each other. A house, or the money it stood for, or the cannibalistic family hungers it symbolized.

I'd run further than I'd realized, perhaps a third of a mile. Eventually the house loomed up through the trees. The yard was empty. Everything was remarkably still. One of the french doors was standing open. I went in. The dining-room had a curious atmosphere, unlived in and unlivable, like one of those three-walled rooms laid out in a museum behind silk rope: Provincial California Spanish, Pre-Atomic Era. The living-room, with its magazines and dirty glasses and Hollywood-Cubist furniture, had the same deserted quality.

I crossed the hallway and opened the door of a study lined with books and filing cabinets. The venetian blinds were drawn. The room had a musty smell. A dark oil portrait of a bald old man hung on one wall. His eyes peered through the dimness at me, out of a lean rapacious face. Senator Hallman, I presumed. I closed the study door on him.

I went through the house from front to back, and finally found two human beings in the kitchen. Mrs. Hutchinson was sitting at the kitchen table, with Martha on her knee.

The elderly woman started at my voice. Her face had sharpened in the quarter-hour since I'd seen her. Her eyes were bleak and accusing.

"What happened next?" Martha said.

"Well, the little girl went to the nice old lady's house, and they had tea-cakes." Mrs. Hutchinson's eyes stayed on me, daring me to speak. "Tea-cakes and chocolate ice cream, and the old lady read the little girl a story."

"What was the little girl's name?"

"Martha, just like yours."

"She couldn't eat chocolate ice cream, 'cause of her algery."

"They had vanilla. We'll have vanilla, too, with strawberry jam on top."

"Is Mummy coming?"

"Not right away. She'll be coming later."

"Is Daddy coming? I don't want Daddy to come."

"Daddy won't—" Mrs. Hutchinson's voice broke off. "That's the end of the story, dear."

"I want another story."

"We don't have time." She set the child down. "Now run into the living-room and play."

"I want to go into the greenhouse." Martha ran to an inner door, and rattled the knob.

"No! Stay here! Come back here!"

Frightened by the woman's tone, Martha returned, dragging her feet.

"What's the matter?" I said, though I thought I knew. "Where is everybody?"

Mrs. Hutchinson gestured toward the door that Martha had tried to open. I heard a murmur of voices beyond it, like bees behind a wall. Mrs. Hutchinson rose heavily and beckoned me to her. Conscious of the child's unwavering gaze, I leaned close to the woman's mouth. She said:

"Mr. Hallman was ess aitch oh tee. He's dee ee ay dee."

"Don't spell! You mustn't spell!"

In a miniature fury, the child flung herself between us and struck the old woman on the hip. Mrs. Hutchinson drew her close. The child stood still with her face in the flowered lap, her tiny white arms embracing the twin pillars of the woman's legs.

I left them and went through the inner door. An unlit passageway lined with shelves ended in a flight of steps. I stumbled down them to a second door, which I opened.

The edge of the door struck softly against a pair of hind quarters. These happened to belong to Sheriff Ostervelt. He let out a little snort of angry surprise, and turned on me, his hand on his gun.

"Where do you think you're going?"

"Coming in."

"You're not invited. This is an official investigation."

I looked past him into the greenhouse. In the central aisle, between rows of massed cymbidiums, Mildred and Zinnie and Grantland were grouped around a body which lay face up. The face had been covered by a gray silk handkerchief, but I knew whose body it was. Jerry's fuzzy tweeds, his rotundity, his helplessness, gave him the air of a defunct teddy bear.

Zinnie stood above him, incongruously robed in ruffled white nylon. Without makeup, her face was almost as colorless as the robe. Mildred stood near her, looking down at the dirt floor. A little apart, Dr. Grantland leaned on one of the planters, controlled and watchful.

Zinnie's face worked stiffly: "Let him come in if he wants to, Ostie. We can probably use all the help we can get."

Ostervelt did as she said. He was almost meek about it. Which reminded me of the simple fact that Zinnie had just fallen heir to the Hallman ranch and whatever power went with it. Grantland didn't seem to need reminding. He leaned close to whisper in her ear, with something proprietory in the angle of his head.

She silenced him with a sidewise warning glance, and edged away from him. Acting on impulse—at least it looked like impulse from where I stood—Zinnie put her arm around Mildred and hugged her. Mildred made as if to pull away, then leaned on Zinnie and closed her eyes. Through the white-painted glass roof, daylight fell harsh and depthless on their faces, sistered by shock.

Ostervelt missed these things, which happened in a moment. He was fiddling with the lid of a steel box that stood on a workbench behind the door. Getting it open, he lifted out a piece of shingle to which a small gun was tied with twine.

"Okay, so you want to be a help. Take a look at this."

It was a small, short-barreled revolver, of about .25 caliber, probably of European make. The butt was sheathed in mother-of-pearl, and ornamented with silver filagree work. A woman's gun, not new: the silver was tarnished. I'd never seen it, or a gun like it, and I said so.

"Mrs. Hallman, Mrs. *Carl* Hallman, said you had some trouble with her husband this morning. He stole your car, is that right?"

"Yes, he took it."

"Under what circumstances?"

"I was driving him back to the hospital. He came to my house early this morning, with some idea I might be able to help him. I figured the best thing I could do for him was talk him into going back in. It didn't quite work."

"What happened?"

"He took me by surprise—overpowered me."

"What do you know?" Ostervelt smirked. "Did he pull this little gun on you?"

"No. He had no gun that I saw. I take it this is the gun that killed Hallman."

"You take it correct, mister. This is also the gun the brother had, according to Yogan's description of it. The doctor found it right beside the body. Two shells fired, two holes in the man's back. The doctor said he died instantly, that right, Doctor?"

"Within a few seconds, I'd say." Grantland was cool and professional. "There was no external bleeding. My guess is that one of the bullets pierced his heart. Of course it will take an autopsy to establish the exact cause of death."

"Did you discover the body, Doctor?"

"I did, as a matter of fact."

"I'm interested in matters of fact. What brought you out to the greenhouse?"

"The shots, of course."

"You heard them?"

"Very clearly. I was taking Martha's clothes out to the car."

Zinnie said wearily: "We all heard them. I thought at first that Jerry—" She broke off.

"Jerry what?" Ostervelt said.

"Nothing. Ostie? Do we have to go through this again—all this palaver? I'm very anxious to get Martha out of the house. God knows what this is doing to her. And wouldn't you accomplish more if you went out after Carl?"

"I got every free man in the department looking for him now. I can't leave until the deputy coroner gets here."

"Does that mean we have to wait?"

"Not right here, if it's getting you down. I think you ought to stick around the house, though."

"I've told you all I can," Grantland said. "And I have patients waiting. In addition to which, Mrs. Hallman has asked me to drive her daughter and her housekeeper into Purissima."

"All right. Go ahead, Doctor. Thanks for your help."

Grantland went out the back door. The two women came down the funereal aisle between the rows of flowers, bronze and green and blood-red. They walked with their arms around each other, and passed through the door that led toward the kitchen. Before the door closed, one of them broke into a storm of weeping.

The noise of grief is impersonal, and I couldn't be sure which one of them it was. But I thought it must have been Mildred. Her loss was the worst. It had been going on for a long time, and was continuing.

chapter 12

THE back door of the greenhouse opened, and two men came in. One was the eager young deputy who excelled at cross-country running. Carmichael's blouse was dark with sweat, and he was still breathing deeply. The other man was a Japanese of indeterminate age. When he saw the dead man on the floor, he stood still, with his head bowed, and took off his soiled cloth hat. His sparse gray hair stood erect on his scalp, like magnetized iron filings.

The deputy squatted and lifted the gray handkerchief over the dead man's face. His held breath came out.

"Take a good long look, Carmichael," the sheriff said. "You were supposed to be guarding this house and the people in it."

Carmichael stood up, his mouth tight. "I did my best."

"Then I'd hate to see your worst. Where in Christ's name did you go?"

"I went after Carl Hallman, lost him in the groves. He must of circled around and come back here. I ran into Sam Yogan back of the bunkhouse, and he told me he heard some shots."

"You heard the shots?"

The Japanese bobbed his head. "Yessir. Two shots." He had a mouthy old-country accent, and some trouble with his esses.

"Where were you when you heard them?"

"In the bunkhouse."

"Can you see the greenhouse from there?"

"Back door, you can."

"He must of left by the back door, Grantland was at the front, and the women came in the side here. You see him, going or coming?"

"Mr. Carl?"

"You know I mean him. Did you see him?"

"No sir. Nobody."

"Did you look?"

"Yessir. I looked out the door of the bunkhouse."

"But you didn't come and look in the greenhouse."

"No sir."

"Why?" The sheriff's anger, flaring and veering like fire in the wind, was turned on Yogan now. "Your boss was lying shot in here, and you didn't move a muscle."

"I looked out the door."

"But you didn't move a muscle to help him, or apprehend the killer."

"He was probably scared," Carmichael said. With the heat removed from him, he was relaxing into camaraderie.

Yogan gave the deputy a look of calm disdain. He extended his hands in front of his body, parallel and close together, as though he was measuring off the limits of his knowledge:

"I hear two guns—two shots. What does it mean? I see guns all morning. Shooting quail, maybe?"

"All right," the sheriff said heavily. "Let's get back to this morning. You told me Mr. Carl was a very good friend of yours, and that was the reason you weren't scared of him. Is that correct, Sam?"

"I guess so. Yessir."

"How good a friend, Sam? Would you let him shoot his brother and get away? Is that how good a friend?"

Yogan showed his front teeth in a smile which could have meant anything. His flat black eyes were opaque.

"Answer me, Sam."

Yogan said without altering his smile: "Very good friend."

"And Mr. Jerry? Was he a good friend?"

"Very good friend."

"Come off it, Sam. You don't like any of us, do you?"

Yogan grinned implacably, like a yellow skull.

Ostervelt raised his voice:

"Wipe the smile off, tombstone-teeth. You're not fooling anybody. You don't like me, and you don't like the Hallman family. Why the hell you came back here, I'll never know."

"I like the country," Sam Yogan said.

"Oh sure, you like the country. Did you think you could con the Senator into giving you your farm back?"

The old man didn't answer. He looked a little ashamed, not for himself. I gathered that he had been one of the Japanese farmers bought out by the Senator and relocated during the war. I gathered further that he made Ostervelt nervous, as though his presence was an accusation. An accusation which had to be reversed:

"You didn't shoot Mr. Jerry Hallman yourself, by any chance?"

Yogan's smile brightened into scorn.

Ostervelt moved to the workbench and picked up the shingle with the pearl-handled gun attached to it. "Come here, Sam."

Yogan stayed immobile.

"Come here, I said. I won't hurt you. I ought to kick those big white teeth down your dirty yellow throat, but I'm not gonna. Come here."

"You heard the sheriff," Carmichael said, and gave the small man a push.

Yogan came one step forward, and stood still. By sheer patience, his slight figure had become the central object in the room. Having nothing better to do, I went and stood beside him. He smelled faintly of fish and earth. After a while the sheriff came to him.

"Is this the gun, Sam?"

Yogan drew in his breath in a little hiss of surprise. He took the shingle and examined the gun minutely, from several angles.

"You don't have to eat it." Ostervelt snatched it away. "Is this the gun Mr. Carl had?"

"Yessir. I think so."

"Did he pull it on you? Threaten you with it?"

"No sir."

"Then how'd you happen to see it?"

"Mr. Carl showed it to me."

"He just walked up to you and showed you the gun?"

"Yessir."

"Did he say anything?"

"Yessir. He said, hello Sam, how are you, nice to see you. Very polite. Also, where is my brother? I said he went to town."

"Anything about the gun, I mean."

"Said did I recognize it. I said, yes."

"You recognized it?"

"Yessir. It was Mrs. Hallman's gun."

"Which Mrs. Hallman?"

"Old lady Mrs. Hallman, Senator's wife."

"This gun belonged to her?"

"Yessir. She used to bring it out to the back garden, shoot at the blackbirds. I said she wanted a better one, a shotgun. No, she said, she didn't want to hit them. Let them live."

"That must of been a long time ago."

"Yessir, ten-twelve years. When I came back here on the ranch, put in her garden for her."

"What happened to the gun?"

"I dunno."

"Did Carl tell you how *he* got it?"

"No sir. I didn't ask."

"You're a close-mouthed s.o.b., Sam. You know what that means?"

"Yessir."

"Why didn't you tell me all this this morning?"

"You didn't ask me."

The sheriff looked up at the glass roof, as if to ask for comfort and help in his deep tribulations. The only apparent result was the arrival of a moon-faced young man wearing shiny rimless spectacles and a shiny blue suit. I needed no intuition to tab him as the deputy coroner. He carried a black medical bag, and the wary good humor of men whose calling is death.

Surveying the situation from the doorway, he raised his hand to the sheriff and made a beeline for the body. A sheriff's captain with a tripod camera followed close on his heels. The sheriff joined them, issuing a steady flux of orders.

Sam Yogan bowed slightly to me, his forehead corrugated, his eyes bland. He picked up a watering can, filled it at a tin sink in the corner, and moved with it among the cymbidiums. Disregarding the flashbulbs, he was remote as a gardener bent in ritual over flowers in a print.

chapter 13

I WALKED around to the front of the house and rapped on the screen door. Zinnie answered. She had changed to a black dress without ornament of any kind. Framed in the doorway, she looked like a posed portrait of a young widow, carefully painted in two dimensions. The third dimension was in her eyes, which had green fire in their depths.

"Are you still here?"

"I seem to be."

"Come in if you like."

I followed her into the living-room, noticing how corseted her movements had become. The room had altered, too, though there was no change in its physical arrangement. The murder in the greenhouse had killed something in the house. The bright furnishings looked cheap and out of place in the old room, as if somebody had tried to set up modern housekeeping in an ancestral cave.

"Sit down if you like."

"Am I wearing out my welcome?"

"Everybody is," she said, a little obscurely. "I don't even feel at home here myself. Come to think of it, maybe I never did. Well, it's a little late to go into that now."

"Or a little early. No doubt you'll be selling."

"Jerry was planning to sell out himself. The papers are practically all drawn up."

"That makes it convenient."

Facing me in front of the dead hearth, she looked into my eyes for a long minute. Being a two-way experience, it wasn't unpleasant at all. The pain she'd just been through, or something else, had wiped out a certain crudity in her good looks and left them pretty dazzling. I hoped it wasn't the thought of a lot of new money shining in her head.

"You don't like me," she said.

"I hardly know you."

"Don't worry, you never will."

"There goes another bubble, iridescent but ephemeral."

"I don't think I like you, either. That's quite a spiel you have, for a cheap private detective. Where do you come from, Los Angeles?"

"Yep. How do you know I'm cheap?"

"Mildred couldn't afford you if you weren't."

"Unlike you, eh? I could raise my prices."

"I bet you could. And I was wondering when we were going to get around to that. It didn't take long, did it?"

"Get around to what?"

"What everybody wants. Money. The *other* thing that everybody wants." She turned, handling her body contemptuously and provocatively, identifying the first thing. "You might as well sit down and we'll talk about it."

"It will be a pleasure."

I sat on the end of a white *bouclé* oblong, and she perched tightly on the other end, with her beautiful legs crossed in front of her. "What I ought to do is tell Ostie to throw you the hell out of here."

"For any particular reason. Or just on general principles?"

"For attempted blackmail. Isn't blackmail the idea?"

"It never crossed my mind. Until now."

"Don't kid me. I know your type. Maybe you like to wrap it up in different words. I pay you a retainer to protect my interests or something like that. It's still blackmail, no matter how you wrap it."

"Or baloney, no matter how you slice it. But go on. It's a long time since anybody offered me some free money. Or is this only a daydream?"

She sneered, not very sophisticatedly. "How dare you try to be funny, with my husband not yet cold in his grave?"

"He isn't in it yet. And you can do better than that, Zinnie. Try another take."

"Have you no respect for a woman's emotions—no respect for anything?"

"Show me some real ones. You have them."

"What do you know about it?"

"I'd have to be blind and deaf not to. You go around shooting them off like fireworks."

She was silent. Her face was unnaturally calm, except for the deep dimension of the eyes. "You mean that scene on the front porch, no doubt. It didn't mean a thing. Not a thing." She sounded like a child repeating a lesson. "I was frightened and upset, and Dr. Grantland is an old friend of the family. Naturally I turned to him in trouble. You'd think even Jerry would understand that. But he's always been irrationally jealous. I can't even look at a man."

She sneaked a look at me to see if I believed her. Our eyes met.

"You can now."

"I tell you I'm not in the least interested in Dr. Grantland. Or anybody else."

"You're young to retire."

Her eyes narrowed rather prettily, like a cat's. Like a

cat, she was kind of smart, but too self-centered to be really smart. "You're terribly cynical, aren't you? I hate cynical men."

"Let's stop playing games, Zinnie. You're crazy about Grantland. He's crazy about you. I hope."

"What do you mean, you hope?" she said, laying my last doubt to rest.

"I hope Charlie is crazy about you."

"He is. I mean, he would be, if I let him. What makes you think he isn't?"

"What makes you think it?"

She put her hands over her ears and made a monkey face. Even then, she couldn't look ugly. She had such good bones, her skeleton would have been an ornament in any closet.

"All this talky-talk," she said. "I get mixed up. Could we come down to cases? That business on the porch, I know it looks bad. I don't know how much you heard?"

I put on my omniscient expression. She was still coming to me, pressed by a fear that made her indiscreet.

"Whatever you heard, it doesn't mean I'm glad that Jerry is dead. I'm sorry he's dead." She sounded surprised. "I felt *sorry* for the poor guy when he was lying there. It wasn't his fault he didn't have it—that we couldn't make it together— Anyway, I had nothing to do with his death, and neither did Charlie."

"Who said you did?"

"Some people would say it, if they knew about that silly fuss on the porch. Mildred might."

"Where is Mildred now, by the way?"

"Lying down. I talked her into taking some rest before she goes back to town. She's emotionally exhausted."

"That was nice of you."

"Oh, I'm not a total all-round bitch. And I don't blame her for what her husband did."

"*If* he did." With nothing much to go on, I threw that in to test her reaction.

She took it personally, almost as an insult. "Is there any doubt he did it?"

"There always is, until it's proved in court."

"But he hated Jerry. He had the gun. He came here to kill Jerry, and we know he was here."

"We know he was here, all right. Maybe he still is. The rest is your version. I'd kind of like to hear his, before we find him guilty and execute him on the spot."

"Who said anything about executing him? They don't execute crazy people."

"They do, though. More than half the people who go to the gas-chamber in this state are mentally disturbed—medically insane, if not legally."

"But they'd never convict Carl. Look what happened last time."

"What did happen last time?"

She put the back of her hand to her mouth and looked at me over it.

"You mean the Senator's death, don't you?" I was frankly fishing, fishing in the deep green of her eyes.

She couldn't resist the dramatic thing. "I mean the Senator's murder. Carl murdered him. Everybody knows it, and they didn't do a thing to him except send him away."

"The way I heard it, it was an accident."

"You heard it wrong then. Carl pushed him down in the bathtub and held him until he drowned."

"How do you know?"

"He confessed the very next day."

"To you?"

"To Sheriff Ostervelt."

"Ostervelt told you this?"

"Jerry told me. He talked the sheriff out of laying charges. He wanted to protect the family name."

"Is that all he was trying to protect?"

"I don't know what you mean by that. Why did Mildred bring you out here, anyway?"

"For the ride. My main idea was to get my car back."

"When you get it, will you be satisfied?"

"I doubt it. I've never been yet."

"You mean you're going to poke around and twist the facts and try to prove that Carl didn't do—what he did do?"

"I'm interested in facts, as I told Dr. Grantland."

"What's he got to do with it?"

"I'd like an answer to that. Maybe you can tell me."

"I know he didn't shoot Jerry. The idea is ridiculous."

"Perhaps. It was your idea. But let's kick it around a little. If Yogan's telling the truth, Carl had the pearl-handled gun, or one like it. We don't know for certain that it killed your husband. We won't until we get ballistic evidence."

"But Charlie found it in the greenhouse, right beside the—poor Jerry."

"Charlie could have planted it. Or he could have fired it himself. That would make it easy for him to find."

"You're making this up."

But she was frightened. She didn't seem to know for sure that it hadn't happened that way.

"Did Ostervelt show you the gun?"

"I saw it."

"Did you ever see it before?"

"No." Her answer was emphatic and quick.

"Did you know it belonged to your mother-in-law?"

"No." But Zinnie asked no questions, showed no surprise, and took my word for it.

"Did you know she had a gun?"

"No. Yes. I guess I did. But I never saw it."

"I heard your mother-in-law committed suicide. Is that right?"

"Yes. Poor Alicia walked into the ocean, about three years ago."

"Why would she commit suicide?"

"Alicia had had a lot of illness."

"Mental?"

"I suppose you'd call it that. The menopause hit her very hard. She never came back, entirely. She was practically a hermit the last few years. She lived in the east wing by herself, with Mrs. Hutchinson to look after her. These things seem to run in the family."

"Something does. Do you know what happened to her gun?"

"Evidently Carl got hold of it, some way. Maybe she gave it to him before she died."

"And he's been carrying it all these years?"

"He could have hid it right here on the ranch. Why ask me? I don't know anything about it."

"Or who fired it in the greenhouse?"

"You know what I think about that. What I *know*."

"I believe you said you heard the shots."

"Yes. I heard them."

"Where were you, at the time?"

"In my bathroom. I'd just finished taking a shower." With never-say-die eroticism, she tried to set up a diversion: "If you want proof of that, examine me. I'm clean."

"Some other time. Stay clean till then. Is that the same bathroom your father-in-law was murdered in?"

"No. He had his own bathroom, opening off his bedroom. I wish you wouldn't use that word murder. I didn't mean to tell you that. I said it in confidence."

"I didn't realize that. Would you mind showing me that bathroom? I'd like to see how it was done."

"I don't know how it was done."

"You did a minute ago."

Zinnie took time out to think. Thinking seemed to come hard to her. "I only know what people tell me," she said.

"Who told you that Carl pushed his father down in the bathtub?"

"Charlie did, and he ought to know. He was the old man's doctor."

"Did he examine him after death?"

"Yes, he did."

"Then he must have known that the Senator didn't die of a heart attack."

"I told you that. Carl killed him."

"And Grantland knew it?"

"Of course."

"You realize what you've just said, Mrs. Hallman? Your good friends Sheriff Ostervelt and Dr. Grantland conspired to cover up a murder."

"No!" She flung the thought away from her with both hands. "I didn't mean it that way."

"How did you mean it?"

"I don't really know anything about it. I was lying."

"But now you're telling the truth."

"You've got me all twisted up. Forget what I said, eh?"

"How can I?"

"What are you looking for? Money? You want a new car?"

"I'm sort of attached to the old one. We'll get along better if you stop assuming I can be bought. It's been tried by experts."

She rose and stood over me, looking down in mingled fear and hatred. Making a great convulsive effort, she swallowed both. In the same effort, she changed her approach, and practically changed her personality. Her shoulders and breasts slumped, her belly arched forward, one of her hips tilted up. Even her eyes took on a melting-iceberg look.

"We *could* get along, quite nicely."

"Could we?"

"You wouldn't want to make trouble for little old me. Why don't you make us a shakerful of Gibsons instead? We'll talk it over?"

"Charlie wouldn't like it. And your husband's not yet cold in his grave, remember?"

There was a greenhouse smell in the room, the smell of flowers and earth and trapped heat. I got up facing her. She placed her hands on my shoulders and let her body come forward until it rested lightly against me. It moved in small intricate ways.

"Come on. What's the matter? Are you scared? I'm not. And I'm very good at it, even if I am out of practice."

In a way, I was scared. She was a hard blonde beauty fighting the world with two weapons, money and sex. Both of them had turned in her hands and scarred her. The scars were invisible, but I could sense the dead tissue. I wanted no part of her.

She exploded against me hissing like an angry cat, fled across the room to one of the deep windows. Her clenched hand jerked spasmodically at the curtains, like somebody signaling a train to stop.

Footsteps whispered on the floor behind me. It was Mildred, small and waiflike in her stocking feet.

"What on earth's the matter?"

Zinnie glared at her across the room. Except for her thin red lips and narrow green eyes, her face was carved from chalk. In one of those instinctive female shifts that are always at least partly real, Zinnie released her fury on her sister-in-law:

"So there you are—spying on me again. I'm sick of your

spying, talking behind my back, throwing mud at Charlie Grantland, just because you wanted him yourself—"

"That's nonsense," Mildred said in a low voice. "I've never spied on you. As for Dr. Grantland, I barely know him."

"No, but you'd like to, wouldn't you? Only you know that you can't have him. So you'd like to see him destroyed, wouldn't you? You hired this man to ruin him."

"I did no such thing. You're upset, Zinnie. *You* should lie down and have a rest."

"I should, eh? So you can carry on your machinations without any interference?"

Zinnie crossed the room in an unsteady rush. I stayed between her and Mildred.

"Mildred didn't hire me," I said. "I have no instructions from her. You're away off the beam, Mrs. Hallman."

"You lie!" She screamed across me at Mildred: "You dirty little sneak, you can get out of my house. Keep your maniac husband away from here or by God I'll have him shot down. Take your bully-boy along with you. Go on, get out, both of you."

"I'll be glad to."

Mildred turned to the door in weary resignation, and I went out after her. I hadn't expected the armistice to last.

chapter 14

I WAITED for Mildred on the front veranda. There were several more cars in the driveway. One of them was my Ford convertible, gray with dust but looking none the worse for wear. It was parked behind a black panel truck with county markings.

A deputy I hadn't seen before was in the front seat of another county car, monitoring a turned-up radio. The rest of the sheriff's men were still in the greenhouse. Their shadows moved on its translucent walls.

"Attention all units," the huge voice of the radio said. "Be on the lookout for following subject wanted as suspect in murder which occurred at Hallman ranch in Buena Vista Valley approximately one hour ago: Carl Hallman, white, male, twenty-four, six-foot-three, two hundred pounds, blond hair, blue eyes, pale complexion, wearing blue cotton workshirt and trousers. Suspect may be armed and is considered dangerous. When last seen he was traveling across country on foot."

Mildred came out, freshly groomed and looking fairly brisk in spite of her wilted-violet eyes. Her head moved in a small gesture of relief as the screen door slammed behind her.

"Where do you plan to go?" I asked her.

"Home. It's too late to think of going back to work. I have to see to Mother, anyway."

"Your husband may turn up there. Have you thought of that possibility?"

"Naturally. I hope he does."

"If he does, will you let me know?"

She gave me a clear cold look. "That depends."

"I know what you mean. Maybe I better make it plain that I'm in your husband's corner. I'd like to get to him before the sheriff does. Ostervelt seems to have his mind made up about this case. I haven't. I think there should be further investigation."

"You want me to pay you, is that it?"

"Forget about that for now. Let's say I like the old-fashioned idea of presumption of innocence."

She took a step toward me, her eyes brightening. Her hand rested lightly on my arm. "You don't believe he shot Jerry, either."

"I don't want to build up your hopes with nothing much to go on. I'm keeping an open mind until we have more information. You heard the shots that killed Jerry?"

"Yes."

"Where were you at the time? And where were the others?"

"I don't know about the others. I was with Martha on the other side of the house. The child seemed to sense what had happened, and I had a hard time calming her. I didn't notice what other people were doing."

"Was Ostervelt anywhere around the house?"

"I didn't see him if he was."

"Was Carl?"

"The last I saw of Carl was in the grove there."

"Which way did he go when he left you?"

"Toward town, at least in that general direction."

"What was his attitude when you talked to him?"

"He was upset. I begged him to turn himself in, but he seemed frightened."

"Emotionally disturbed?"

"It's hard to say. I've seen him much worse."

"Did he show any signs of being dangerous?"

"Certainly not to me. He never has. He was a little rough when I tried to hold him, that's all."

"Has he often been violent?"

"No. I didn't say he was violent. He simply didn't want to be held. He pushed me away from him."

"Did he say why?"

"He said something about following his own road. I didn't have time to ask him what he meant."

"Do you have any idea what he meant?"

"No." But her eyes were wide and dark with possibility.

"I'm certain, though, he didn't mean anything like shooting his brother."

"There's another question that needs answering," I said. "I hate to throw it at you now."

She squared her slender shoulders. "Go ahead. I'll answer it if I can."

"I've been told your husband killed his father. Deliberately drowned him in the bathtub. Have you heard that?"

"Yes. I've heard that."

"From Carl?"

"Not from him, no."

"Do you believe it?"

She took a long time to answer. "I don't know. It was just after Carl was hospitalized—the same day. When a tragedy cuts across your life like that, you don't know what to believe. The world actually seemed to fly apart. I could recognize the pieces, but all the patterns were unfamiliar, the meanings were different. They still are. It's an awful thing for a human being to admit, but I don't know *what* I believe. I'm waiting. I've been waiting for six months to find out where I stand in the world, what sort of a life I can count on."

"You haven't really answered my question."

"I would if I could. I've been trying to explain why I can't. The circumstances were so queer, and awful." The thought of them, whatever they were, pinched her face like cold.

"Who told you about this alleged confession?"

"Sheriff Ostervelt did. I thought at the time he was lying, for reasons of his own. Perhaps I was rationalizing, simply because I couldn't face the truth—I don't know."

Before she trailed off into further self-doubts, I said: "What reasons would he have for lying to you?"

"I can tell you one. It isn't very modest to say it, but he's been interested in me for quite a long time. He was always hanging around the ranch, theoretically to see the Senator, but looking for excuses to talk to me. I knew what he wanted; he was about as subtle as an old boar. The day we took Carl to the hospital, Ostervelt made it very clear, and very ugly." She shut her eyes for a second. A faint dew had gathered on her eyelids, and at her temples. "So ugly that I'm afraid I can't talk about it."

"I get the general idea."

But she went on, in a chilly trance of memory which seemed to negate the place and time: "He was to drive Carl to the hospital that morning, and naturally I wanted to go along. I wanted to be with Carl until the last possible minute before the doors closed on him. You don't know how a woman feels when her husband's being taken away like that, perhaps forever. I was afraid it was forever. Carl didn't say a word on the way. For days before he'd been talking constantly, about everything under the sun—the plans he had for the ranch, our life together, philosophy, social justice, and the brotherhood of man. Suddenly it was all over. Everything was over. He sat in the car, between me and the sheriff, as still as a dead man.

"He didn't even kiss me good-by at the admissions door. I'll never forget what he did do. There was a little tree growing beside the steps. Carl picked one of the leaves and folded it in his hand and carried it into the hospital with him.

"I didn't go in. I couldn't bear to, that day, though I've been there often enough since. I waited outside in the sheriff's car. I remember thinking that this was the end of the line, that nothing worse could ever happen to me. I was wrong.

"On the way back, Ostervelt began to act as if he owned me. I didn't give him any encouragement; I never had. In fact, I told him what I thought of him.

"It was then he got really nasty. He told me I'd better be

careful what I said. That Carl had confessed the murder of his father, and he was the only one who knew. He'd keep it quiet if I'd be nice to him. Otherwise there'd be a trial, he said. Even if Carl wasn't convicted we'd be given the kind of publicity that people can't live through." Her voice sank despairingly. "The kind of publicity we're going to have to live through now."

Mildred turned and looked out across the green country as if it were a wasteland. She said, with her face averted:

"I didn't give in to him. But I was afraid to reject him as flatly as he deserved. I put him off with some sort of a vague promise, that we might get together sometime in the future. I haven't kept the promise, needless to say, and I never will." She said it calmly enough, but her shoulders were trembling. I could see the rim of one of her ears, between silky strands of hair. It was red with shame or anger. "The horrible old man hasn't forgiven me for that. I've lived in fear for the last six months, that he'd take action against Carl—drag him back to stand trial."

"He didn't, though," I said, "which means that the confession was probably a phony. Tell me one thing, could it have happened the way Ostervelt claimed? I mean, did your husband have the opportunity?"

"I'm afraid the answer is yes. He was roaming around the house most of the night, after the quarrel with his father. I couldn't keep him in bed."

"Did you ask him about it afterwards?"

"At the hospital? No, I didn't. They warned me not to bring up disturbing subjects. And I was glad enough to let sleeping dogs lie. If it was true, I felt better not knowing than knowing. There's a limit to what a person can bear to know."

She shuddered, in the chill of memory.

The front door of the greenhouse was flung open suddenly. Carmichael backed out, bent over the handles of a covered stretcher. Under the cover, the dead man huddled lumpily. The other end of the stretcher was supported by the deputy coroner. They moved awkwardly along the flagstone path toward the black panel truck. Against the sweep of the valley and the mountains standing like monuments in the sunlight, the two upright men and the prostrate man seemed equally small and transitory. The living men hoisted the dead man into the back of the truck and slammed the double doors. Mildred jumped at the noise.

"I'm terribly edgy, I'd better get out of here. I shouldn't have gone into—all that. You're the only person I've ever told."

"It's safe with me."

"Thank you. For everything, I mean. You're the only one who's given me a ray of hope."

She raised her hand in good-by and went down the steps into sunlight which gilded her head. Ostervelt's senescent passion for her was easy to understand. It wasn't just that she was young and pretty, and round in the right places. She had something more provocative than sex: the intense grave innocence of a serious child, and a loneliness that made her seem vulnerable.

I watched the old Buick out of sight and caught myself on the edge of a sudden hot dream. Mildred's husband might not live forever. His chances of surviving the day were not much better than even. If her husband failed to survive, Mildred would need a man to look after her.

I gave myself a mental kick in the teeth. That kind of thinking put me on Ostervelt's level. Which for some reason made me angrier at Ostervelt.

chapter 15

The deputy coroner had lit a cigar and was leaning against the side of the panel truck, smoking it. I strolled over and took a look at my car. Nothing seemed to be missing. Even the key was in the ignition. The additional mileage added up, so far as I could estimate, to the distance from the hospital to Purissima to the ranch.

"Nice day," the deputy coroner said.

"Nice enough."

"Too bad Mr. Hallman isn't alive to enjoy it. He was in pretty good shape, too, judging from a superficial examination. I'll be interested in what his organs have to say."

"You're not suggesting he died of natural causes."

"Oh, no. It's merely a little game I play with myself to keep the interest up." He grinned, and the sunlight glinted on his spectacles in cold mirth. "Not every doctor gets a chance to know his patients inside and out."

"You're the coroner, aren't you?"

"Deputy coroner. Ostervelt's the coroner—he wears two hats. Actually I do, too. I'm pathologist at the Purissima Hospital. Name's Lawson."

"Archer." We shook hands.

"You from one of the L.A. papers? I just got finished talking to the local man."

"I'm a private investigator, employed by a member of the family. I was wondering about your findings."

"Haven't got any yet. I know there're two bullets in him because they went in and didn't come out. I'll get 'em when I do the autopsy."

"When will that be?"

"Tonight. Ostervelt wants it quick. I ought to have it wrapped up by midnight, sooner maybe."

"What happens to the slugs after you remove them?"

"I turn 'em over to the sheriff's ballistics man."

"Is he any good?"

"Oh, yeah, Durkin's a pretty fair technician. If it gets too tough, we send the work up to the L.A. Police Lab, or to Sacramento. But this isn't a case where the physical evidence counts for much. We pretty well know who did it. Once they catch him, he shouldn't be hard to get a story out of. Ostervelt may not bother doing anything with the slugs. He's a pretty easy-going guy. You get that way after twenty-five or thirty years in office."

"Worked for him long?"

"Four-five years. Five." He added, a little defensively: "Purissima's a nice place to live. The wife won't leave it. Who can blame her?"

"Not me. I wouldn't mind settling here myself."

"Talk to Ostervelt, why don't you? He's understaffed—always looking for men. You have any police experience?"

"A few years back. I got tired of living on a cop's salary. Among other things."

"There are always ways of padding it out."

Not knowing how he meant me to take that, I looked into his face. He was sizing me up, too. I said:

"That was one of the other things I got tired of. But you wouldn't think there'd be much of that in this county."

"More than you think, brother, more than you think. We won't go into that, though." He took a bite out of the tip of his cigar and spat it into the gravel. "You say you've working for the Hallman family?"

I nodded.

"Ever been in Purissima before?"

"Over the years, I have."

He looked at me with curiosity. "Are you one of the detectives the Senator brought in when his wife drowned?"

"No."

"I just wondered. I spent several hours with one of them—a smart old bulldog named Scott. You wouldn't happen to know him? He's from L.A. Glenn Scott?"

"I know Scott. He's one of the old masters in the field. Or he was until he retired."

"My impression exactly. He knew more about pathology than most medical students. I never had a more interesting conversation."

"What about?"

"Causes of death," he said brightly. "Drowning and asphyxiation and so on. Fortunately I'd done a thorough post-mortem. I was able to establish that she died by drowning; she had sand and fragments of kelp in her bronchial tubes, and the indicated saline solution in her lungs."

"There wasn't any doubt of it, was there?"

"Not after I got through. Scott was completely satisfied. Of course I couldn't entirely rule out the possibility of murder, but there were no positive indications. It's almost certain that the contusions were inflicted after death."

"Contusions?" I prompted softly.

"Yeah, the contusions on the back and head. You often get them in drownings along this coast, with the rocks and the heavy surf. I've seen some cadavers that were absolutely macerated, poor things. At least they got Mrs. Hallman before that happened to her. But she was bad enough. They ought to print a few of my pictures in the papers. There wouldn't be so many suicides walking into the water. Not so many women, anyway, and most of them *are* women."

"Is that what Mrs. Hallman did, walk into the water?"

"Probably. Or else she jumped from the pier. Of

course there's always an outside chance that she fell, and that's how she got the contusions. The Coroner's Jury called it an accident, but that was mainly to spare the family's feelings. Elderly women don't normally go down to the ocean at night and accidentally fall in."

"They don't normally commit suicide, either."

"True enough, only Mrs. Hallman wasn't what you'd call exactly normal. Scott talked to her doctor after it happened and he said she'd been having emotional trouble. It's not fashionable these days to talk about hereditary insanity, but you can't help noticing certain family tie-ups. This one in the Hallman family, for instance. It isn't pure chance when a woman subject to depression has a son with a manic-depressive psychosis."

"Mother had blue genes, eh?"

"Ouch."

"Who was her doctor?"

"G.P. in town named Grantland."

"I know him slightly," I said. "He was out here today. He seems like a good man."

"Uh-huh." In the light of the medical code that inhibits doctors from criticizing each other, his grunt was eloquent.

"You don't think so?"

"Hell, it's not for me to second-guess another doctor. I'm not one of these medical hotshots with the big income and the bedside manner. I'm purely and simply a lab man. I did think at the time he should have referred Mrs. Hallman to a psychiatrist. Might have saved her life. After all, he knew she was suicidal."

"How do you know that?"

"He told Scott. Until he did, Scott thought it could be murder, in spite of the physical evidence. But when he found out she'd tried to shoot herself—well, it all fitted into a pattern."

"When did she try to shoot herself?"

"A week or two before she drowned, I think." Lawson stiffened perceptibly, as if he realized that he'd been talking very freely. "Understand me, I'm not accusing Grantland of negligence or anything like that. A doctor has to use his own judgment. Personally I'd be helpless if I had to handle one of these—"

He noticed that I wasn't listening, and peered into my face with professional solicitude. "What's the trouble, fellow? You got a cramp?"

"No trouble." At least no trouble I wanted to put into words. It was the Hallman family that really had trouble: father and mother dead under dubious circumstances, one son shot, the second being hunted. And at each high point of trouble, Grantland cropped up. I said:

"Do you know what happened to the gun?"

"What gun?"

"The one she tried to shoot herself with."

"I'm afraid I don't know. Maybe Grantland would."

"Maybe he would."

Lawson tapped the lengthening ash from his cigar. It splattered silently on the gravel between us. He drew on the cigar, its glowing end pale salmon in the sun, and blew out a cloud of smoke. The smoke ascended lazily, almost straight up in the still air, and drifted over my head toward the house.

"Or Ostervelt," he said. "I wonder what's keeping Ostervelt. I suppose he's trying to make an impression on Slovekin."

"Slovekin?"

"The police reporter from the Purissima paper. He's talking to Ostervelt in the greenhouse. Ostervelt loves to talk."

Ostervelt wasn't the only one, I thought. In fifteen or twenty minutes, a third of a cigar length, Lawson had given me more information than I knew what to do with.

"Speaking of causes of death," I said, "did you do the autopsy on Senator Hallman?"

"There wasn't any," he said.

"You mean no autopsy was ordered?"

"That's right, there was no question about cause of death. The old man had a heart history. He'd been under a doctor's care practically from day to day."

"Grantland again?"

"Yes. It was his opinion the Senator died of heart failure, and I saw no reason to question it. Neither did Ostervelt."

"Then there was no indication of drowning?"

"Drowning?" He looked at me sharply. "You're thinking about his wife, aren't you?"

His surprise seemed real, and I had no reason to doubt his honesty. He wore the glazed suit and frayed shirt of a man who lived on his salary.

"I must have got my signals switched," I said.

"It's understandable. He did die in the bathtub. But not of drowning."

"Did you examine the body?"

"It wasn't necessary."

"Who said it wasn't necessary?"

"The family, the family doctor, Sheriff Ostervelt, everybody concerned. I'm saying it now," he added with some spirit.

"What happened to the body?"

"The family had it cremated." He thought about this for a moment, behind his glasses. "Listen, if you're thinking that there was foul play involved, you're absolutely wrong. He died of heart failure, in a locked bathroom. They had to break in to get to him." Then, perhaps to put his own doubts to rest: "I'll show you where it happened, if you like."

"I would like."

Lawson pressed out his cigar against the sole of his shoe, and dropped the smelly butt in his side pocket. He led me through the house to a large rear bedroom. With blinds drawn, dust covers on the bed and the other furniture, the room had a ghostly air.

We went into the adjoining bathroom. It contained a six-foot tub supported on cast-iron feet. Lawson switched on the lofty ceiling fixture above it.

"The poor old man was lying in here," he said. "They had to force the window to get to him." He indicated the single window high above the basin.

"Who had to force the window?"

"The family. His two sons, I believe. The body was in the bathtub most of the night."

I examined the door. It was thick and made of oak. The lock was the old-fashioned kind that has to be turned with a key. The key was in the keyhole.

I turned it back and forth several times, then pulled it out and looked at it. The heavy, tarnished key told me nothing in particular. Either Lawson was misinformed, or the Senator had died alone. Or I had a locked-room mystery to go with the other mysteries in the house.

I tried a skeleton key on the door, and after a little jiggling around, it worked. I turned to Lawson. "Was the key in the lock when they found him?"

"I couldn't say, really. I wasn't here. Maybe Ostervelt could tell you."

chapter 16

WE ran into Ostervelt in the front hallway, ran into him almost literally as he came out of the living-room. He pushed between us, his belly projecting like a football concealed in his clothes. His jowls became convulsive:

"What goes on?"

"Mr. Archer wanted to see the Senator's bathroom," Lawson said. "You remember the morning they found him, Chief. Was the key in the lock?"

"What lock, for Christ sake?"

"The lock on the bathroom door."

"I don't know." Ostervelt's head jerked as he hammered out the words: "I'll tell you what I do know, Lawson. You don't talk official business to strangers. How many times do we have to go into that?"

Lawson removed his glasses and wiped them with the inside of his tie. Without them, his face looked unformed and vulnerable. But he had guts and some professional poise:

"Mr. Archer isn't a stranger, exactly. He's employed by the Hallman family."

"To do what? Pick your brains, if you have any?"

"You can't talk to me like that."

"What do you think you're going to do about it? Resign?"

Lawson turned on his heel, stiffly, and walked out. Ostervelt called after him:

"Go ahead and resign. I accept your resignation."

Feeling some compunction, since I had been picking Lawson's brains, I said to Ostervelt:

"Lay off him. What's the beef?"

"The beef is you. Mrs. Hallman said you asked her for money, made a pass at her."

"Did she rip her dress open at the neck? They usually rip their dresses open at the neck."

"It's no joke. I could put you in jail."

"What are you waiting for? The suit for false arrest will make my fortune."

"Don't get flip with me." Under his anger, Ostervelt seemed to be badly shaken. His little eyes were dirty with dismay. He took out his gun to make himself feel better.

"Put it away," I said. "It takes more than a Colt revolver to change a Keystone cop into an officer."

Ostervelt raised the Colt and laid it raking and burning across the side of my head. The ceiling slanted, then rose away from me as I went down. As I got up, a thin young man in a brown corduroy jacket appeared in the doorway. Ostervelt started to raise the gun for another blow. The thin young man took hold of his arm and almost ascended with it.

Ostervelt said: "I'll cut him to pieces. Get away from me, Slovekin."

Slovekin held onto his arm. I held onto my impulse to hit an old man. Slovekin said:

"Wait a minute, Sheriff. Who is this man, anyway?"

"A crooked private dick from Hollywood."

"Are you arresting him?"

"You're damn right I'm arresting him."

"What for? Is he connected with this case?"

Ostervelt shook him off. "That's between him and I. You stay out of it, Slovekin."

"How can I, when I'm assigned to it? I'm just doing my

job, the same as you are, Sheriff." The black eyes in Slovekin's sharp young face glittered with irony. "I can't do my job if you give me no information. I have to fall back on reporting what I see. I see a public official beating a man with a gun, naturally I'm interested."

"Don't try to blackmail me, you little twerp."

Slovekin stayed cool and smiling. "You want me to deliver that message to Mr. Spaulding? Mr. Spaulding's always looking for a good local topic for an editorial. This could be just what he needs."

"Screw Spaulding. You know what you can do with that rag you work for, too."

"That's pretty language from the top law-enforcement official in the county. An elected official, at that. I suppose you don't mind if I quote you." Slovekin produced a notebook from a side pocket.

Ostervelt's face tried various colors and settled for a kind of mottled purple. He put his gun away. "Okay, Slovekin. What else do you want to know?" His voice was a rough whisper.

"Is this man a suspect? I thought Carl Hallman was the only one."

"He is, and we'll have him in twenty-four hours. Dead or alive. You can quote me on that."

I said to Slovekin: "You're a newspaperman, are you?"

"I try to be." He looked at me quizzically, as if he wondered what I was trying to be.

"I'd like to talk to you about this murder. The sheriff's got Hallman convicted already, but there are certain discrepancies—"

"The hell there are!" Ostervelt said.

Slovekin whipped out a pencil and opened his notebook. "Clue me in."

"Not now. I need more time to pin them down."

"He's bluffing," Ostervelt said. "He's just trying to make

me look bad. He's one of these jokers, tries to make a hero out of himself."

Disregarding him, I said to Slovekin: "Where can I get in touch with you, tomorrow, say?"

"You're not going to be here tomorrow," Ostervelt put in. "I want you out of this county in one hour, or else."

Slovekin said mildly: "I thought you were arresting him."

Ostervelt was getting frantic. He began to yammer: "Don't get too cocky, Mr. Slovekin. Bigger men than you thought they could cross me, and lost their jobs."

"Oh, come off it, Sheriff. Do you go to movies much?" Slovekin unwrapped a piece of gum, put it in his mouth, and began to chew it. He said to me: "You can reach me through the paper any time—Purissima *Record.*"

"You think so, eh?" Ostervelt said. "After today you won't be working there."

"Phone 6328," Slovekin said. "If I'm not there, talk to Spaulding. He's the editor."

"I can go higher than Spaulding, if I have to."

"Take it to the Supreme Court, Sheriff." Slovekin's chewing face had an expression of pained superiority which made him look like an intellectual camel. "I'd certainly like to get what you have now. Spaulding's holding the city edition for this story."

"I'd like to give it to you, but it hasn't jelled."

"You see?" Ostervelt said. "He's got nothing to back it up. He's only trying to make trouble. You're crazy if you take his word against mine. Christ, he may even be in cahoots with the psycho. He let Hallman use his car, remember."

"It's getting pretty noisy in here," I said to Slovekin, and moved toward the door.

He followed me outside to my car. "What you said about the evidence—you weren't kidding?"

"No. I think there's a good chance that Hallman's getting the dirty end of the stick."

"I hope you're right. I rather like the guy, or used to before he got sick."

"You know Carl, do you?"

"Ever since high school. I've known Ostervelt for quite a long time, too. But this is no time to go into Ostervelt." He leaned on the car window, smelling of Dentyne chewing gum. "Do you have another suspect in mind?"

"Several."

"Like that, eh?"

"Like that. Thanks for the assist."

"Don't mention it." His black gaze shifted to the side of my head. "Did you know you've got a torn ear? You should see a doctor."

"I intend to."

chapter 17

I DROVE into Purissima and checked in at a waterfront motel named the Hacienda. Not being on expense account and having forty-odd dollars in my wallet to tide me over until I qualified for the old-age pension, I picked the cheapest one I could find with telephones in the rooms. The room I paid eight dollars for in advance contained a bed and a chair and a limed-oak veneer chest of drawers, as well as a telephone. The window overlooked a parking lot.

The room surprised me into a sharp feeling of pain and loss. The pain wasn't for Carl Hallman, though his fugitive image continually crossed my mind. Perhaps the pain was for myself; the loss was of a self I had once imagined.

Peering out through the slats of the dusty blind, I felt like a criminal hiding out from the law. I didn't like the feeling, so I clowned it away. All I needed was a suitcase full of hot money and an ash-blonde moll whining for mink and diamonds. The closest thing to an ash-blonde moll I knew was Zinnie, and Zinnie appeared to be somebody's else's moll.

I was kind of glad that Zinnie wasn't my moll. It was a small room, and the printed notice under the glass top of the chest of drawers said that the room rented for fourteen dollars double. Checkout time was twelve noon. Lighting an ash-blond cigarette, I calculated that I had about twenty-four hours to wrap up the case. I wasn't going to pay for another day out of my own pocket. That would be criminal.

Try listening to yourself sometime, alone in a transient room in a strange town. The worst is when you draw a blank, and the ash-blonde ghosts of the past carry on long twittering long-distance calls with your inner ear, and there's no way to hang up.

Before I made a long-distance call of my own, I went into the bathroom and examined my head in the mirror over the sink. It looked worse than it felt. One ear was cut, and half full of drying blood. There were abrasions on temple and cheek. One eye was slightly blackened, and made me appear more dissipated than I was. When I smiled at a thought that struck me, the effect was pretty grim.

The thought that struck me sent me back to the bedroom. I sat down on the edge of the bed and looked up Zinnie's doctor friend in the local directory. Grantland maintained an office on upper Main Street and a residence on Seaview Road. I made a note of the addresses and telephone numbers, and called his office number. The girl who answered gave me, after some persuasion, an emergency appointment for five-thirty, the end of office hours.

If I hurried, and if Glenn Scott was at home, I should have time to see him and get back for my appointment with Grantland. Glenn had retired to an avocado ranch in the Malibu hinterland. I'd driven up two or three times in the last two years to play chess with him. He always beat me at chess, but his whisky was good. Also, I happened to like him. He was one of the few survivors of the Hollywood rat race who knew how to enjoy a little money without hitting other people over the head with it.

I thought as I put through the call to his house that money happened to Glenn the way poverty happened to a lot of others. He'd worked hard all his life, of course, but he'd never knocked himself out for money. He used to say that he'd never tried to sell himself for fear that somebody might be tempted to buy him.

The maid who'd been with the Scotts for twenty years answered the telephone. Mr. Scott was outside watering his trees. Far as she knew, he'd be there all afternoon, and he'd be glad to see me, far as she knew.

I found him about a half-hour later, wielding a hose on the side of a sunburnt hill. The rocky barrenness of the hillside was accentuated by the rows of scrawny young avocado trees. Glenn's jeep was at the side of the road. Turning and parking behind it, I could look down on the gravel roof of his cantilevered redwood house, and further down on the long white curve of the beach rimming the sea. I felt a twinge of envy as I crossed the field toward him. It seemed to me that Glenn had everything worth having: a place in the sun, wife and family, enough money to live on.

Glenn gave me a smile that made me ashamed of my thoughts. His keen gray eyes were almost lost in his sun-wrinkles. His wide-brimmed straw hat and stained khaki coveralls completed his resemblance to a veteran farmhand. I said:

"Hi, farmer."

"You like my protective coloration, eh?" He turned off the water and began to coil the hose. "How you been, Lew? Still brawling, I see."

"I ran into a door. You're looking well."

"Yeah, the life suits me. When I get bored, Belle and I go in to the Strip for dinner and take a quick look around and beat it the hell back home."

"How is Belle?"

"Oh, she's fine. Right now she's in Santa Monica with the kids. Belle had her first grandson last week, with a little help from the daughter-in-law. Seven and a half pounds, built like a middleweight, they're going to call him Glenn. But you didn't make a special trip to ask me about my family."

"Somebody else's family. You had a case in Purissima about three years ago. Elderly woman committed suicide by drowning. Husband suspected murder, called you in to check."

"Uh-huh. I wouldn't call Mrs. Hallman elderly. She was probably in her early fifties. Hell, I'm older than that myself, and I'm not elderly."

"Okay, grandpa," I said with subtle flattery. "Are you willing to answer a couple of questions about the Hallman case?"

"Why?"

"It seems to be kind of reopening itself."

"You mean it was homicide?"

"I wouldn't go that far. Not yet. But the woman's son was murdered this afternoon."

"Which son? She had two."

"The older one. His younger brother escaped from a

mental ward last night, and he's prime suspect. He was at the ranch shortly before the shooting—"

"Jesus," Glenn breathed. "The old man was right."

I waited, with no result, and finally said: "Right about what?"

"Let's skip that, Lew. I know he's dead now, but it's still a confidential case."

"I get no answers, eh?"

"You can ask the questions, I'll use my judgment about answering 'em. First, though, who are you representing in Purissima?"

"The younger son. Carl."

"The psycho?"

"Should I give my clients a Rorschach before I take them on?"

"I didn't mean that. He hire you to clear him?"

"No, it's my own idea."

"Hey, you're not off on one of your crusades."

"Hardly," I said with more hope than I felt. "If my hunch pans out, I'll get paid for my time. There's a million or two in the family."

"More like five million. I get it. You're on a contingency basis."

"Call it that. Do I get to ask you any questions?"

"Go ahead. Ask them." He leaned against a boulder and looked inscrutable.

"You've answered the main one already. That drowning could have been homicide."

"Yeah. I finally ruled it out at the time because there were no positive indications—nothing you could take to court, I mean. Also on account of the lady's background. She was unstable, been on barbiturates for years. Her doctor wouldn't admit she was hooked on them, but that was the picture I got. In addition to which, she'd attempted suicide before. Tried to shoot herself right in the doctor's office, a few days before she drowned."

"Who told you this?"

"The doctor told me himself, and he wasn't lying. She wanted a bigger prescription from him. When he wouldn't give it to her, she pulled a little pearl-handled revolver out of her purse and pointed it at her head. He knocked it up just in time, and the slug went into the ceiling. He showed me the hole it made."

"What happened to the gun?"

"Naturally he took it away from her. I think he told me he threw it into the sea."

"That's a funny way to handle it."

"Not so funny, under the circumstances. She begged him not to tell her husband about the attempt. The old man was always threatening to stash her away in a snake-pit. The doctor covered for her."

"You get any confirmation of this?"

"How could I? It was strictly between him and her." He added with a trace of irritation: "The guy didn't have to tell me anything. He was sticking his neck out, telling me what he did. Speaking of necks, mine is out a mile right now."

"Then you might as well stick it out some more. What do you think of the local law?"

"In Purissima? They have a good police force. Undermanned, like most, but one of the better small-city departments, I'd say."

"I was thinking more of the county department."

"Ostervelt, you mean? We got along. He co-operated fine." Glenn smiled briefly. "Naturally he co-operated. Senator Hallman swung a lot of votes."

"Is Ostervelt honest?"

"I never saw any evidence that he wasn't. Maybe some

graft crept in here and there. He isn't as young as he used to be, and I heard a rumor or two. Nothing big, you understand. Senator Hallman wouldn't stand for it. Why?"

"Just checking." Very tentatively, I said: "I don't suppose I could get a peek at your report on the case?"

"Not even if I had one. You know the law as well as I do."

"You didn't keep a copy?"

"I didn't make a written report. The old man wanted it word-of-mouth, and that was the way I gave it to him. I can tell you what I said in one word. Suicide." He paused. "But maybe I was wrong, Lew."

"Do you think you were wrong?"

"Maybe I was. If I did make a mistake, like La Guardia said, it was a beaut: they don't come often like that. I know I shouldn't admit it to an ex-competitor. On the other hand, you were never a very serious competitor. They went to you when they couldn't afford me." Scott was trying to carry it off lightly, but his face was heavy. "On the other hand, I wouldn't want you to climb way out on a limb, and get it sawed off from under you."

"So?"

"So take a piece of advice from an old pro who started in the rack—in the business, before you learned toilet control. You're wasting your time on this one."

"I don't think so. You gave me what I need."

"Then I better give you something you don't need, just so you won't get elated." Scott looked the opposite of elated. His voice dragged slower and slower. "Don't start to spend your piece of that five million until after you deposit the check. You know there's a little rule of law that says a murderer can't benefit from the estate of his victim."

"Are you trying to tell me Carl Hallman murdered his father?"

"I heard the old man died of natural causes. I didn't investigate his death. It looks as if somebody ought to."

"I intend to."

"Sure, but don't be surprised if you come up with an answer you don't like."

"Such as?"

"You said it a minute ago yourself."

"You've got some inside information?"

"Only what you told me, and what the old man told me when his lawyer sent for me. You know why he wanted me to make a confidential investigation of that drowning?"

"He didn't trust the local law."

"Maybe. The main reason was, he suspected his own son of knocking out the mother and throwing her in the water. And I'm beginning to think that's what actually happened."

I'd seen it coming from a long way off, but it hit me hard, with the weight of Glenn Scott's integrity behind it.

"Do you know what the Senator's suspicions were based on?"

"He didn't tell me much about that. I assumed he knew his own boy better than I did. I never even got to meet the boy. I talked to the rest of the family, though, and I gathered that he was very close to his mother. Too close for comfort, maybe."

"Close like Oedipus?"

"Could be. There was apronstring trouble, all right. The mother raised a hell of a stink when he went away to college. She was a clutcher, for sure, and not very stable, like I said. Could be he thought he had to kill her to get free. There've been cases like that. I'm only brainstorming, understand. You won't quote me."

"Not even to myself. Where was Carl when she died?"

"That's just the trouble, I don't know. He was going to school in Berkeley at the time, but he left there about a week before it happened. Dropped out of sight for maybe ten days, all told."

"What did he say he was doing?"

"I don't know. The Senator wouldn't even let me ask him. It wasn't a very satisfactory case to work on. As you'll discover."

"I already have."

chapter 18

I PARKED on upper Main Street, in front of a flat-topped building made of pink stucco and glass brick. An imitation flagstone walk led through well-trimmed shrubbery to a door inset in one corner. A small bronze plate beside the door announced discreetly: J. Charles Grantland, M.D.

The waiting-room was empty, except for a lot of new-looking furniture. A fairly new-looking young woman popped up behind a bleached oak counter in the far corner beside an inner door. She had dark, thin good looks which needed a quick paint job.

"Mr. Archer?"

"Yes."

"I'm sorry, doctor's still busy. We're behind schedule today. Do you mind waiting a few minutes?"

I said I didn't mind. She took down my address.

"Were you in an accident, Mr. Archer?"

"You could call it that."

I sat in the chair nearest her, and took a folded newspaper out of my jacket pocket. I'd bought it on the street a few minutes earlier, from a Mexican newsboy crying murder. I spread it out on my knees, hoping that it might make a conversation piece.

The Hallman story had Eugene Slovekin's by-line under a banner heading: Brother Sought in Shooting. There was a three-column picture of the Hallman brothers in the middle of the page. The story began in a rather stilted atmospheric style which made me wonder if Slovekin had been embarrassed by the writing of it:

"In a tragedy which may parallel the ancient tragedy of Cain and Abel, violent death paid a furtive and shocking visit today to a well-known local family. Victim of the apparent slaying was Jeremiah Hallman, 34, prominent Buena Vista Valley rancher. His younger brother, Carl Hallman, 24, is being sought for questioning in the shooting. Mr. Hallman, son of the recently deceased Senator Hallman, was found dead at approximately one o'clock this afternoon by his family physician, Dr. Charles Grantland, in the conservatory of the Hallman estate.

"Mr. Hallman had been shot twice in the back, and apparently died within seconds of the shooting. A pearl-handled revolver, with two cartridges discharged, was found beside the body, lending a touch of fantastic mystery to the case. According to family servants the murder gun formerly belonged to the late Mrs. Alicia Hallman, mother of the victim.

"Sheriff Duane Ostervelt, who was on the scene within minutes of the shooting, stated that the murder weapon was known to be in the possession of Carl Hallman. Young Hallman was seen on the ranch immediately prior to the shooting. He escaped last night from the State Hospital, where he had been a patient for some months. According to members of the family, young Hallman has been a long-time victim of mental illness. An all-points search is being made for him, by the local sheriff's department and city and state police.

"Contacted by long-distance telephone, Dr. Brockley of the State Hospital staff said that young Hallman was suffering from manic-depressive psychosis when admitted to the hospital six months ago. According to Dr. Brockley, Hallman was not considered dangerous, and was thought to be 'well on the road to recovery.' Dr. Brockley expressed surprise and concern at the tragic outcome of Hallman's escape. He said that the local authorities were informed of the escape as soon as it occurred, and expressed the hope that the public would 'take a calm view of the situation. There is no violence in Hallman's hospital record,' Dr. Brockley said. 'He is a sick boy who needs medical care.'

"A similar view was expressed by Sheriff Ostervelt, who says that he is organizing a posse of a hundred or more local citizens to supplement the efforts of his department in the search. The public is asked to be on the lookout for Hallman. He is six feet three inches tall, of athletic build, blue-eyed, with light hair cut very short. When last seen he was wearing a blue work shirt and blue dungaree trousers. According to Sheriff Ostervelt, Hallman may be accompanied by Thomas Rica, alias Rickey, a fellow-escapee from . . ."

The story was continued on the second page. Before turning over, I took a close look at the picture of the two brothers. It was a stiffly posed portrait of the sort that photographers make to commemorate weddings. Both brothers wore boiled shirts and fixed smiles. Their resemblance was accentuated by this, and by the fact that Jerry hadn't grown fat when the picture was taken. The caption was simply: "The Hallman brothers (Carl on the right)."

The dark girl coughed insinuatingly. I looked up and

saw her leaning far out over her counter, slightly cross-eyed with desire to break the silence.

"Terrible, isn't it? What makes it worse, I know him." She shivered, and hunched her thin shoulders up. "I talked to him just this morning."

"Who?"

"The murderer." She rolled the "r's" like an actress in melodrama.

"He telephoned here?"

"He *came* here, personally. He was standing right here in front of me." She pointed at the floor between us with a fingernail from which the red polish was flaking. "I didn't know him from Adam, but *I* could tell there was something funny. He had that wild look they have in their eyes." Her own look was slightly wild, in a girlish way, and she'd forgotten her receptionist's diction: "Jeeze, it bored right through me."

"It must have been a frightening experience."

"*You're* not kidding. 'Course I had no way of knowing he was going to shoot somebody, he only *looked* that way. 'Where's the doctor?' he said, just like that. I guess he thought he was Napoleon or something. Only he was dressed like any old bum. You'd never think he was a Senator's son. His brother used to come in here, and *he* was a real gentleman, always nicely dressed in the height of fashion—cashmere jackets and stuff. It's too bad about him. I feel sorry for his wife, too."

"You know her?"

"Oh yes, Mrs. Hallman, she comes in all the time for her sinuses." Her eyes took on the waiting birdlike expression of a woman naming another woman she happens not to like.

"Did you get rid of him all right?"

"The crazy-man? I tried to tell him doctor wasn't in, but he wouldn't take no for an answer. So I called out Dr.

Grantland, *he* knows how to handle them, Dr. Grantland hasn't got a nerve in his body." The birdlike expression subtly changed to the look of adoration which very young receptionists reserve for their doctor-employers. " 'Hello, old man, what brings you here?' the doctor says, like they were buddy-buddy from way back. He put his arm around him, calm as anything, and off they went into the back room. I guess he got rid of him out the back way, 'cause that was the last I saw of him. 'Least I hope that's the last. Anyway, doctor told me not to worry about it, that things like that come up in every office."

"Have you worked here long?"

"Just three months. This is my first real job. I filled in for other girls before, when they went on vacation, but I consider this the real start of my career. Dr. Grantland is wonderful to work for. Most of his patients are the nicest people you'd ever want to meet."

As though to illustrate this boast, a fat woman wearing a small flat hat and a mink neckpiece emerged through the inner door. She was followed by Grantland looked professional in a white smock. She had the vaguely frightened eyes of a hypochondriac, and she clutched a prescription slip in her chubby hand. Grantland escorted her to the front door and opened it, bowing her out. She turned to him on the threshold:

"Thank you so much, doctor. I know I'll be able to sleep tonight."

chapter 19

GRANTLAND closed the door and saw me. The lingering smile on his face gave up the ghost entirely. Shoved by a gust of anger, he crossed the room toward me. His fists were clenched.

I rose to meet him. "Hello, doctor."

"What are you doing here?"

"I have an appointment with you."

"Oh no you haven't." He was torn between anger and the need to be charming to his receptionist. "Did you make an appointment for this—this gentleman?"

"Why not?" I said, since she was speechless. "Are you retiring from practice?"

"Don't try to tell me you're here as a patient."

"You're the only doctor I know in town."

"You didn't tell me you knew Dr. Grantland," the receptionist said accusingly.

"I must have forgotten to."

"Very likely," Grantland said. "You can go now, Miss Cullen, unless you've made some more of these special appointments for me."

"He told me it was an emergency."

"I said you can go."

She went, with a backward look from the doorway. Grantland's face was trying various attitudes: outrage, dignified surprise, bewildered innocence.

"What are you trying to pull on me?"

"Not a thing. Look, if you don't want to treat me, I can find another doctor."

He weighed the advantages and disadvantages of this,

and decided against it. "I don't do much in the surgical line, but I guess I can fix you up. What happened to you, anyway—did you run into Hallman again?" Zinnie had briefed him well, apparently.

"No. Did you?"

He let that go by. We went through a consulting-room furnished in mahogany and blue leather. There were sailing prints on the walls, and above the desk a medical diploma from a college in the middle west. Grantland switched on the lights in the next room and asked me to remove my coat. Washing his hands at the sink in the corner, he said over his shoulder:

"You can get up on the examination table if you like. I'm sorry my nurse has gone home—I didn't know I'd be wanting to use her."

I stretched out on the leatherette top of the metal table. Lying flat on the back wasn't a bad position for self-defense, if it came to that.

Grantland crossed the room briskly and leaned over me, turning on a surgical light that extended on retractable arms from the wall. "You get yourself gun-whipped?"

"Slightly. Not every doctor would recognize the marks."

"I interned at Hollywood Receiving. Did you report this to the police?"

"I didn't have to. Ostervelt did it to me."

"You're not a fugitive, for God's sake?"

"No, for God's sake."

"Were you resisting arrest?"

"The sheriff just lost his temper. He's a hot-headed old youth."

Grantland made no comment. He went to work cleaning my cuts with swabs dipped in alcohol. It hurt.

"I'm going to have to put some clamps in that ear. The other cut ought to heal itself. I'll simply put an adhesive bandage over it."

Grantland went on talking as he worked: "A regular surgeon could do a better job for you, especially a plastic surgeon. That's why I was a little surprised when you came to me. You're going to have a small scar, I'm afraid. But that's all right with me if it's all right with you." He pressed a series of clamps into my torn ear. "That ought to do it. You ought to have a doctor look at it in a day or two. Going to be in town long?"

"I don't know." I got up, and faced him across the table. "It could depend on you."

"Any doctor can do it," he said impatiently.

"You're the only one who can help me."

Grantland caught the implication, and glanced at his watch. "I'm late for an appointment now—"

"I'll make it as fast as I can. You saw a pearl-handled gun today. You didn't mention that you'd seen it before."

He was a very quick study. Without a second's hesitation, he said: "I like to be sure of my facts before I sound off. I'm a medical man, after all."

"What are your facts?"

"Ask your friend the sheriff. He knows them."

"Maybe. I'm asking you. You might as well tell a straight story. I've been in touch with Glenn Scott."

"Glenn who?" But he remembered. His gaze flickered sideways.

"The detective Senator Hallman hired to investigate the murder of his wife."

"Did you say murder?"

"It slipped out."

"You're mistaken. She committed suicide. If you talked to Scott, you know she was suicidal."

"Suicidal people can be murdered."

"No doubt, but what does that prove?" A womanish petulance tugged at his mouth, disrupting his false calm. "I'm sick and tired of being badgered about it, simply because she happened to be my patient. Why, I saved her life the week before she drowned. Did Scott bother to tell you that?"

"He told me what you told him. That she attempted suicide in this office."

"It was in my previous office. I moved last year."

"So you can't show me the bullethole in the ceiling."

"Good Lord, are you questioning that? I got that gun away from her at the risk of my own life."

"I don't question it. I wanted to hear it from you, though."

"Well, now you've heard it. I hope you're satisfied." He took off his smock and turned to hang it up.

"Why did she try to commit suicide in your office?"

He was very still for an instant, frozen in the act of placing the white garment on a hook. Between the shoulderblades and under the arms, his gray shirt was dark with sweat. It was the only indication that I was giving him a hard time. He said:

"She wanted something I wasn't prepared to give her. A massive dose of sleeping pills. When I refused, she pulled this little revolver out of her purse. It was touch and go whether she was going to shoot me or herself. Then she pointed it at her head. Fortunately I managed to reach her, and take the gun away." He turned with a bland and doleful look on his face.

"Was she on a barb kick?"

"You might call it that. I did my best to keep it under control."

"Why didn't you have her put in a safe place?"

"I miscalculated, I admit it. I don't pretend to be a psychiatrist. I didn't grasp the seriousness of her condition. We doctors make mistakes, you know, like everybody else."

He was watching me like a chess-player. But his sympathy gambit was a giveaway. Unless he had something important to cover up, he'd have ordered me out of his office long ago.

"What happened to the gun?" I said.

"I kept it. I intended to throw it away, but never got around to it."

"How did Carl Hallman get hold of it?"

"He lifted it out of my desk drawer." He added disarmingly: "I guess I was a damn fool to keep it there."

I'd been holding back my knowledge of Carl Hallman's visit to his office. It was disappointing to have the fact conceded. Grantland said with a faint sardonic smile:

"Didn't the sheriff tell you that Carl was here this morning? I telephoned him immediately. I also got in touch with the State Hospital."

"Why did he come here?"

Grantland turned his hands palms outward. "Who can say? He was obviously disturbed. He bawled me out for my part in having him committed, but his main animus was against his brother. Naturally I tried to talk him out of it."

"Naturally. Why didn't you hold on to him?"

"Don't think I didn't try to. I stepped into the dispensary for a minute to get him some thorazine. I thought it might calm him down. When I came back to the office, he was gone. He must have run out the back way here." Grantland indicated the back door of the examination room. "I heard a car start, but he was gone before I could catch him."

I walked over to the half-curtained window and looked out. Grantland's Jaguar was parked in the paved lot. Back of the lot, a dirt lane ran parallel with the street. I turned back to Grantland: "You say he took your gun?"

"Yes, but I didn't know it at the time. It wasn't exactly *my* gun, either. I'd practically forgotten it existed. I didn't even think of it till I found it in the greenhouse beside poor Jerry's body. Then I couldn't be sure it was the same one, I'm no expert on guns. So I waited until I got back here this afternoon, and had a chance to check the drawer of my desk. When I found it gone I got in touch with the sheriff's department right away—much as I hated to do it."

"Why did you hate to do it?"

"Because I'm fond of the boy. He used to be my patient. You'd hardly expect me to get a kick out of proving that he's a murderer."

"You've proved that, have you?"

"You're supposed to be a detective. Can you think of any other hypothesis?"

I could, but I kept it to myself. Grantland said:

"I can understand your feeling let down. Ostervelt told me you're representing poor Carl, but don't take it too hard, old man. They'll take his mental condition into account. I'll see to it personally that they do."

I wasn't as sad as I looked. Not that I was happy about the case. Every time I moved, I picked up another link in the evidence against my client. But this happened with such clockwork regularity that I was getting used to it and beginning to discount it. Besides, I was encouraged by the firm and lasting faith which I was developing in Dr. Grantland's lack of integrity.

chapter 20

TWILIGHT was thickening in the street outside. The white-walled buildings, fluorescent with last light, had taken on the beauty and mystery of a city in Africa or someplace else I'd never been. I nosed my car out into a break in the traffic, turned right at the next intersection, and parked a hundred feet short of the entrance to Grantland's back lane. I hadn't been there five minutes when his Jaguar came bumping along the lane. It arced out into the street on whining tires.

Grantland didn't know my car. I followed him fairly closely, two blocks south, then west on a boulevard that slanted toward the sea. I almost lost him when he made a left turn onto the highway on the tail end of a green light. I followed through on the yellow as it turned red.

From there the Jaguar was easy to keep in sight. It headed south on the highway through the outskirts where marginal operators purveyed chicken-fried steaks and salt-water taffy, Mexican basketry and redwood mementoes. The neon-cluttered sub-suburbs dropped behind. The highway snaked up and along brown bluffs which rose at a steep angle above the beach. The sea lay at their foot, a more somber reflection of the sky, still tinged at its far edge with the sun's red death.

About two miles out of town, as many minutes, the Jaguar's brakelights blazed. It heeled and turned onto a black top shelf overlooking the sea. There was one other car in the turnout, a red Cadillac with its nose against the guard-rail. Before the next curve swept me out of sight, I saw Grantland's car pull up beside the Cadillac.

There was traffic behind me. I found another turnout a quarter of a mile further on. By the time I'd made my turn and got back to the first turnout, the Jaguar was gone and the Cadillac was going.

I caught a glimpse of the driver's face as he turned onto the highway. It gave me the kind of shock you might get from seeing the ghost of someone you'd once known. I'd known him ten years before, when he was a high-school athlete, a big boy, nice looking, full of fermenting energy. The face behind the wheel of the Cadillac: yellow skin stretched over skull, smokily lit by black unfocused eyes: could have belonged to that boy's grandfather. I knew him, though. Tom Rica.

I turned once again and followed him south. He drove erratically, slowing on the straightaway and speeding up on the curves, using two of the four lanes. Once, at better than seventy, he left the road entirely, and veered onto the shoulder. The Cadillac skidded sideways in the gravel, headlights swinging out into gray emptiness. The bumper clipped the steel guardrail, and the Cadillac slewed wildly in the other direction. It regained the road and went on as if nothing had happened.

I stayed close behind, trying to think my way into Tom Rica's brain and along his damaged nerves and do his driving for him. I'd always felt an empathy for the boy. When he was eighteen and his unmaturing youth had begun to go rank, I'd tried to hold him straight, and even run some interference for him. An old cop had done it for me when I was a kid. I couldn't do it for Tom.

The memory of my failure was bitter and obscure, mixed with the ash-blonde memory of a woman I'd once been married to. I put both memories out of my mind.

Tom was steadying down to his driving. The big car held the road, and even stayed in one lane most of the time. The road straightened out, and began to climb. Just beyond the crest of the rise, a hundred feet or more above the invisible sea, a red neon sign flashed at the entrance to a private parking lot: Buenavista Inn.

The Cadillac turned in under the sign. I stopped before I got to it, and left my car on the shoulder of the road. The inn lay below, a pueblo affair with a dozen or more stucco cottages staggered along the shadowy terraces. About half of them had lights behind their blinds. There was a red neon Office sign above the door of the main building beside the parking lot.

Tom parked the Cadillac with several other cars, and left it with its lights burning. I kept the other cars between me and him. I didn't think he saw me, but he began to run toward the main building. He moved in a jerky knock-kneed fashion, like an old man trying to catch a bus which had already left.

The door under the red sign opened before he reached it. A big woman stepped out onto the platform of light projected from the doorway. Her hair was gold, her skin a darker gold. She wore a gold lamé gown with a slashed neckline. Even at a distance, she gave the impression of a shining hardness, as though she'd preserved her body from age by having it cast in metal. Her voice had a metallic carrying quality:

"Tommy! Where've you been?"

If he answered, I couldn't hear him. He stopped on his heels in front of her, feinted to the left, and tried to move past her on the right. The action was a sad parody of the broken-field running he'd once been pretty good at. Her flashing body blocked him in the doorway, and one of her round gold arms encircled his neck. He struggled weakly. She kissed him on the mouth, then looked out over his shoulder across the parking lot.

"You took my car, you naughty boy. And now you left the lights on. Get inside now, before somebody sees you."

She slapped him half-playfully, and released him. He scuttled into the lighted lobby. She marched across the parking lot, an unlikely figure of a woman with a broad serene brow, deep eyes, an ugly hungry tortured mouth, a faint pouch under her chin. She walked as if she owned the world, or had owned it once and lost it but remembered how it felt.

She switched off the lights of the car, removed the ignition key and pulled up her skirt to slip it into the top of her stocking. Her legs were heavy and shapely, with slender ankles. She slammed the door of the Cadillac and said out loud, in a tone of mingled anger and indulgence:

"Silly damn little fool."

She breathed and sighed, and noticed me in the middle of the sigh. Without changing the rhythm of her breathing, she smiled and nodded: "Hello there. What can I do for you?"

"You look as if you could do plenty."

"Kidder." But her smile widened, revealing bright gold inlays in its corners. "Nobody's interested in Maude any more. Except Maude. I'm very much interested in Maude."

"That's because you're Maude."

"You bet your sweet life I am. Who are you?"

I told her as I got out of my car, and added: "I'm looking for a friend."

"A new friend?"

"No, an old friend."

"One of my dolls?"

"Could be."

"Come on inside if you want to."

I followed her in. I'd hoped to find Tom Rica in the lobby, but he'd evidently gone through into the private part of the building.

The lobby was surprisingly well furnished with pastel leather chairs, potted palms. One end wall was covered with a photomural of Hollywood at night, which gave the effect of a picture window overlooking the city. The opposite wall was an actual window overlooking the sea.

Maude went around the curved teakwood counter across from the door. The inner door behind the counter was partly open. She closed it. She unlocked a drawer and took out a typewritten sheet, much interlined.

"I mayn't have her listed any more. My turnover is terrific. The girls get married."

"Good for them."

"But not so good for me. I've had a recruiting problem ever since the war. You'd think I was running a matrimonial bureau or something. Well, if she isn't with me any more I can always get you another one. It's early. What did you say her name was?"

"I didn't say. And it's not a her."

She gave me a slightly disappointed look. "You're in the wrong pew. I run a clean place, strictly from heterosex."

"Who said I had sex on my mind?"

"I thought everybody had," she said with a kind of habitual wiggle.

"All the time?"

She glanced at me from the hard gray surface of her deep-set eyes. "What happened to you?"

"A lot of things. I'm trying to sell the movie rights to my life. Somebody down here hates me."

"I mean your face."

"Oh, that."

"What are you stalling for? My God, don't tell me you're a lamster, too. The woods are crawling with them."

"Could you put me up if I was?"

She took it as the fact, with the gullibility of cynicism: "How hot are you?"

"Not very."

"That car outside belong to you?"

"It's mostly the bank's."

"My God, you robbed a bank?"

"They're robbing me. Ten per cent interest on the money I borrowed to buy the crate."

She leaned forward across the counter, her ringed hands flat on its top, her eyes hard-bright as the cut stones in the rings:

"What kind of a joker are you? If you're thinking of knocking me over, I warn you I got protection, plenty of it."

"Don't get hinky."

"I'm not hinky. I get a little irritated, is all, when a beat-up punk walks into my place and won't tell me what he wants." She moved quickly to a small switchboard at the end of the counter, picked up a headphone, and said over her shoulder: "So get to the point, brother."

"Tom Rica is the friend I'm looking for."

A ripple of nerves went through her. Then she stood heavy and solid again. Her eyes didn't shift, but their bright stare became more intense.

"Who sent you here?"

"I came on my own."

"I doubt that. Whoever it was gave you the wrong information." She put down the phone and returned to the counter. "Come to think of it, there was a boy named Rica worked here a while back. What did you say the first name was?"

"Tom."

"What do you want with him?"

"A chance to talk, that's all."

"What about?"

"Old times."

She struck the countertop with the front of her fist. "Cut the doubletalk, eh? You're no friend of his."

"Better than some he has. I hate to see him poison his brains with heroin. He used to be a smart boy."

"He still is," she said defensively. "It isn't his fault he was sick." In a sudden gesture of self-contempt, self-doubt, she tugged at the pouch of flesh under her chin, and went on worrying it. "Who are you, anyway? Are you from the hospital?"

"I'm a private detective investigating a murder."

"That shooting in the country?" For the first time she seemed afraid. "You can't tie Tom in with it."

"What makes you think I'm trying to?"

"You said you wanted to see him, didn't you? But you're not seeing him. He had nothing to do with that killer."

"They escaped together last night."

"That proves nothing. I got rid of that Hallman character soon as we hit the main road. Him I wanted no part of. I see enough of them in line of business. And Tom hasn't seen him since, or gone anywhere. He's been here all day. With me."

"So you helped them get away from the hospital."

"What if I did?"

"You weren't doing Hallman a favor. Or Tom, either."

"I beg to differ. They were torturing him. They cut him off cold turkey. He had nothing to eat for over a week. You ought to've seen him when I picked him up."

"So you put him back on horse."

"I did not. He begged me to get him some caps, but I wouldn't do it. It's the only one thing I wouldn't do for Tom. I did buy him some bottles of cough medicine with the codeine in it. I couldn't just sit there and watch him suffer, could I?"

"You want him to be a hype for the rest of his life? And die of it?"

"Don't say that."

"What are you trying to do to him?"

"Look after him."

"You think you're qualified?"

"I love the boy," she said. "I did what I could for him. Does that make me so lousy?"

"Nobody said you're lousy."

"Nobody has to say it. I tried to make him happy. I didn't have what it takes."

Fingering her heavy breasts, she looked down at herself in sorrow.

chapter 21

THE door behind her opened. Tom Rica leaned in the opening, with one frail shoulder propped against the doorframe. His sharp tweed jacket hung loosely on him.

"What's the trouble, Maudie?" His voice was thin and dry, denatured. His eyes were puddles of tar.

Maude resumed her smiling mask before she turned to him. "No trouble. Go back in."

She put her hands on his shoulders. He smiled past her at me, detachedly, pathetically, as if there was a thick glass wall between us. She shook him: "Did you get a needle? Is that where you were?"

"Wouldn't you like to know," he said in dull coquetry, using his hollow face as if it was young and charming.

"Where did you get it? Where did you get the money?"

"Who needs money, honey?"

"Answer me." Her shoulders bowed across him. She shook him so that his teeth clicked. "I want to know who gave you the stuff and how much you got and where the rest of it is."

He collapsed against the doorframe. "Lay off me, bag."

"That isn't a bad idea," I said, coming around the counter.

She whirled as if I'd stuck a knife in her back. "You stay out of this, brother. I'm warning you. I've taken enough from you, when all I want is to do what's right for my boy."

"You own him, do you?"

She yelled in a brass tenor: "Get out of my place."

Tom moved between us, like a vaudeville third man. "Don't talk like that to my old buddy." He peered at me through the glass wall. His eyes and speech were more focused, as though the first shock of the drug was passing off. "You still a do-gooder, old buddy? Myself, I'm a do-badder. Every day in every way I'm doing badder and badder, as dear old mother used to say."

"You talk too much," Maude said, laying a heavy arm across his shoulders. "Come in and lie down now."

He turned on her in a sudden spurt of viciousness. "Leave me be. I'm in good shape, having a nice reunion with my old buddy. You trying to break up my friendships?"

"I'm the only friend you got."

"Is that so? Let me tell you something. You'll have dirt in your eyes, and I'll be riding high, living the life of Riley. Who needs you?"

"You need me, Tom," she said, without assurance. "You were on your uppers when I took you in. If it wasn't for me you'd be in the pen. I got your charge reduced, and you know it, and it cost me plenty. So here you go right back on the same crazy kick. Don't you ever learn?"

"I learn, don't worry. All these years I been studying the angles, see, like an apprenticeship. I know the rackets like I know the back of my hand. I know where you stupid hustlers make your stupid mistakes. And I'm not making any. I got a racket of my own now, and it's as safe as houses." His mood had swung violently upward, in anger and elation.

"Houses with bars on the windows," the blonde woman said. "You stick your neck out again, and I can't cover for you."

"Nobody asked you to. I'm on my own now. Forget me."

He turned his back on her and went through the inner door. His body moved loosely and lightly, supported by invisible strings. I started to follow him. Maude turned her helpless anger on me:

"Stay out of there. You got no right in there."

I hesitated. She was a woman. I was in her house. With the toe of her shoe, Maude pressed a faintly worn spot in the carpet behind the counter:

"You better beat it out of here, I'm warning you."

"I think I'll stay for a while."

She folded her arms across her breasts and looked at me like a lioness. A short broad man in a plaid shirt opened the front door and came in quietly. His smile was wide and meaningless under a hammered-in nose. A leather blackjack, polished like a keepsake, swung from his hand.

"Dutch, take this one out," Maude said, standing away.

I went around the counter and took Dutch out instead. Perhaps bouncing drunks had spoiled him. Anyway, he was easy to hit. Between his wild swings, I hit him with a left to the head, a right cross to the jaw, a long left hook to the solar plexus which bent him over into my right coming up. He subsided. I picked up his blackjack and moved past Maude through the inner door. She didn't say a word.

I went through a living-room crowded with overstuffed furniture in a green-and-white jungle design from which eyes seemed to watch me, down a short hallway past a pink satin bedroom which reminded me of the inside of a coffin in disarray, to the open door of a bathroom. Tom's jacket lay across the lighted threshold like the headless torso of a man, flattened by the passage of some enormous engine.

Tom was sitting on the toilet seat with his left shirtsleeve rolled up and a hypodermic needle in his right hand. He was too busy looking for a vein to notice me. The veins he had already used and ruined writhed black up his arm from wrist to wasted biceps. Blue tattoo marks disguised the scars on his wrists.

I took the needle away from him. It was about a quarter full of clear liquid. Upturned in the bright bathroom light, his face set in hard wrinkles like a primitive mask used to conjure evil spirits, its eyeholes full of darkness.

"Give it back. I didn't get enough."

"Enough to kill yourself?"

"It keeps me alive. I almost died without it, there in the hospital. My brains were running out of my ears."

He made a sudden grab for the needle in my hand. I held it out of his reach.

"Go back to the hospital, Tom."

He swung his head slowly from side to side. "There's nothing for me there. Everything I want is on the outside."

"What do you want?"

"Kicks. Money and kicks. What else is there?"

"A hell of a lot."

"You've got it?" He sensed my hesitation, and looked up slyly. "Do-gooder ain't doing so good, eh? Don't go into the old look-to-the-future routine. It makes me puke. It always made me puke. So save it for the birds. *This* is my future, *now.*"

"You like it?"

"If you give me back my needle. It's all I need from you."

"Why don't you kick it, Tom? Use your guts for that. You're too young to go down the drain."

"Save it for the boy scouts, den-father. You want to know why I'm a hype? Because I got bored with double-mouthed bastards like you. You spout the old uplift line, but I never seen a one of you that believed in it for himself. While you're telling other people how to live, you're double-timing your wife and running after gash, drinking like a goddam fish and chasing any dirty nickel you can see."

There was enough truth in what he said to tie my tongue for a minute. The obscure pain of memory came back. It centered in an image in my mind: the face of the woman I had lost. I blotted the image out, telling myself that that was years ago. The important things had happened long ago.

Tom spoke to the doubt that must have showed in my face:

"Give me back my needle. What's to lose?"

"Not a chance."

"Come on," he wheedled. "The stuff is weak. The first shot didn't even give me a lift."

"Then you don't have so far to fall."

He beat his sharp knees with his fists. "Give me my needle, you hot-and-cold-running false-faced mother-lover. You'd steal the pennies off a dead man's eyes and sell his body for soap."

"Is that how you feel? Dead?"

"The hell I am. I'll show you. I can get more."

He got up and tried to push past me. He was frail and light as a scarecrow. I forced him back onto the seat, holding the needle carefully out of his reach.

"Where did you get it in the first place, Tom?"

"Would I tell you?"

"Maybe you don't have to."

"Then why ask?"

"What's this fine new racket of yours that you were warbling about?"

"Wouldn't you like to know."

"Pushing reefers to school kids?"

"You think I'm interested in peanuts?"

"Buying and selling old clothes?"

His ego couldn't stand to be downgraded. The insult blew it up like a balloon. "You think I'm kidding? I got a piece of the biggest racket in the world. Before I'm through I'll be buying and selling peanut-eaters like you."

"By saving green stamps, no doubt."

"By putting on the squeeze, jerk, where the money is.

You get something on somebody, see, and you sell it back a little piece at a time. It's like an annuity."

"Or a death-warrant."

He looked at me imperviously. Dead men never die.

"The good doctor could be very bad medicine."

He grinned. "I got an antidote."

"What have you got on him, Tom?"

"Do I look crazy enough to tell you?"

"You told Carl Hallman."

"Did I? Maybe he thinks I did. I told him any little thing that came into my little pointed head."

"What were you trying to do to him?"

"Just stir him up a little. I had to get out of that ward. I couldn't make it alone."

"Why did you send Hallman to me?"

"Get him off my hands. He was in my way."

"You must have had a better reason than that."

"Sure. I'm a do-gooder." His wise grin turned malign. "I thought you could use the business."

"Carl Hallman's got a murder rap on his hands, did you know that?"

"I know it."

"If I thought you talked him into it—"

"What would you do? Slap my wrist, do-gooder?"

He looked at me through the glass wall with lazy curiosity, and added casually: "Anyway, he didn't shoot his brother. He told me so himself."

"Has he been here?"

"Sure he was here. He wanted Maude to hide him out. She wouldn't touch him with gloves on."

"How long ago was this?"

"A couple of hours, maybe. He took off for town when Maude and Dutch gave him the rush."

"Did he say where he was going in town?"

"No."

"He didn't shoot his brother, you say?"

"That's right, he told me that."

"Did you believe him?"

"I had to believe him, because I did it myself." Tom looked at me dead-pan. "I flew over there by helicopter, see. In my new supersonic helicopter with the synchronized death-ray gun."

"Turn off the stardrive, Tom. Tell me what really happened."

"Maybe I will, if you give me back my needle."

His eyes held a curious mixture of plea and threat. They looked expectantly at the bright instrument in my fist. I was tempted to let him have it, on the chance that he knew something I could use. A few more caps in those black veins wouldn't make any difference. Except to me.

I was sick of the whole business. I threw the needle into the square pink bathtub. It smashed to pieces.

Tom looked at me incredulously, "What did you do that for?"

Sudden fury shook him, too strong for his nerves to carry. It broke through into grief. He flung himself face down on the pink tile floor, sobbing in a voice like fabric tearing.

In the intervals of the noise he made, I heard other noises behind me. Maude was coming through the jungle-colored living-room. A gun gleamed dully blue in her white hand. The man called Dutch was a pace behind her. His grin was broken-toothed. I could see why my knuckles were sore.

"What goes on?" Maude cried. "What did you do to him?"

"Took his needle away. See for yourself."

She didn't seem to hear me. "Come out of there. Leave him alone." She pushed the gun toward my face.

"Let me at him. I'll clobber the bastard," the man behind her lisped in punchy eagerness.

An Argyle sock hung heavy and pendulous from his hand. It reminded me of the blackjack in my pocket. I backed out of the doorway to gain elbowroom, and swung the leather club over and down at Maude's wrist.

She hissed with pain. The gun clanked at her feet. Dutch went down on his hands and knees after it. I hit him on the back of the head with the blackjack, not too hard, just hard enough to stretch him on his face again. The heavy sock fell from his numb hand, some of its sand spilling out.

Maude was scrambling in the doorway for the gun. I pushed her back and picked it up and put it in my pocket. It was a medium-caliber revolver and it made a very heavy pocket. I put the blackjack in my other pocket so that I wouldn't walk lopsided.

Maude leaned on the wall outside the door, holding her right wrist in her left hand. "You're going to be sorry for this."

"I've heard that before."

"Not from me you haven't, or you wouldn't be running around making trouble for people. Don't think it's going to last. I got the top law in this county in my pocket."

"Tell me more," I said. "You have a lovely singing voice. Maybe I can arrange a personal appearance, in front of the Grand Jury."

Her ugly mouth said yah at me. Her left hand came out stiff, its carmine talons pointed at my eyes. It was more of a threat than attempt, but it made me despair of our relationship.

I left her and found a back way out. There were soft lights and loud noises in the cottages on the terraces, music, female laughter, money, kicks.

chapter 22

I DROVE back toward Purissima, keeping a not very hopeful lookout for Carl Hallman. Just outside the city limits, where the highway dipped down from the bluffs toward the sea, I saw a huddle of cars on the shoulder. Two of the cars had red pulsating lights. Other lights were moving on the beach.

I parked across the highway and got the flashlight out of my dash compartment. Before I closed it, I relieved my pockets of the gun and the blackjack and locked them up. I descended a flight of concrete steps which slanted down to the beach. Near their foot, the vestiges of a small fire glowed. Beside it, a blanket was spread on the sand, weighted down by a picnic basket.

Most of the lights were far up the beach by now, bobbing and swerving like big slow fireflies. Between me and the dim thumping line of the surf, a dozen or so people were milling aimlessly. A man detached himself from the shadowy group and trotted toward me, soft-footed in the sand.

"Hey! That's my stuff. It belongs to me."

I flashed my light across him. He was a very young man in a gray sweatshirt with a college letter on the front of it. He moved as though he had won the letter playing football.

"What's the excitement about?" I said.

"I'm not excited. I just don't like people messing around with my stuff."

"Nobody's messing around with your stuff. I mean the excitement up the beach."

"The cops are after a guy."

"What guy is that?"

"The maniac—the one that shot his brother."

"Did you see him?"

"I hope to tell you. I was the one that raised the alarm. He walked right up to Marie when she was sitting here. Lord knows what would have happened if I hadn't been within reach." The boy arched his shoulders and stuck out his chest.

"What did happen?"

"Well, I went up to the car to get some cigarettes, and this guy came out of the dark and asked Marie for a sandwich. It wasn't just a sandwich that he wanted, she could tell. A sandwich was just the thin edge of the wedge. Marie let out a yell, and I came down the bank and threw a tackle at him. I could have held him, too, except that it was dark and I couldn't see what I was doing. He caught me a lucky blow in the face, and got away."

I turned my light on his face. His lower lip was swollen.

"Which way did he go?"

He pointed along the shore to the multicolored lights of the Purissima waterfront. "I would have run him down, only maybe he had confederates, so I couldn't leave Marie here by herself. We drove to the nearest gas station and I phoned in the alarm."

The onlookers on the beach had begun to straggle up the concrete steps. A highway patrolman approached us, the light from his flash stabbing at the pockmarked sand. The boy in the sweatshirt called out heartily:

"Anything else I can do?"

"Not right now there isn't. He got clean away, it looks like."

"Maybe he swam out to sea and went aboard a yacht and they'll put him ashore in Mexico. I heard the family is loaded."

"Maybe," the patrolman said drily. "You're sure you saw the man? Or have you been seeing too many movies?"

The boy retorted hotly: "You think I smacked myself in the mouth?"

"Sure it was the man we're looking for?"

"Of course. Big guy with light-colored hair in dungarees. Ask Marie. She had a real good look at him."

"Where is your girlfriend now?"

"Somebody took her home, she was pretty upset."

"I guess we better have her story. Show me where she lives, eh?"

"I'll be glad to."

While the young man was dousing the fire with sand and collecting his belongings, another car stopped on the roadside above us. It was an old black convertible which looked familiar. Mildred got out and started down the steps. She came so blindly and precipitously that I was afraid she'd fall and plunge headlong. I caught her at the foot of the steps with one arm around her waist.

"Let me go!"

I let her go. She recognized me then, and returned to her mind's single track: "Is Carl here? Have you seen him?"

"No—"

She turned to the patrolman: "Has my husband been here?"

"You Mrs. Hallman?"

"Yes. The radio said my husband was seen on Pelican Beach."

"He's been and gone, ma'am."

"Gone where?"

"That's what we'd like to know. Do you have any ideas on the subject?"

"No. I haven't."

"Has he got any close friends in Purissima—somebody he might go to?"

Mildred hesitated. The faces of curious onlookers strained out of the darkness toward her. The boy in the sweatshirt was breathing on the back of her neck. He spoke as if she were deaf or dead:

"This is the guy's *wife*."

The patrolman looked disgusted. "Break it up, eh? Move along there now." He turned back to Mildred: "Any ideas, ma'am?"

"I'm sorry—it's hard for me to think. Carl had lots of friends in high school. They all dropped away. He didn't see anyone the last year or so." Her voice trailed off. She seemed confused by the lights and the people.

I said, as stuffily as possible: "Mrs Hallman came here to look for her husband. She doesn't have to answer questions."

The patrolman's light came up to my face. "Who are you?"

"A friend of the family. I'm going to take her home."

"All right. Take her home. She shouldn't be running around by herself, anyway."

With a hand under her elbow, I propelled Mildred up the steps and across the highway. Her face was an oval blur in the dark interior of my car, so pale that it seemed luminous.

"Where are you taking me?"

"Home, as I said. Is it far from here?"

"A couple of miles. I have my own car, thank you, and I'm perfectly fit to drive it. After all, I drove it here."

"Don't you think it's time you relaxed?"

"With Carl still being hunted? How can I? Anyway, I've been home all day. You said he might come to the house, but he never did."

Exhaustion or disappointment overcame her. She sat inertly, propped doll-like in the seat. Headlights went by in the road like brilliant forlorn hopes rushing out of darkness into darkness.

"He may be on his way there now," I said. "He's hungry, and he must be bone-tired. He's been on the run for a night and a day." And another night was beginning.

Her hand moved from her mouth to my arm. "How do you know he's hungry?"

"He asked a girl on the beach for a sandwich. Before that he went to a friend, looking for shelter. Friend may be the wrong word. Did Carl ever mention Tom Rica to you?"

"Rica? Isn't that the fellow who escaped with him? His name was in the paper."

"That's right. Do you know anything else about him?"

"Just from what Carl said."

"When was that?"

"The last time I saw him, in the hospital. He told me how this Rica man had suffered in the ward. Carl was trying to make it easier for him. He said that Rica was a heroin addict."

"Did he tell you anything more about him?"

"Not that I remember. Why?"

"Rica saw Carl, not more than a couple of hours ago. If Rica can be believed. He's staying with a woman named Maude, at a place called the Buenavista Inn, just a few miles down the highway. Carl went there looking for a place to hole up."

"I don't understand," Mildred said. "Why would Carl go to a woman like that for help?"

"You know Maude, do you?"

"Certainly not. But everybody in town knows what goes on at that so-called Inn." Mildred looked at me with a kind of terror. "Is Carl mixed up with those people?"

"It doesn't follow. A man on the run will take any out he can think of."

The words didn't sound the way I'd meant them to. Her head went down under the weight of the heavy image they made. She sighed again.

It was hard to listen to. I put my arm around her. She held herself stiff and silent against my shoulder.

"Relax. This isn't a pass."

I didn't think it was. Possibly Mildred knew better. She pulled herself away from me and got out of my car in a single flurry of movement.

Most of the cars across the highway had left as we sat talking. The road was empty except for a heavy truck highballing down the hill from the south. Mildred stood at the edge of the pavement, silhouetted by its approaching lights.

The situation went to pieces, and came together in the rigid formal clarity of a photographed explosion. Mildred was on the pavement, walking head down in the truck's bright path. It bore down on her as tall as a house, braying and squealing. I saw its driver's lantern-slide face high above the road, and Mildred in the road in front of the giant tires.

The truck stopped a few feet short of her. In the sudden vacuum of sound, I could hear the sea mumbling and spitting like a beast under the bank. The truck-driver leaned from his cab and yelled at Mildred in relief and indignation:

"Damn fool woman! Watch where you're going. You damn near got yourself killed."

Mildred paid no attention to him. She climbed into the Buick, waited until the truck was out of the way, and made a sweeping turn in front of me. I was bothered by the way she handled herself and the car. She moved and drove obliviously, like someone alone in black space.

chapter 23

My quasi-paternal instinct followed her home; I went along for the ride. She made it safely, and left the black convertible at the curb. When I pulled in behind it, she stopped in the middle of the sidewalk:

"What are you trying to do?"

"Seeing Millie home."

Her response was flat. "Well, I'm home."

The old house leaned like a tombstone on the night. But there were lights inside, behind cracked blinds, and the sound of a broken soprano voice. I got out and followed Mildred up the walk:

"You almost got yourself run over."

"Did I?" She turned at the top of the veranda steps. "I don't need a keeper, thank you. In fact, all I want is to be let alone."

"The deep tangled wildwood," the lost and strident voice sang from the house. "And all the loved songs that my infancy knew."

"Is your mother all right, Mildred?"

"Mother's just dandy, thank you. She's been drinking all day." She looked up and down the dark street and said in a different voice: "Even the crummy people who live on this street look down their noses at us. I can't put up a front any more. I'd simply like to crawl into a hole and die."

"You need some rest."

"How can I get any rest? With all this trouble on my shoulders? And that?"

Cast by the light from one of the front windows, her

shadow lay broken on the steps. She gestured toward the window. Behind it her mother had finished her song and was playing some closing bars on a badly tuned piano.

"Anyway," Mildred said, "I have to go to work tomorrow morning. I can't miss another half day."

"Who do you work for, Simon Legree?"

"I don't mean that. Mr. Haines is very nice. It's just, if I go off schedule, I'm afraid I'll never get back on."

She fumbled in her black plastic bag for her key. The doorknob turned before she touched it. The outside light came on over our heads. Mrs. Gley opened the door, smiling muzzily:

"Bring your friend in, dear. I've said it before and I'll say it again. Your mother's always pleased and proud to entertain your friends."

Mrs. Gley didn't seem to recognize me; I was part of the indiscriminate past blurred out by the long day's drinking. She was glad to see me anyway.

"Bring your friend in, Mildred. I'll pour him a drink. A young man likes to be entertained; that's something you've got to learn. You've wasted too much of your youth on that good-for-nothing husband—"

"Stop making a fool of yourself," Mildred said coldly.

"I am not making a fool of myself. I am expressing the feelings of my womanly heart. Isn't that so?" she appealed to me. "You'll come in and have a drink with me, won't you?"

"Be glad to."

"And I'll be glad to have you."

Mrs. Gley spread her arms out in a welcoming gesture, and toppled toward me. I caught her under the arms. She giggled against my shirt front. With Mildred's help, I walked her into the sitting-room. She was awkward to handle in her draperies, like a loosely shrouded corpse.

But she managed to sit upright on the sofa and say in gracious tones:

"Excuse me. I was overcome by dizziness for a moment. The shock of the night air, you know."

Like someone struck by a bullet, invisible and inaudible, she fell softly sideways. Very soon, she began to snore.

Mildred straightened our her mother's legs, smoothed her purplish red hair and put a cushion under her head. She took off her own cloth coat and covered the lower part of her mother's body. She did these things with neutral efficiency, without tenderness and without anger, as though she'd done them many times before and expected to do them many times again.

In the same neutral way, like an older woman speaking to a younger, she said: "Poor mother, have sweet dreams. Or no dreams. I wish you no dreams at all."

"Can I help to get her upstairs?" I said.

"She can sleep here. She often has. This happens two or three times a week. We're used to it."

Mildred sat at her mother's feet and looked around the room as if to memorize its shabby contents. She stared at the empty eye of the television set. The empty eye stared back at her. She looked down at her mother's sleeping face. My feeling that their ages were reversed was stronger when she spoke again:

"Poor redhead. She used to be a genuine redhead, too. I give her money to have it dyed. But she prefers to dye it herself, and save the money for drinking. I can't really blame her. She's tired. She ran a boarding-house for fourteen years and then she got tired."

"Is your mother a widow?"

"I don't know." She raised her eyes to my face. "It hardly matters. My father took off when I was seven years old. He had a wonderful chance to buy a ranch in Nevada for very little down. Father was always getting those wonderful chances, but this was the one that was really going to pay off. He was supposed to come back for us in three weeks or a month, when everything was settled. He never did come back. I heard from him just once. He sent me a present for my eighth birthday, a ten-dollar gold piece from Reno. There was a little note along with it, that I wasn't to spend it. I was to keep it as a token of his love. I didn't spend it, either. Mother did."

If Mildred felt resentment, she didn't show it. She sat for a time, silent and still. Then she twitched her slender shoulders, as though to shake off the dead hand of the past:

"I don't know how I got off on the subject of Father. Anyway, it doesn't matter." She changed the subject abruptly: "This man Rica, at the Buenavista Inn, what kind of a person is he?"

"Pretty dilapidated. There's not much left but hunger. He's been on dope for years. As a witness he may be useless."

"As a witness?"

"He said that Carl told him he didn't shoot Jerry."

Faint color rose in her face, and her eyes brightened. "Why didn't you tell *me* that?"

"You didn't give me a chance to. You seemed to have a rendezvous with a truck."

Her color deepened. "I admit I had a bad reaction. You oughtn't to have put your arm around me."

"I meant it in a friendly way."

"I know. It just reminded me of something. We were talking about those people at the Inn."

"I thought you didn't know them."

"I don't know them. I don't want to know them." She hesitated. "But don't you think you should inform the police about what that man said?"

"I haven't made up my mind."

"Did you believe what he said?"

"With reservations. I never did think that Carl shot his brother. But my opinion isn't based on Rica's testimony. He's a dream-talker."

"What is it based on?"

"It's hard to say. I had a strange feeling about the events at the ranch today. They had an unreal quality. Does that fit in with anything you noticed?"

"I think so, but I couldn't pin it down. What do you mean, exactly?"

"If I could say exactly, I'd know what happened out there. I don't know what happened, not yet. Some of the things I saw with my own eyes seemed as if they'd been staged for my benefit. Your husband's movements don't make sense to me, and neither do some of the others. That includes the sheriff."

"It doesn't mean Carl is guilty."

"That's just my point. He did his best to try and prove that he was, but I'm not convinced. You're familiar with the situation, the people involved. And if Carl didn't shoot Jerry, somebody else did. Who had a motive?"

"Zinnie had, of course. Only the idea of Zinnie is impossible. Women like Zinnie don't shoot people."

"Sometimes they do if the people are their husbands, and if they have strong enough motives. Love and money are a strong combination."

"You know about her and Dr. Grantland? Yes, of course, you must. She's pretty obvious."

"How long has it been going on?"

"Not long, I'm sure of that. Whatever there is between them started after I left the ranch. I heard rumors downtown. One of my best friends is a legal secretary. She told me two or three months ago that Zinnie wanted a divorce from Jerry. He wasn't willing to give it to her, though. He threatened to fight her for Martha, and apparently she dropped the whole idea. Zinnie would never do anything that would lose her Martha."

"Shooting Jerry wouldn't lose her Martha," I said, "unless she was caught."

"You're not suggesting that Zinnie did shoot him? I simply don't believe it."

I didn't believe it, either. I didn't disbelieve it. I held it in my mind and turned it around to see how it looked. It looked as ugly as sin.

"Where's Zinnie now, do you know?"

"I haven't seen her since I left the ranch."

"What about Martha?"

"I suppose she's with Mrs. Hutchinson. She spends a lot of her life with Mrs. Hutchinson." Mildred added in a lower tone: "If I had a little girl like Martha, I'd stay with her and look after her myself. Only I haven't."

Her eyes brightened with tears. I realized for the first time what her barren broken marriage meant to her.

The telephone rang like an alarm clock in the hall. Mildred went to answer it.

"This is Mildred Hallman speaking." Her voice went higher. "No! I don't want to see you. You have no right to harass me. . . . Of course he hasn't. I don't need anyone to protect me."

I heard her hang up, but she didn't come back to the sitting-room. Instead she went into the front of the house. I found her in a room off the hallway, standing in the dark by the window.

"What's the trouble?"

She didn't answer. I found the light switch by the door, and pressed it. A single bulb winked on in the old brass chandelier. Against the opposite wall, an ancient piano grinned at me with all its yellow keys. An empty gin bottle stood on top of it.

"Was that Sheriff Ostervelt on the telephone?"

"How did you know?"

"The way you react to him. The Ostervelt reaction."

"I hate him," she said. "I don't like her, either. Ever since Carl's been in the hospital, she's been acting more and more as if she owns him."

"I seem to have lost the thread. Who are we talking about?"

"A woman called Rose Parish, a social worker at the State Hospital. She's with Sheriff Ostervelt, and they both want to come here. I don't want to see them. They're people-eaters."

"What does that mean?"

"They're people who live on other people's troubles. I hope I headed them off. I've had enough bites taken out of me."

"I think you're wrong about Miss Parish."

"You know her?"

"I met her this morning, at the hospital. She seemed very sympathetic to your husband's case."

"Then what's she doing with Sheriff Ostervelt?"

"Probably straightening him out, if I know Miss Parish."

"He can use some straightening out. If he comes here, I won't let him in."

"Are you afraid of him?"

"I suppose I am. No. I hate him too much to be afraid of him. He did a dreadful thing to me."

"You mean the day you took Carl to the hospital?"

Mildred nodded. Pale and heavy-eyed, she looked as if her youth had run out through the unstopped wound of that day.

"I'd better tell you what actually happened. He tried to make me his—his whore. He tried to take me to Buenavista Inn."

"That same day?"

"Yes, on the way back from the hospital. He'd already made three or four stops, and every time he came back to the car he was drunker and more obnoxious. Finally I asked him to let me off at the nearest bus station. We were in Buena Vista by then, just a little way from home, but I couldn't put up with him any longer.

"I was forced to, however. Instead of taking me to the bus station, he drove out the highway to the Inn, and parked above it. The owner was a friend of his, he said—a wonderful woman, very broad-minded. If I wanted to stay there with her, she'd give me a suite to myself, and it wouldn't cost me a cent. I could take a week's vacation, or a month's—as long as I liked—and he would come and keep me company at night.

"He said he'd had this in mind for a long time, ever since his wife passed away, before that. Now that Carl was out of the way, he and I could get together at last. You should have heard him, trying to be romantic. The great lover. Leaning across me with his bald head, sweating and breathing hard and smelling of liquor."

Anger clenched in my stomach like a fist. "Did he try to use force on you?"

"He tried to kiss me. I was able to handle him, though, when he saw how I felt about him. He didn't assault me, not physically, if that's what you're getting at. But he treated me as if I—as if a woman whose husband was sick was fair game for anybody."

"What about Carl's alleged confession? Did he try to use it to make you do what he wanted?"

"Yes, he did. Only please don't do anything about it. The situation is bad enough already."

"It could get worse for him. Abuse of office cuts two ways."

"You mustn't talk like that. It will only make things worse for Carl."

A car purred somewhere out of sight. Then its headlights entered the street.

"Turn off the light," Mildred whispered, "I have a feeling it's them."

I pressed the switch and crossed to the window where she stood. A black Mercury Special pulled in to the curb behind my convertible. Ostervelt and Miss Parish got out of the back seat. Mildred pulled down the blind and turned to me:

"Will you talk to them? I don't want to see them."

"I don't blame you for not wanting to see Ostervelt. You ought to talk to Miss Parish, though. She's definitely on our side."

"I'll talk to her if I have to. But she'll have to give me a chance to change my clothes."

Their footsteps were on the porch. As I went to answer the door, I heard Mildred running up the stairs behind me.

chapter 24

Miss Parish and the sheriff were standing in uncomfortable relation to each other. I guessed they'd had an argument. She looked official and rather imposing in a plain blue coat and hat. Ostervelt's face was shadowed by his wide hatbrim, but I got the impression that he was feeling subdued. If there had been an argument, he'd lost.

"What are you doing here?" He spoke without force, like an old actor who has lost faith in his part.

"I've been holding Mrs. Hallman's hand. Hello, Miss Parish."

"Hello." Her smile was warm. "How *is* Mrs. Hallman?"

"Yeah," Ostervelt said. "How is she? She sounded kind of upset on the telephone. Did something happen?"

"Mrs. Hallman doesn't want to see you unless it's necessary."

"Hell, I'm just interested in her personal safety." He looked sideways at Miss Parish and added for her benefit, in an injured-innocent tone: "What's Mildred got against me?"

I stepped outside and shut the door behind me. "Are you sure you want an answer?"

I couldn't keep the heat out of my voice. In reflex, Ostervelt put his hand on his gun-butt.

"Good heavens!" Miss Parish said with a forced little laugh. "Haven't we got enough trouble, gentlemen?"

"I want to know what he means by that. He's been needling me all day. I don't have to take that stuff from any keyhole cop." Ostervelt sounded almost querulous. "Not in my own county I don't."

"You ought to be ashamed of yourself, Mr. Archer." She stepped between us, turning her back on me and her full maternal charm on Ostervelt. "Why don't you wait for me in the car, Sheriff? I'll talk to Mrs. Hallman if she'll let me. It's obvious that her husband hasn't been here. That's all you wanted to know, isn't it?"

"Yeah, but—" He glared at me over her shoulder. "I didn't like that crack."

"You weren't intended to. Make something out of it."

The situation was boiling up again. Miss Parish poured cool words on it: "I didn't hear any crack. Both you men are under a strain. It's no excuse for acting like boys with a chip on your shoulder." She touched Ostervelt's shoulder, and let her hand linger there. "You will go and wait in the car, won't you? I'll only be a few minutes."

With a kind of caressing firmness, she turned Ostervelt around and gave him a gentle push toward the street. He took it, and he went. She gave me a bright, warm look.

"How did you get him eating out of your hand?"

"Oh, that's my little secret. Actually, something came up."

"What came up?"

She smiled. "I did. Dr. Brockley couldn't make it; he had an important meeting. So he sent me instead. I asked him to."

"To check up on Ostervelt?"

"I have no official right to do anything like that." The door of the Mercury slammed in the street. "We'd better go inside, don't you think? He'll know we're talking about him."

"Let him."

"You men. Sometimes I feel as though the whole world were a mental hospital. It's certainly a safe enough assumption to act on."

After the day I'd put in, I wasn't inclined to argue. I opened the door and held it for her. She faced me in the lighted hallway.

"I didn't expect to find you here."

"I got involved."

"I understand you have your car back."

"Yes." But she wasn't interested in my car. "If you're asking the question I think you are, I'm working for your friend Carl. I don't believe he killed his brother, or anybody else."

"Really?" Her bosom rose under her coat. She unbuttoned the coat to give it the room it needed. "I just got finished telling Sheriff Ostervelt the same thing."

"Did he buy it?"

"I'm afraid not. The circumstances are very much against Carl, aren't they? I did manage to cool the old man off a bit."

"How did you manage that?"

"It's official business. Confidential."

"Having to do with Carl?"

"Indirectly. The man he escaped with, Tom Rica. I really can't give you any more information, Mr. Archer."

"Let me guess. If I'm right, I know it already. If I'm wrong, there's no harm done. Ostervelt got Rica off with a state-hospital commitment when under the law he should have been sent to the pen."

Miss Parish didn't say I was wrong. She didn't say anything.

I ushered her into the front room. Her dark awareness took it in at a glance, staying on the empty bottle on top of the piano. There was a family photograph beside it, in a tarnished silver frame, and a broken pink conch shell.

Miss Parish picked up the bottle and sniffed it and set it down with a rap. She looked suspiciously toward the door. Her bold profile and mannish hat reminded me of a female operative in a spy movie.

"Where's the little wife?" she whispered.

"Upstairs, changing her clothes."

"Is she a drinker?"

"Never touches the stuff. Her mother drinks for both of them."

"I see."

Miss Parish leaned forward to examine the photograph. I looked at it over her shoulder. A smiling man in shirt-sleeves and wide suspenders stood under a palm tree with a strikingly pretty woman. The woman held a long-dressed child on her arm. The picture had been amateurishly tinted by hand. The tree was green, the woman's bobbed hair was red, the flowers in her dress were red. All the colors were fading.

"Is this the mother-in-law?"

"Apparently."

"Where is she now?"

"Dreamland. She passed out."

"Alcoholic?"

"Mrs. Gley is working at it."

"What about the father?"

"He dropped away long ago. He may be dead."

"I'm surprised," Miss Parish murmured. "I understood Carl came from quite a wealthy—quite a good background."

"Wealthy, anyway. His wife doesn't."

"So I gather." Miss Parish looked around the mortuary room where the past refused to live or die. "It helps to fill in the picture."

"What picture?" Her patronizing attitude irked me.

"My understanding of Carl and his problems. The type of family a sick man marries into can be very significant. A person who feels socially inadequate, as sick people do, will often lower himself in the social scale, deliberately declass himself."

"Don't jump to conclusions too fast. You should take a look at his own family."

"Carl's told me a great deal about them. You know, when a person breaks down, he doesn't do it all by himself. It's something that happens to whole families. The terrible thing is when one member cracks up, the rest so often make a scapegoat out of him. They think they can solve their own problems by rejecting the sick one—locking him up and forgetting him."

"That applies to the Hallmans," I said. "It doesn't apply to Carl's wife. I think her mother would like to see him put away for good, but she doesn't count for much."

"I know, I mustn't let myself be unfair to the wife. She seems to be quite a decent little creature. I have to admit she stayed with it when the going was rough. She came to see Carl every week, never missed a Sunday. Which is more than you can say for a lot of them." Miss Parish cocked her head, as if she could hear a playback of herself. She flushed slowly. "Good heavens, listen to me. It's such a temptation to identify with the patients and blame the relatives for everything. It's one of our worst occupational hazards."

She sat down on the piano stool and took out a cigarette, which I lit for her. Twin lights burned deep in her eyes. I could sense her emotions burning behind her professional front, like walled atomic fires. They didn't burn for me, though.

Just to have something burning for me, I lit a cigarette of my own. Miss Parish jumped at the snap of the lighter; she had nerves, too. She turned on the stool to look up at me:

"I know I identify with my patients. Especially Carl. I can't help it."

"Isn't that doing it the hard way? If I went through the wringer every time one of my clients does—" I lost interest in the sentence, and let it drop. I had my own identification with the hunted man.

"I don't *care* about myself." Miss Parish crushed out her cigarette rather savagely, and moved to the doorway. "Carl is in serious jeopardy, isn't he?"

"It could be worse."

"It may be worse than you think. I talked to several people at the courthouse. They're raking up those other deaths in his family. He did a lot of talking, you know, at the time he was committed. Completely irrational talking.

You don't take what a disturbed person says at its face value. But a lot of men in law enforcement don't understand that."

"Did the sheriff tell you about Carl's alleged confession?"

"He hinted around about it. I'm afraid he gives it a lot of weight. As if it proved anything."

"You sound as if you've heard it all before."

"Of course I have. When Carl was admitted six months ago he had himself convinced that he was the criminal of the century. He accused himself of killing both his parents."

"His mother, too?"

"I think his guilt-feelings originated with her suicide. She drowned herself several years ago."

"I knew that. But I don't understand why he'd blame himself."

"It's a typical reaction in depressed patients to blame themselves for everything bad that happens. Particularly the death of people they love. Carl was devoted to his mother, deeply dependent on her. At the same time he was trying to break away and have a life of his own. She probably killed herself for reasons that had no connection with Carl. But he saw her death as a direct result of his disloyalty to her, what he thought of as disloyalty. He felt as though his efforts to cut the umbilical cord had actually killed her. From there it was only a step to thinking that he was a murderer."

It was tempting doctrine, that Carl's guilt was compounded of words and fantasies, the stuff of childhood nightmares. It promised to solve so many problems that I was suspicious of it.

"Would a theory like that stand up in court?"

"It isn't theory, it's fact. Whether or not it was accepted as fact would depend on the human element: the judge, the jury, the quality of the expert witnesses. But there's no reason why it should ever come to court." Her eyes were watchful, ready to be angry with me.

"I'd still like to get my hands on firm evidence that he didn't do these crimes, that somebody else did. It's the only certain way to prove that his confession was a phony."

"But it definitely was. We know his mother was a suicide. His father died of natural causes, or possibly by accident. The story Carl told about that was pure fantasy, right out of the textbook."

"I haven't read the textbook."

"He said that he broke into his father's bathroom when the old man was in the tub, knocked him unconscious, and held him under water until he was dead."

"Do you know for a fact that it didn't happen that way?"

"Yes," she said. "I do. I have the word of the best possible witness, Carl himself. He knows now that he had no direct connection with his father's death. He told me that several weeks ago. He's developed remarkable insight into his guilt-feelings, and his reasons for confessing something he didn't do. He knows now that he wanted to punish himself for his father-killing fantasies. Every boy has the Oedipus fantasies, but they seldom come out so strongly, except in psychotic breakthrough.

"Carl had a breakthrough the morning he and his brother found their father in the bathtub. The night before, he'd had a serious argument with his father. Carl was very angry, murderously angry. When his father actually did die, he felt like a murderer. The guilt of his mother's death came up from the unconscious and reinforced this new guilt. His mind invented a story to explain his terrible guilt-feelings, and somehow deal with them."

"Carl told you all this?" It sounded very complicated and tenuous.

"We worked it out together," she said softly and gravely. "I don't mean to take credit to myself. Dr. Brockley directed the therapy. Carl simply happened to do his talking-out to me."

Her face was warm and bright again, with the pride a woman can take in being a woman, exerting peaceful power. It was hard to hold on to my skepticism, which seemed almost like an insult to her calm assurance.

"How can you tell the difference between true confessions and fantasies?"

"That's where training and experience come in. You get a feeling for unreality. It's partly in the tone, and partly in the content. Often you can tell by the very enormity of the fantasy, the patient's complete insistence on his guilt. You wouldn't believe the crimes I've had confessed to me. I've talked to a Jack the Ripper, a man who claimed he shot Lincoln, several who killed Christ himself. All these people feel they've done evil—we all do in some degree—and unconsciously they want to punish themselves for the worst possible crimes. As the patient gets better, and can face his actual problems, the need for punishment and the guilty fantasies disappear together. Carl's faded out that way."

"And you never make a mistake about these fantasies?"

"I don't claim that. There's no mistake about Carl's. He got over them, and that's proof positive that they were illusory."

"I hope he got over them. This morning when I talked to him, he was still hung up on his father's death. In fact, he wanted to hire me to prove that somebody else murdered his father. I guess that's some improvement over thinking he did it himself."

Miss Parish shook her head. She brushed past me and moved to the window, stood there with her thumbnail between her teeth. Her shadow on the blind was like an enlarged image of a worried child. I sensed the doubts and fears that had kept her single and turned her love toward the sick.

"He's had a setback," she said bitterly. "He should never have left the hospital so soon. He wasn't ready to face these dreadful things."

I laid my hand on one of her bowed shoulders. "Don't let it get *you* down. He's depending on people like you to help him out of it." Whether or not he's guilty, the words ran on unspoken in my head.

I looked out past the edge of the blind. The Mercury was still in the street. I could hear the squawk of its radio faintly through the glass.

"I'd do anything for Carl," Miss Parish said close to my ear. "I suppose that's no secret to you."

I didn't answer her. I was reluctant to encourage her intimacy. Miss Parish alternated between being too personal and too official. And Mildred was a long time coming down.

I went to the piano and picked out a one-finger tune. I quit when I recognized it: "Sentimental Journey." I took the conch shell and set it to my ear. Its susurrus sounded less like the sea than the labored breathing of a tiring runner. No doubt I heard what I was listening for.

chapter 25

I SAW the reason for Mildred's delay when she appeared finally. She'd brushed her hair shining, changed to a black jersey dress which molded her figure and challenged comparison with it, changed to heels which added three inches to her height. She stood in the doorway, holding out both her hands. Her smile was forced and brilliant:

"I'm so glad to see you, Miss Parish. Forgive me for keeping you waiting. I know how precious your time must be, with all your nursing duties."

"I'm not a nurse." Miss Parish was upset. For a moment she looked quite ugly, with her black brows pulled down and her lower lip pushed out.

"I'm sorry, did I make a mistake? I thought Carl mentioned you as one of his nurses. He has mentioned you, you know."

Miss Parish rose rather awkwardly to the occasion. I gathered that the two young women had crossed swords or needles before. "It doesn't matter, dear. I know you've had a bad day."

"You're so sympathetic, Rose. Carl thinks so, too. You don't mind if I call you Rose? I've felt so close to you, through Carl."

"I *want* you to call me Rose. I'd love nothing better than for you to regard me as a big sister, somebody you can lean on."

Like other forthright people, Miss Parish got very phony when she got phony at all. I guessed that she'd come with some notion of mothering Mildred, the next best thing to mothering Mildred's husband. Clumsily, she tried to embrace the smaller woman. Mildred evaded her:

"Won't you sit down? I'll make you a cup of tea."

"Oh, no thanks."

"You must take something. You've come such a long way. Let me get you something to eat."

"Oh, no."

"Why not?" Mildred stared frankly at the other woman's body. "Are you dieting?"

"No. Perhaps I ought to." Large and outwitted and rebuffed, Miss Parish sank into a chair. Its springs creaked satirically under her weight. She tried to look small. "Perhaps, if I could have a drink?"

"I'm sorry." Mildred glanced at the bottle on the piano, and met the issue head-on. "There's nothing in the house. My mother happens to drink too much. I try to keep it unavailable. I don't always succeed, as you doubtless know. You hospital workers keep close tabs on the patients' relatives, don't you?"

"Oh, no," Miss Parish said. "We don't have the staff—"

"What a pity. But I can't complain. You've made an exception for me. I think it's marvelous of you. It makes me feel so looked-after."

"I'm sorry you feel that way. I just came by to help in any way I could."

"How thoughtful of you. I hate to disappoint you. My husband is not here."

Miss Parish was being badly mauled. Although in a way she'd asked for it, I felt sorry for her.

"About that drink," I said with faked cheerfulness. "I could use a drink, too. What do you say we surge out and find one, Rose?"

She looked up gratefully, from the detailed study she had been making of her fingernails. I noticed that they had been bitten short. Mildred said:

"Please don't rush away. I could have a bottle sent in from the liquor store. Perhaps my mother will join you. We could have a party."

"Lay off," I said to her under my breath.

She answered with her brilliant smile: "I hate to appear inhospitable."

The situation was getting nowhere except on my nerves. It was terminated abruptly by a scuffle of feet on the porch, a knock on the door. The two women followed me to the door. It was Carmichael, the sheriff's deputy. Behind him in the street, the sheriff's car was pulling away from the curb.

"What is it?" Mildred said.

"We just got a radio report from the Highway Patrol. A man answering your husband's description was sighted at the Red Barn drive-in. Sheriff Ostervelt thought you ought to be warned. Apparently he's headed in this direction."

"I'm glad if he is," Mildred said.

Carmichael gave her an astonished look. "Just the same, I'll keep guard on the house. Inside if you want."

"It isn't necessary. I'm not afraid of my husband."

"Neither am I," Miss Parish said behind her. "I know the man thoroughly. He isn't dangerous."

"A lot of people think different, ma'am."

"I know Sheriff Ostervelt thinks different. What orders did he give you, concerning the use of your gun?"

"I use my own discretion if Hallman shows. Naturally I'm not going to shoot him if I don't have to."

"You'd be wise to stick to that, Mr. Carmichael." Miss Parish's voice had regained its authority. "Mr. Hallman is a suspect, not a convict. You don't want to do something that you'll regret to the end of your days."

"She's right," I said. "Take him without gunfire if you can. He's a sick man, remember."

Carmichael's mouth set stubbornly. I'd seen that expression on his face before, in the Hallman greenhouse. "His brother Jerry is sicker. We don't want any more killings."

"That's my point exactly."

Carmichael turned away, refusing to argue further. "Anyway," he said from the steps, "I'm keeping guard on the house. Even if you don't see me, I'll be within call."

The low augh of a distant siren rose to an ee. Mildred

shut the door on the sound, the voice of the treacherous night. Behind her freshly painted mask her face was haggard.

"They want to kill him, don't they?"

"Nonsense," Miss Parish said in her heartiest voice.

"I think we should try to get to him first," I said.

Mildred leaned on the door. "I wonder—it's barely possible he's trying to reach Mrs. Hutchinson's house. She lives directly across the highway from the Red Barn."

"Who on earth is Mrs. Hutchinson?" Miss Parish said.

"My sister-in-law's housekeeper. She has Zinnie's little girl with her."

"Why don't you phone Mrs. Hutchinson?"

"She has no phone, or I'd have been in touch long ago. I've been worried about Martha. Mrs. Hutchinson means well, but she's an old woman."

Miss Parish gave her a swift, dark look. "You don't seriously think there's any danger to the child?"

"I don't know."

None of us knew. On a deeper level than I'd been willing to recognize till now, I experienced fear. Fear of the treacherous darkness around us and inside of us, fear of the blind destruction that had wiped out most of a family and threatened the rest.

"We could easily check on Martha," I said, "or have the police check."

"Let's keep them out of it for now," Miss Parish said. "What's this Mrs. Hutchinson's address?"

"Fourteen Chestnut Street. It's a little white frame cottage between Elmwood and the highway." Mildred opened the door and pointed down the street. "I can easily show you."

"No. You better stay here, dear."

Rose Parish's face was dismal. She was afraid, too.

chapter 26

MRS. HUTCHINSON'S cottage was the third of three similar houses built on narrow lots between Elmwood and the highway. Only one side of the short block was built up. The other side was vacant ground overgrown with scrub oaks. A dry creek, brimming with darkness, cut along the back of the empty lots. Beyond the continuous chain-lightning of the highway headlights, I could see the neon outline of the Red Barn, with cars clustered around it.

A softer light shone through lace curtains in Mrs. Hutchinson's front window. When I knocked on the door, a heavy shadow moved across the light. The old woman spoke through the closed door:

"Who is that?"

"Archer. We talked this morning at the Hallman ranch."

She opened the door cautiously and peered out. "What do you want?"

"Is Martha with you?"

"Sure she is. I put her to bed in my room. It looks like she's spending the night."

"Has anyone else been here?"

"The child's mother was in and out. She didn't waste much time on us, I can tell you. Mrs. Hallman has more important things on her mind than her little orphan daughter. But don't let me get started on that or I'll keep you standing on the steps all night." She glanced inquiringly at Rose Parish. With the excessive respect for privacy of her class, she had avoided noticing her till now.

"This is Miss Parish, from the state hospital."

"Pleased to meet you, I'm sure. You folks come inside, if you want. I'll ask you to be as quiet as you can. Martha isn't asleep yet. The poor child's all keyed up."

The door opened directly into the front room. The room was small and neat, warmed by rag rugs on the floor, an afghan on the couch. Embroidered mottoes on the plasterboard walls went with the character lines in the old woman's face. A piece of wool with knitting needles in it lay on the arm of a chair. She picked it up and hid it in a drawer, as if it was evidence of criminal negligence in her housekeeping.

"Sit down, if you can find a place to sit. Did you say you were from the state hospital? They offered me a job there once, but I always liked private work better."

Rose Parish sat beside me on the couch. "Are you a nurse, Mrs. Hutchinson?"

"A special nurse. I started to train for an R.N. but I never got my cap. Hutchinson wouldn't wait. Would you be an R.N., Miss?"

"I'm a psychiatric social worker. I suppose that makes me a sort of nurse. Carl Hallman was one of my patients."

"You wanted to ask me about him? Is that it? I say it's a crying shame what happened to that boy. He used to be as nice as you could want. There in that house, I watched him change right in front of my eyes. I could see his mother's trouble coming out in him like a family curse, and not one of them made a move to help him until it was too late."

"Did you know his mother?" I said.

"Know her? I nursed her for over a year. Waited on her hand and foot, day and night. I should say I did know her. She was the saddest woman you ever want to see, specially toward the end there. She got the idea in her head that nobody loved her, nobody ever *did* love her. Her husband didn't love her, her family didn't love her, even her poor dead parents didn't love her when they were alive. It became worse when Carl went away to school. He was always her special darling, and she depended on him. After he left home, she acted like there was nothing for her in life except those pills she took."

"What kind of pills?" Rose Parish said. "Barbiturates?"

"Them, or anything else she could get her hands on. She was addicted for many years. I guess she ran through every doctor in town, the old ones and then the new ones, ending up with Dr. Grantland. It isn't for me to second-guess a doctor, but I used to think those pills he let her have were her main trouble. I got up my nerve and told him so, one day toward the end. He said that he was trying to limit her, but Mrs. Hallman would be worse off without them."

"I doubt that," Rose Parish said. "He should have committed her; he might have saved her life."

"Did the question ever come up, Mrs. Hutchinson?"

"Between me and her it did, when doctor first sent me out there to look after her. I had to use *some* kind of leverage on her. She was a sad, spoiled woman, spoiled rotten all her life. She was always hiding her pills on me, and taking more than her dosage. When I bawled her out for it, she pulled out that little gun she kept under her pillow. I told her she'd have to give up those shenanigans, or the doctor would have to commit her. She said he better not. She said if he tried it on her, she'd kill herself and ruin him. As for me, I'd never get another job in this town. Oh, she could be a black devil when she was on the rampage."

Breathing heavily with remembered anger, Mrs. Hutchinson looked up at the wall above her armchair. An embroidered motto there exhorted Christian charity. It calmed her visibly. She said:

"I don't mean she was like that all the time, just when

she had a spell. Most of the time she wasn't a bad sort of lady to have to deal with. I've dealt with worse. It's a pity what had to happen to her. And not only her. You young people don't read the Bible any more. I know that. There's a line from the Word keeps running in my head since all this trouble today. 'The fathers have eaten sour grapes, and the children's teeth are set on edge'."

"Right out of Freud," Rose Parish said in a knowing undertone.

I thought she was putting the cart in front of the horse, but I didn't bother arguing. The Old Testament words reverberated in my mind. I cut their echo short, and brought Mrs. Hutchinson back to the line of questioning I'd stumbled upon:

"It's funny they'd let Mrs. Hallman have a gun."

"All the ranch women have them, or used to have. It was a hangover from the old days when there were a lot of hoboes and outlaws wandering around in the west. Mrs. Hallman told me once her father sent her that gun, all the way from the old country—he was a great traveler. She took a pride in it, the way another kind of woman would take pride in a piece of jewelry. It was something like a gewgaw at that—a short-barreled little thing with a pearl handle set in filigree work. She used to spend a lot of time cleaning and polishing it. I remember the fuss she made when the Senator wanted to take it away from her."

"I'm surprised he didn't," Rose Parish said. "We don't even permit nailfiles or bottles on our closed wards."

"I know that, and I told the Senator it was a danger to her. He was a hard man to understand in some ways. He couldn't really admit to himself that there was anything the matter with her mind. It was the same with his son later. He believed that their troubles were just notions, that all they wanted was to attract some attention to themselves. He let her keep that gun in her room, and the box of shells that went with it, right up to the day of her death. You'd almost think," she added with the casual insight of the old, "you'd almost think he wanted her to do herself a harm. Or somebody else."

"Somebody else?" I said.

Mrs. Hutchinson reddened and veiled her eyes. "I didn't mean anything, I was only talking."

"You said Mrs. Hallman had that gun right up to the day of her death. Do you know that for a fact?"

"Did I say that? I didn't mean it that way."

There was a breathing silence.

"How did you mean it?"

"I wasn't trying to pin down any exact time. What I said was in a general manner of speaking."

"*Did* she have it on the day of her death?"

"I can't remember. It was a long time ago—more than three years. It doesn't matter, anyway." Her statement had the force of a question. Her gray head turned toward me, the skin of her neck stretched in diagonal folds like recalcitrant material being twisted under great pressure.

"Do you know what happened to Mrs. Hallman's gun?"

"I never was told, no. For all I know it's safe at the bottom of the ocean."

"Mrs. Hallman had it the night she drowned herself?"

"I didn't say that. I don't know."

"Did she drown herself?"

"Sure she did. But I couldn't swear to it. I didn't see her jump in." Her pale gaze was still on me, cold and watchful under slack folded lids. "What is it that's so important about her gun? Do you know where it is?"

"Don't you?"

The strain was making her irritable. "I wouldn't be asking you if I knew all about it, would I?"

"The gun is in an evidence case in the sheriff's office. It

was used to shoot Jerry Hallman today. It's strange you don't know that, Mrs. Hutchinson."

"How would *I* know what they shot him with?" But the color of confusion had deepened in her face. Its vessels were purplish and congested with the hot shame of an unpracticed barefaced liar. "I didn't even hear the shot, let alone see it happen."

"There were two shots."

"That's news to me. I didn't hear either one of them. I was in the front room with Martha, and she was playing with that silver bell of her mother's. It drowned out everything."

The old woman sat in a listening attitude, screwing up her face as if she was hearing the shots now, after a long delay. I was certain that she was lying. Apart from the evidence of her face, there was at least one discrepancy in her story. I scanned back across the rush and welter of the day, trying to pin it down, but without success. Too many words had been spilled. The sense of discrepancy persisted in my mind, a gap in the known through which the darkness threatened, like sea behind a dike.

Mrs. Hutchinson shuffled her slippered feet in token flight. "Are you trying to tell me I shot him?"

"I made no such accusation. I have to make one, though. You're hiding something."

"Me hide something? Why should I do that?"

"It's the question I'm asking myself. Perhaps you're protecting a friend, or think you are."

"My friends don't get into that kind of trouble," she said angrily.

"Speaking of friends, have you known Dr. Grantland long?"

"Long enough. That doesn't mean we're friends." She corrected herself hastily: "A special nurse doesn't consider herself friends with her doctors, not if she knows her place."

"I gather he got you your job with the Hallmans."

"He recommended me."

"And he drove you into town today, shortly after the shooting."

"He wasn't doing it for me. He was doing it for *her*."

"I know that. Did he mention the shooting to you?"

"I guess he did. Yes. He mentioned it, said it was a terrible thing."

"Did he mention the gun that was used?"

She hesitated before answering. The color left her face. Otherwise she was completely immobile, concentrating on what she would say and its possible implications. "No. Martha was with us, and all. He didn't say anything about the gun."

"It still seems queer to me. Grantland saw the gun. He told me himself that he recognized it, but wasn't certain of the identification. He must have known that you were familiar with it."

"I'm no expert on guns."

"You gave me a good description of it just now. In fact, you probably knew it as well as anyone alive. But Grantland didn't say a word to you about it, ask you a single question. Or did he?"

There was another pause. "No. He didn't say a word."

"Have you seen Dr. Grantland since this afternoon?"

"What if I have?" she answered stolidly.

"Has Grantland been here tonight?"

"What if he was? Him coming here had nothing to do with me."

"Who did it have to do with? Zinnie?"

Rose Parish stirred on the couch beside me, nudging my knee with hers. She made a small coughing noise of distress. This encouraged Mrs. Hutchinson, as perhaps it was intended to. I could practically see her resistance solidifying. She sat like a monument in flowered silk:

"You're trying to make me talk myself out of a job. I'm too old to get another job. I've got too much property to qualify for the pension, and not enough to live on." After a pause, she said: "No! I'm falsifying myself. I could always get along someway. It's Martha that keeps me on the job. If it wasn't for her, I would have quit that house long ago."

"Why?"

"It's a bad-luck house, that's why. It brings bad luck to everybody who goes there. Yes, and I'd be happy to see it burn to the ground like Sodom. That may sound like a terrible thing for a Christian woman to say. No loss of life; I wouldn't wish that on them; there's been loss of life enough. I'd just like to see that house destroyed, and that family scattered forevermore."

I thought without saying it that Mrs. Hutchinson was getting her awesome wish.

"What are you leading up to?" I said. "I know the doctor and Zinnie Hallman are interested in each other. Is that the fact you're trying to keep from spilling? Or is there more?"

She weighed me in the balance of her eyes. "Just who are you, Mister?"

"I'm a private detective—"

"I know that much. Who're you detecting for? And who against?"

"Carl Hallman asked me to help him."

"Carl did? How could that be?"

I explained briefly how it could be. "He was seen in your neighborhood tonight. It's why Miss Parish and I came here to your house, to head off any possible trouble."

"You think he might try and do something to the child?"

"It occurred to us as a possibility," Rose Parish said. "I wouldn't worry about it. We probably went off half-cocked. I honestly don't believe that Carl would harm anyone."

"What about his brother?"

"I don't believe he shot his brother." She exchanged glances with me. "Neither of us believes it."

"I thought, from the paper and all, they had it pinned on him good."

"It nearly always looks like that when they're hunting a suspect," I said.

"You mean it isn't true?"

"It doesn't have to be."

"Somebody else did it?"

Her question hung unanswered in the room. An inner door at the far end was opening slowly, softly. Martha slipped in through the narrow aperture. Elfin in blue sleepers, she scampered into the middle of the room, stood and looked at us with enormous eyes.

Mrs. Hutchinson said: "Go back to bed, you minx."

"I won't. I'm not sleepy."

"Come on, I'll tuck you in."

The old woman rose ponderously and made a grab for the child, who evaded her.

"I want Mommy to tuck me in. I want my Mommy."

In the middle of her complaint, Martha stopped in front of Rose Parish. A reaching innocence, like an invisible antenna, stretched upward from her face to the woman's face, and was met by a similar reaching innocence. Rose opened her arms. Martha climbed into them.

"You're bothering the lady," Mrs. Hutchinson said.

"She's no bother, are you, honey?"

The child was quiet against her breast. We sat in silence for a bit. The tick of thought continued like a tiny stitching in my consciousness or just below it, trying to piece together the rags and bloody tatters of the day. My thoughts threatened the child, the innocent one, perhaps the only one who was perfectly innocent. It wasn't fair that her milk teeth should be set on edge.

chapter 27

NOISES from outside, random voices and the scrape of boots, pulled me out of my thoughts and to the door. A guerrilla formation of men carrying rifles and shotguns went by in the street. A second, smaller group was fanning out across the vacant lots toward the creekbed, probing the tree-clotted darkness with their flashlights.

The man directing the second group wore some kind of uniform. I saw when I got close to him that he was a city police sergeant.

"What's up, Sergeant?"

"Manhunt. We got a lunatic at large in case you don't know it."

"I know it."

"If you're with the posse, you're supposed to be searching farther up the creek."

"I'm a private detective working on this case. What makes you think that Hallman's on this side of the highway?"

"The carhop at the Barn says he came through the culvert. He came up the creek from the beach, and the chances are he's following it right on up. He may be long gone by now, though. She was slow in passing the word to us."

"Where does the creekbed lead to?"

"Across town." He pointed east with his flashlight. "All the way to the mountains, if you stay with it. But he won't get that far, not with seventy riflemen tracking him."

"If he's gone off across town, why search around here?"

"We can't take chances with him. He may be lying doggo. We don't have the trained men to go through all the houses and yards, so we're concentrating on the creek." His light came up to my face for a second. "You want to pitch in and help?"

"Not right now." With seventy hunters after a single buck, conditions would be crowded. "I left my red hat home."

"Then you're taking up my time, fellow."

The sergeant moved off among the trees. I walked to the end of the block and crossed the highway, six lanes wide at this point.

The Red Barn was a many-windowed building which stood in the center of a blacktop lot on the corner. Its squat pentagonal structure was accentuated by neon tubing along the eaves and corners. Inside this brilliant red cage, a tall-hatted short-order cook kept several waitresses running between his counter and the cars in the lot. The waitresses wore red uniforms and little red caps which made them look like bellhops in skirts. The blended odors of gasoline fumes and frying grease changed in my nostrils to a foolish old hot-rod sorrow, nostalgia for other drive-ins along roads I knew in prewar places before people started dying on me.

It seemed that my life had dwindled down to a series of one-night stands in desolate places. Watch it, I said to myself; self-pity is the last refuge of little minds and aging professional hardnoses. I knew the desolation was my own. Brightness had fallen from my interior air.

A boy and a girl in a hand-painted lavender Chevrolet coupé made me feel better, for some reason. They were sitting close, like a body with two ducktailed heads, taking alternate sips of malted milk from the same straw, germ-free with love. Near them in a rusty Hudson a man in a workshirt, his dark and hefty wife, three or four children whose eyes were brilliant and bleary with drive-in-movie memories, were eating mustard-dripping hot dogs with the rapt solemnity of communicants.

Among the half-dozen other cars, one in particular interested me. It was a fairly new Plymouth two-door with Purissima *Record* lettered across the door. I walked over for a closer look.

A molded prewar Ford with a shackled rear end and too much engine came off the highway on banshee tires and pulled up beside the Plymouth. The two boys in the front seat looked me over with bold and planless eyes and forgot about me. I was a pedestrian, earth-borne. While they were waiting for a carhop, they occupied themselves with combing and rearranging their elaborate hair-structures. This process took a long time, and continued after one of the waitresses came up to the side of their car. She was a little blonde, pert-breasted in her tight uniform.

"Drive much?" she said to the boys. "I saw you come into the lot. You want to kill it before it multiplies."

"A lecture," the boy at the wheel said.

The other boy leaned toward her. "It said on the radio Gwen saw the killer."

"That's right, she's talking to the reporter now."

"Did he pull a gun on her?"

"Nothing like that. She didn't even know he *was* the killer."

"What did he *do*?" the driver said. He sounded very eager, as if he was seeking some remarkable example to emulate.

"Nothing. He was poking around in the garbage pails. When he saw her, he took off. Listen, kids, I'm busy. What'll it be?"

"You got a big George, George?" the driver asked his passenger.

"Yeah, I'm loaded. We'll have the usual, barbecued baby and double martinis. On second thought, make it a couple of cokes."

"Sure, kids, have yourselves a blast." She came around the Plymouth to me. "What can I do for you, sir?"

I realized I was hungry. "Bring me a hamburger, please."

"Deluxe, Stackburger, or Monarch? Monarchburger is the seventy-five-center. It's bigger, and you get free potatoes with it."

"Free potatoes sounds good."

"You can eat it inside if you want."

"Is Gwen inside? I want to talk to her."

"I wondered if you were plainclothes. Gwen's out behind with Gene Slovekin from the paper. He wanted to take her picture."

She indicated an open gate in the grapestake fence that surrounded the rear of the lot. There were several forty-gallon cans beside the gate. I looked into the nearest one. It was half full of a greasy tangle of food and other waste. Carl Hallman was hard-pressed.

On the other side of the gate, a footpath led along the bank of the creek. The dry bed of the creek was lined with concrete here, and narrowed down to a culvert which ran under the highway. This was high enough for a man to walk upright through it.

Slovekin and the carhop were coming back along the path toward me. She was thirtyish and plump; her body looked like a ripe tomato in her red uniform. Slovekin was carrying a camera with a flashbulb attachment. His tie was twisted, and he walked as if he was tired. I waited for them beside the gate.

"Hello, Slovekin."

"Hello, Archer. This is a mad scramble."

The carhop turned to him. "If you're finished with me, Mr. Slovekin, I got to get back to work. The manager'll be docking me, and I got a kid in school."

"I was hoping to ask you a couple of questions," I said.

"Gee, I dunno about that."

"I'll fill you in," Slovekin said, "if it doesn't take too long. Thanks, Gwen."

"You're more than welcome. Remember you promised I could have a print. I haven't had my picture taken since God made little green apples."

She touched the side of her face, delicately, hopefully, and hustled into the building on undulating hips. Slovekin deposited the camera in the back seat of his press car. We got into the front.

"Did she see Hallman enter the culvert?"

"Not actually," Slovekin said. "She made no attempt to follow him. She thought he was just a bum from the jungle on the other side of the tracks. Gwen didn't catch onto who he was until the police got here and asked some questions. They came up the creekbed from the beach, incidentally, so he couldn't have gone that way."

"What was his condition?"

"Gwen's observations aren't worth much. She's a nice girl, but not very bright. Now that she knows who he is, he was seven feet tall with horns and illuminated revolving eyeballs." Slovekin moved restlessly, turning the key in the ignition. "That's about all there is here. Can I drop you anywhere? I'm supposed to cover the movements of the sheriff's posse." His intonation satirized the phrase.

"Wear your bulletproof vest. Turning seventy hunters loose in a town is asking for double trouble."

"I agree. So does Spaulding, my editor. But we report the news, we don't make it. You got any for me, by any chance?"

"Can I talk off the record?"

"I'd rather have it on. It's getting late, and I don't mean late at night. We've never had a lynching in Purissima, but it could happen here. There's something about insanity, it frightens people, makes *them* irrational, too. Their worst aggressions start popping out."

"You sound like an expert in mob psychology," I said.

"I sort of am. It runs in the family. My father was an Austrian Jew. He got out of Vienna one jump ahead of the storm troopers. I also inherited a prejudice in favor of the underdog. So if you know something that will let Hallman off the hook, you better spill it. I can have it on the radio in ten minutes."

"He didn't do it."

"Do you know he didn't for certain?"

"Not quite. I'd stake my reputation on it, but I have to do better than that. Hallman's being used as a patsy, and a lot of planning went into it."

"Who's behind it?"

"There's more than one possibility. I can't give you any names."

"Not even off the record?"

"What would be the use? I haven't got enough to prove a case. I don't have access to the physical evidence, and I can't depend on the official interpretation of it."

"You mean it's been manipulated?"

"Psychologically speaking, anyway. There may have been some actual tampering. I don't know for sure that the gun that was found in the greenhouse fired the slugs in Jerry Hallman."

"The sheriff's men think so."

"Have they run ballistics tests?"

"Apparently. The fact that it was his mother's gun has generated a lot of heat downtown. They're going into ancient history. The rumor's running around that Hallman killed his mother, too, and possibly his father, and the family money got him off and hushed it up." He gave me a quick, sharp look. "Could there be anything in that?"

"You sound as if you're buying it yourself."

"I wouldn't say that, but I know some things it could jibe with. I went to see the Senator last Spring, just a few days before he died." He paused to organize his thoughts, and went on more slowly. "I had dug up certain facts about a certain county official whose re-election was coming up in May. Spaulding thought the Senator ought to know these facts, because he'd been supporting this certain official for a good many years. So had the paper, as a matter of fact. The paper generally went along with Senator Hallman's ideas on county government. Spaulding didn't want to change that policy without checking with Senator Hallman. He was a big minority stockholder in the paper, and you might say the local elder statesman."

"If you're trying to say he was county boss and Ostervelt was one of his boys, why beat around the bush?"

"It wasn't quite that simple, but that's the general picture. All right, so you know." Slovekin was young and full of desire, and his tone became competitive: "What you don't know is the nature of my facts. I won't go into detail, but I was in a position to prove that Ostervelt had been taking regular payoff money from houses of prostitution. I showed Senator Hallman my affidavits. He was an old man, and he was shocked. I was afraid for a while that he might have a heart attack then and there. When he calmed down, he said he needed time to think about the problem, perhaps talk it over with Ostervelt himself. I was to come back in a week. Unfortunately, he died before the week was up."

"All very interesting. Only I don't see how it fits in with the idea that Carl killed him."

"It depends on how you look at it. Say Carl did it and Ostervelt pinned it on him, but kept the evidence to himself. It would give Ostervelt all the leverage he needed to keep the Hallman family in line. It would also explain what happened afterwards. Jerry Hallman went to a lot of trouble to quash our investigation. He also threw all his weight behind Ostervelt's re-election."

"He might have done that for any number of reasons."

"Name one."

"Say he killed his father himself, and Ostervelt knew it."

"You don't believe that," Slovekin stated.

He looked around nervously. The little blonde ankled up to the side of the car with my Monarchburger. I said, when she was out of hearing:

"This is supposed to be a progressive county. How does Ostervelt keep his hold on it?"

"He's been in office a long time, and, as you know, he's got good political backing, at least until now. He knows where the bodies are buried. You might say he's buried a couple of them himself."

"Buried them himself?"

"I was speaking more or less figuratively." Slovekin's voice had sunk to a worried whisper. "He's shot down one or two escaping prisoners—shootings that a lot of the townspeople didn't think were strictly necessary. The reason I mention it—I wouldn't want to see *you* end up with a hole in the back."

"That's a hell of a thought, when I'm eating a sandwich."

"I wish you'd take me seriously, Archer. I didn't like what happened between you this afternoon."

"Neither did I."

Slovekin leaned toward me. "Those names you have in mind that you won't give me—is Ostervelt one of them?"

"He is now. You can write it down in your little black book."

"I already have, long ago."

chapter 28

I WAITED for the green light and walked back across the highway. Chestnut Street was empty again, except for my car at the curb, and another car diagonally across from it near the corner of Elmwood. It hadn't been there before, or I would have noticed it.

It was a new red station wagon very like the one I had seen in the drive of the Hallman ranch-house. I went up the street and looked in at the open window on the driver's side. The key was in the ignition. The registration slip on the steering-post had Jerry Hallman's name on it.

Evidently Zinnie had come back to tuck her baby in. I glanced across the roof of the wagon toward Mrs. Hutchinson's cottage. Her light shone steadily through the lace-veiled windows. Everything seemed peaceful and as it should be. Yet a sense of disaster came down on me like a ponderous booby trap.

Perhaps I'd glimpsed and guessed the meaning of the blanket-covered shape on the floor at the rear of the wagon. I opened the back door and pulled the blanket away. So white that it seemed luminous, a woman's body lay huddled in the shadow.

I turned on the ceiling light and Zinnie jumped to my vision. Her head was twisted toward me, glaring at me open-eyed. Her grin of fear and pain had been fixed in the rictus of death. There were bloody slits in one of her breasts and in her abdomen. I touched the unwounded breast, expecting a marble coldness. The body was still warm, but unmistakably dead. I drew the blanket over it again, as if that would do any good.

Darkness flooded my mind for an instant, whirling like black water in which three bodies turned unburied. Four. I lost my Monarchburger in the gutter. Sweating cold, I looked up and down the street. Across the corner of the vacant lot, a concrete bridge carried Elmwood Street over the creekbed. Further up the creek, around a bend, I could see the moving lights of the sergeant and his men.

I could tell them what I had found, or I could keep silent. Slovekin's talk of lynching was fresh in my thought. Under it I had an urge to join the hunt, run Hallman down and kill him. Because I distrusted that urge, I made a decision which probably cost a life. Perhaps it saved another.

I closed the door, left the wagon as it stood, and went back to Mrs. Hutchinson's house. The sight of me seemed to depress her, but she invited me in. Before I stepped inside, I pointed out the red wagon:

"Isn't that Mrs. Hallman's car?"

"I believe so. I couldn't swear to it. She drives one like it."

"Was she driving it tonight?"

The old woman hesitated. "She was in it."

"You mean someone else was driving?"

She hesitated again, but she seemed to sense my urgency.

When her words finally came, they sounded as if an inner dam had burst, releasing waves of righteous indignation:

"I've worked in big houses, with all sorts of people, and I learned long ago to hold my tongue. I've done it for the

Hallmans, and I'd go on doing it, but there's a limit, and I've reached mine. When a brand-new widow goes out on the town the same night her husband was killed—"

"Was Dr. Grantland driving the car? This is important, Mrs. Hutchinson."

"You don't have to tell me that. It's a crying shame. Away they go, as gay as you please, and the devil take the hindmost. I never did think much of her, but I used to consider him a fine young doctor."

"What time were they here?"

"It was Martha's suppertime, round about six-fifteen or six-thirty. I know she spoiled the child's evening meal, running in and out like that."

"Did Grantland come in with her?"

"Yes, he came in."

"Did he say anything? Do anything?"

Her face closed up on me. She said: "It's chilly out here. Come in if you want to talk."

There was nobody else in the living-room. Rose Parish's coat lay on the couch. I could hear her behind the wall, singing a lullaby to the child.

"I'm glad for a little help with that one. I get tired," the old woman said. "Your friend seems to be a good hand with children. Does she have any of her own?"

"Miss Parish isn't married, that I know of."

"That's too bad. I was married myself for nearly forty years, but I never had one of my own either. I never had the good fortune. It was a waste of me." The wave of her indignation rose again: "You'd think that those that had would look after their own flesh and bone."

I seated myself in a chair by the window where I could watch the station wagon. Mrs. Hutchinson sat opposite me:

"Is *she* out there?"

"I want to keep an eye on her car."

"What did you mean, did Dr. Grantland say anything?"

"How did he act toward Zinnie?"

"Same as usual. Putting on the same old act, as if he wasn't interested in her, just doing his doctor's duty. As if I didn't know all about them long ago. I guess he thinks I'm old and senile, but I've got my eyes and my good ears. I've watched that woman playing him like a big stupid fish, ever since the Senator died. She's landing him, too, and he acts like he's grateful to her for slipping the gaff to him. I thought he had more sense than to go for a woman like that, just because she's come into a wad of money."

With my eye on the painted red wagon in which her body lay, I felt an obscure need to defend Zinnie:

"She didn't seem like a bad sort of woman to me."

"You talk about her like she was dead," Mrs. Hutchinson said. "Naturally you wouldn't see through her, you're a man. But I used to watch her like the flies on the wall. She came from nothing, did you know that? Mr. Jerry picked her up in a nightclub in Los Angeles, he said so in one of the arguments they had. They had a lot of arguments. She was a driving hungry woman, always hungry for something she didn't have. And when she got it, she wasn't satisfied. An unsatisfied wife is a terrible thing in this life.

"She turned against her husband after the child was born, and then she went to work to turn the child against him. She even had the brass to ask me to be a divorce-court witness for her, so's she could keep Martha. She wanted me to say that her husband treated her cruel. It would have been a lie, and I told her so. It's true they didn't get along, but he never raised a hand to her. He suffered in silence. He went to his death in silence."

"When did she ask you to testify?"

"Three-four months ago, when she thought that a divorce was what she wanted."

"So she could marry Grantland?"

"She didn't admit it outright, but that was the idea. I was surprised, surprised and ashamed for him, that he would fall for her and her shabby goods. I could have saved my feelings. They make a pair. He's no better than she is. He may be a lot worse."

"What makes you say so?"

"I *hate* to say it. I remember him when he first moved to town, an up-and-coming young doctor. There was nothing he wouldn't do for his patients. He told me once it was the great dream of his life to be a doctor. His family lost their money in the depression, and he put himself through medical school by working in a garage. He went through the college of hard knocks as well as medical college, and it taught him something. In those early days, six-eight years ago, when his patients couldn't pay him he went right on caring for them. That was before he got his big ideas."

"What happened, did he get a whiff of money?"

"More than that happened to him. Looking back, I can see that the big change in him started about three years ago. He seemed to lose interest in his medical practice. I've seen the same thing with a few other doctors, something runs down in them and something else starts up, and they go all out for the money. All of a sudden they're nothing more than pill-pushers, some of them living on their own pills."

"What happened to Dr. Grantland three years ago?"

"I don't know for sure. I can tell you it happened to more people than him, though. Something happened to me, if you want the truth."

"I do want the truth. I think you've been lying to me."

Her head jerked up as if I'd tightened a rope. She narrowed her eyes. They watched me with a faded kind of guile. I said:

"If you know something important about Alicia Hallman's death, it's your duty to bring it out."

"I've got a duty to myself, too. This thing I've kept locked up in my breast—it don't make me look good."

"You could look worse, if you let an innocent man take the blame for murder. Those men that went by in the street are after him. If you hold back until they find him and shoot him down, it's going to be too late. Too late for Carl Hallman and too late for you."

Her glance followed mine out to the street. Except for my car and Zinnie's, it was still empty. Like the street's reflection, her eyes grew dark with distant lights in them. Her mouth opened, and shut in a grim line.

"You can't sit and hold back the truth while a whole family dies off, or is killed off. You call yourself a good woman—"

"Not any more, I don't."

Mrs. Hutchinson lowered her head and looked down at her hands in her lap. On their backs the branched blue veins showed through the skin. They swelled as her fingers retracted into two clenched fists. Her voice came out half-choked, as though the moral noose had tightened on her:

"I'm a wicked woman. I did lie about that gun. Dr. Grantland brought it up on the way into town today. He brought it up again tonight when she was with the child."

"What did he say to you?"

"He said if anybody asked me about that gun, that I was to stick to my original story. Otherwise I'd be in a peck of trouble. Which I am."

"You're in less trouble than you were a minute ago. What was your original story?"

"The one he told me to tell. That she didn't have the gun the night she died. That I hadn't seen it for at least a week, or the box of shells, either."

"What happened to the shells?"

"He took them. I was to say that he took the gun and the shells away from her for her own protection."

"When did he feed you this story?"

"That very same night when he came out to the ranch."

"It was his story. Why did you buy it from him?"

"I was afraid," she said. "That night when she didn't come home and didn't come home, I was afraid she'd done herself a harm, and I'd be blamed."

"Who would blame you?"

"Everybody would. They'd say I was too old to go on nursing." The blue-veined hands opened and shut on her thighs. "I blamed myself. It was my fault. I should have stayed with her every minute, I shouldn't have let her go out. She'd had a phone call from Berkeley the evening before, something about her son, and she was upset all day. Talking about killing herself because her family deserted her and nobody loved her. She blamed it all on the Doomsters."

"The what?"

"The Doomsters. She was always talking about those Doomsters of hers. She believed her life was ruled by evil fates like, and they had killed all the love in the world the day that she was born. It was true, in a way, I guess. Nobody did love her. I was getting pretty sick of her myself. I thought if she did die it would be a relief to her and a good riddance. I took it upon myself to make that judgment which no human being has a right to do."

Her eyes seemed to focus inward, on an image in her memory. She blinked, as though the image lay under brilliant light:

"I remember the very minute I made that judgment and washed my hands of her. I walked into her room with her dinner tray, and there she was in her mink coat in front of the full-length mirror. She was loading the gun and talking to herself, about how her father abandoned her—he didn't, he just died, but she took it personally—and how her children were running out on her. She pointed the gun at herself in the mirror, and I remember thinking she ought to turn it around and put an end to herself instead of just talking about it. I didn't blame her son for running away. She was a burden on him, and on the whole family.

"I know that's no excuse for me," she added stonily. "A wicked thought is a wicked act, and it leads to wicked acts. I heard her sneak out a few minutes later, when I was making her coffee in the kitchen. I heard the car drive up and I heard it drive away. I didn't lift a finger to stop her. I just let her go, and sat there drinking coffee with the evil wish in my heart."

"Who was driving the car?"

"Sam Yogan. I didn't see him go but he was back in less than an hour. He said he dropped her off at the wharf, which was where she wanted to go. Even then, I didn't phone the police."

"Did Yogan often drive her into town?"

"She didn't go very often, but Sam did a lot of her driving for her. He's a good driver, and she liked him. He was about the only man she ever liked. Anyway, he was the only one available that night."

"Where were the rest of the family?"

"Away. The Senator and Jerry had gone to Berkeley, to try and find out where Carl was. Zinnie was staying with some friends in town here. Martha was only a few months old at the time."

"Where was Carl?"

"Nobody knew. He kind of disappeared for a while. It turned out afterwards he was in the desert all the time, over in Death Valley. At least that was his story."

"He could have been here in town?"

"He could have been, for all I know. He didn't report in to me, or anybody else for that matter. Carl didn't show up until after they found his mother in the sea."

"When did they find her?"

"Next day."

"Did Grantland come to see you before they found her?"

"Long before. He got to the ranch around midnight. I was still awake, I couldn't sleep."

"And Mrs. Hallman had left the house around dinner time?"

"Yes, around seven o'clock. She always ate at seven. That night she didn't eat, though."

"Had Grantland seen her between dinner time and midnight?"

"Not that I know of. I took it for granted he was looking for her. I never thought to ask him. I was so full of myself, and the guilt I felt. I just spilled out everything about her and the gun and me letting her go without a by-your-leave, and my wicked thoughts. Dr. Grantland said I was overexhausted, and blaming myself too much. She'd probably turn up all right. But if she didn't I was to say that I didn't know anything about any gun. That she just slipped out on me, and I took it for granted she went to town for something, maybe to see her grandchild, I didn't know what. I wasn't to mention him coming out here either. That way, they'd be more likely to believe me. Anyway, I did what Dr. Grantland said. He was a doctor. I'm only a special nurse. I don't pretend to be smart."

She let her face fall into slack and stupid folds, as if to relieve herself of responsibility. I couldn't blame her too much. She was an old woman, worn out by her ordeal of conscience, and it was getting late.

chapter 29

ROSE PARISH came quietly into the room. She looked radiant and slightly disorganized.

"I finally got her to sleep. Goodness, it's past eleven. I didn't mean to keep you waiting so long."

"It's all right. You didn't keep me waiting."

I spent most of my working time waiting, talking and waiting. Talking to ordinary people in ordinary neighborhoods about ordinary things, waiting for truth to come up to the surface. I'd caught a glimpse of it just now, and it must have showed in my eyes.

Rose glanced from me to Mrs. Hutchinson. "Has something happened?"

"I talked his arm off, that's what happened." The old woman's face had resumed its peculiar closed look. "Thank you for helping out with the child. You ought to have some of your own to look after."

Rose flushed with pleasure, then shook her head quite sharply, as if to punish herself for the happy thought. "I'd settle for Martha any day. She's a little angel."

"Sometimes," Mrs. Hutchinson said.

A rattle in the street drew my attention back to the window. An old gray pickup had come off the highway. It slowed down as it passed the house, and stopped abreast of the station wagon. A slight, wiry figure got out of the truck on the righthand side and walked around the back of it to the wagon. I recognized Sam Yogan by his quick unhurried movements.

The truck was rattling away on Elmwood by the time I reached the wagon. Yogan was behind the wheel, trying to start it. It wouldn't start for him.

"Where are you going, Sam?"

He looked up and smiled when he saw me. "Back to the ranch. Hello."

He turned the motor over again, but it refused to catch. It sounded as though it was out of gas.

"Leave it, Sam. Get out and leave it."

His smile widened and became resistant. "No, sir. Mrs. Hallman says take it back to the ranch."

"Did she tell you herself?"

"No, sir. Garageman phoned Juan, Juan told me."

"Garageman?"

"Yessir. He said Mrs. Hallman said to pick up the car on Chestnut Street."

"How long ago did he call?"

"Not so long. Garageman says hurry up. Juan brought me in right away."

He tried the motor again, without success. I reached across him and removed the ignition key.

"You might as well get out, Sam. The fuel line's probably cut."

He got out and started for the front of the hood. "I fix it, eh?"

"No. Come here."

I opened the back door and showed him Zinnie Hallman. I watched his face. There was nothing there but an imperturbable sorrow. If he had guilty knowledge, it was hidden beyond my reach. I didn't believe he had.

"Do you know who killed her?"

His black eyes looked up from under his corrugated forehead. "No, sir."

"It looks like whoever did it tried to blame it on you. Doesn't that make you mad?"

"No, sir."

"Don't you have any idea who it was?"

"No, sir."

"Do you remember the night old Mrs. Hallman died?"

He nodded.

"You let her off on the wharf, I believe."

"The street in front of the wharf."

"What was she doing there?"

"Said she had to meet somebody."

"Did she say who?"

"No, sir. She told me go away, don't wait. She didn't want me to see, maybe."

"Did she have her gun?"

"I dunno."

"Did she mention Dr. Grantland?"

"I don't think."

"Did Dr. Grantland ever ask you about that night?"

"No, sir."

"Or give you a story to tell?"

"No, sir." He gestured awkwardly toward the body. "We ought to tell the police."

"You're right. You go and tell them, Sam."

He nodded solemnly. I handed him the key to the wagon and showed him where to find the sergeant's party. As I was starting my own car, Rose came out of the house and got in beside me. I turned onto Elmwood, bumped over the bridge, and accelerated. The arching trees passed over us with a whoosh, like giant dark birds.

"You're in an awful hurry," she said. "Or do you always drive like this?"

"Only when I'm frustrated."

"I'm afraid I can't help you with that. Did I do something to make you angry?"

"No."

"Something *has* happened, hasn't it?"

"Something is going to. Where do you want to be dropped off?"

"I don't want to be."

"There may be trouble. I think I can promise it."

"I didn't come to Purissima with the idea of avoiding trouble. I didn't come to get killed in an auto accident, either."

The lights at the main-street intersection were flashing red. I braked to a hard stop. Rose Parish didn't go with the mood I was in. "Get out."

"I will not."

"Stop asking questions then." I turned east toward the hills.

"I will not. Is it something about Carl?"

"Yes. Now hold the thought."

It was an early-to-bed town. There was practically no traffic. A few drunks drifted and argued on the pavement in front of the bars. Two night-blooming tarts or their mothers minced purposefully toward nothing in particular. A youth on a stepladder was removing the lettering from the shabby marquee of the Mexican movie house. AMOR was the only word that was left. He started to take that down.

In the upper reaches of the main street there was no one on foot at all. The only human being in sight was the attendant of an all-night gas station. I pulled in to the curb just below Grantland's office. A light shone dimly inside, behind the glass bricks. I started to get out. Some kind of animal emerged from the shrubbery and crawled toward me onto the sidewalk.

It was a human kind of animal, a man on his hands and knees. His hands left a track of blood, black as oil drippings under my headlights. His arms gave away and he fell on his side. His face was the dirty gray of the pavement. Rica again.

Rose went to her knees beside him. She gathered his head and shoulders into her lap.

"Get him an ambulance. I think he's cut his wrists."

Rica struggled feebly in her arms. "Cut my wrists hell. You think I'm one of your psychos?"

His red hands struck at her. Blood daubed her face and smeared the front of her coat. She held him, talking softly in the voice she used for Martha:

"Poor man, you hurt yourself. How did you hurt yourself?"

"There was wire in the window-glass. I shouldn't have tried to bust it with my hands."

"Why did you want to bust it?"

"I didn't want to. He made me. He gave me a shot in the back office and said he'd be back in a minute. He never did come back. He turned the key on me."

I squatted beside him. "Grantland locked you up?"

"Yeah, and the bastard's going to pay for it." Rica's eyes swiveled toward me, heavy and occulted like ball bearings dusted with graphite. "I'm going to lock him up in San Quentin death row."

"How are you going to do that?"

"He killed an old lady, see, and I'm a witness to it. I'll stand up in any court and swear to it. You ought to've seen his office after he did it. It was a slaughterhouse, with that poor old lady lying there in the blood. And he's a dirty butcher."

"Hush now," Rose said. "Be quiet now. Take it easy."

"Don't tell him that. Do you know who she was, Tom?"

"I found out. It was old lady Hallman. He beat her to death and tossed her in the drink. And I'm the one that's gonna see him gassed for it."

"What were you doing there?"

His face became inert. "I don't remember."

Rose gave me a look of pure hatred. "I forbid you to question him. He's half out of his mind. God knows how much drug he's had, or how much blood he's lost."

"I want his story now."

"You can get it tomorrow."

"He won't be talking tomorrow. Tom, what were you doing in Grantland's office that night?"

"Nothing. I was cruising. I needed a cap, so I just dropped by to see if I could con him out of one. I heard this shot, and then this dame came out. She was dripping blood."

Tom peered at his own hands. His eyes rolled up and went blind. His head rolled loosely sideways.

I shouted in his ear: "What dame? Can you describe her?"

Rose cradled his head in her arms protectively. "We have to get him to a hospital. I believe he's had a massive overdose. Do you want him to die?"

It was the last thing I wanted. I drove back to the all-night station and asked the attendant to call an ambulance.

He was a bright-looking boy in a leather windbreaker. "Where's the accident?"

"Up the street. There's an injured man on the sidewalk in front of Dr. Grantland's office."

"It isn't Dr. Grantland?"

"No."

"I just wondered. He came in a while ago. Buys his gas from us."

The boy made the call and came out again. "They ought to be here pretty quick. Anything else I can do?"

"Did you say Dr. Grantland was here tonight?"

"Sure thing." He looked at the watch on his wrist. "Not more than thirty minutes ago. Seemed to be in a hurry."

"What did he stop for?"

"Gas. Cleaning gas, not the regular kind. He spilt something on his rug. Gravy, I think he said. It must've been a mess. He was real upset about it. The doc just got finished building himself a nice new house with wall-to-wall carpeting."

"Let's see, that's on Seaview."

"Yeah." He pointed up the street toward the ridge. "It runs off the boulevard to the left. You'll see his name on the mailbox if you want to talk to him. Was he involved in the accident?"

"Could be."

Rose Parish was still on the sidewalk with Tom Rica in her arms. She looked up as I went by, but I didn't stop. Rose threatened something in me which I wanted to keep intact at least a little longer. As long as it would take to make Grantland pay with everything he had.

chapter 30

HIS house stood on a terraced lot near the crest of the ridge. It was a fairly extensive layout for a bachelor, a modern redwood with wide expanses of glass and many lights inside, as though to demonstrate that its owner had nothing to hide. His Jaguar was in the slanting driveway.

I turned and stopped in the woven shadow of a pepper tree. Before I left my car, I took Maude's gun out of the dash compartment. It was a .32 caliber automatic with a full clip and an extra shell in the chamber, ready to fire. I walked down Grantland's driveway very quietly, with my hand in my heavy pocket.

The front door was slightly ajar. A rasping radio voice

came from somewhere inside the house. I recognized the rhythmic monotonous clarity of police signals. Grantland had his radio tuned to the CHP dispatching station.

Under cover of the sound, I moved along the margin of the narrow light that fell across the doorstep. A man's legs and feet, toes down, were visible through the opening. My heart skipped a beat when I saw them, another beat when one of the legs moved. I kicked the door wide open and went in.

Grantland was on his knees with a red-stained cloth in his hand. There were deeper stains in the carpet which he had been scrubbing. He whirled like an animal attacked from the rear. The gun in my hand froze him in mid-action.

He opened his mouth wide as if he was going to scream at the top of his lungs. No sound came from him. He closed his mouth. The muscles dimpled along the line of his jaw. He said between his teeth:

"Get out of here."

I closed the door behind me. The hallway was full of the smell of gasoline. Beside a telephone table against the opposite wall, a gallon can stood open. Spots of undried gasoline ran the length of the hallway.

"Did she bleed a lot?" I said.

He got up slowly, watching the gun in my hand. I patted his flanks. He was unarmed. He backed against the wall and leaned there chin down, folding his arms across his chest, like a man on a cold night.

"Why did you kill her?"

"I don't know what you're talking about."

"It's a little late for that gambit. Your girl's dead. You're a dead pigeon yourself. But they can always use good hospital orderlies in the pen. Maybe you'll get some consideration if you talk."

"Who do you think you are? God?"

"I think maybe you did, Grantland. The big dream is over now. The best you have to hope for is a little consideration from a jury."

He looked down at the spotted carpet under his feet. "Why would I kill Zinnie? I loved her."

"Sure you did. You fell in love with her as soon as she got within one death of five million dollars. Only now she's one death past it, no good to you, no good to anybody."

"Do you have to grind my nose in it?" His voice was dull with the after-boredom of shock.

I felt a flicker of sympathy for him, which I repressed. "Come off it. If you didn't cut her yourself, you're covering for the ripper."

"No. I swear I'm not. I don't know who it was. I wasn't here when it happened."

"But Zinnie was?"

"Yes, she was. She was tired and ill, so I put her to bed in my room. I had an emergency patient, and had to leave the house." His face was coming to life as he talked, as though he saw an opening that he could slip through. "When I returned, she was gone. I was frantic. All I could think of was getting rid of the blood."

"Show me the bedroom."

Reluctantly, he detached himself from the support of the wall. I followed him through the door at the end of the hallway, into the lighted bedroom. The bed had been stripped. The bloody bedclothes, sheets and electric blanket, lay in the middle of the floor with a heap of women's clothes on top of them.

"What were you going to do with these? Burn them?"

"I guess so," he said with a wretched sidewise look. "There was nothing between us, you understand. My part in all this was perfectly innocent. But I knew what would happen if I didn't get rid of the traces. I'd be blamed."

"And you wanted someone else to be blamed, as usual So you bundled her body into her station wagon and left it in the lower town, near where Carl Hallman was seen You kept track of his movements by tuning in the police band. In case he wasn't available for the rap, you phoned the ranch and brought Zinnie's servants in, as secondary patsies."

Grantland's face took on its jaundiced look. He sat on the edge of the mattress with his head down. "You've been keeping track of my movements, have you?"

"It's time somebody did. Who was the emergency patient who called you out tonight?"

"It doesn't matter. Nobody you know."

"You're wrong again. It matters, and I've known Tom Rica for a good many years. You gave him an overdose of heroin and left him to die."

Grantland sat in silence. "I gave him what he asked for."

"Sure. You're very generous. He wanted a little death. You gave him the whole works."

Grantland began to speak rapidly, surrounding himself with a protective screen of words:

"I must have made a mistake in the dosage. I didn't know how much he was used to. He was in a bad way, and I had to give him something for temporary relief. I intended to have him moved to the hospital. I see now I shouldn't have left him without an attendant. Apparently he was worse off than I realized. These addicts are unpredictable."

"Lucky for you they are."

"Lucky?"

"Rica isn't quite dead. He was even able to do some talking before he lost consciousness."

"Don't believe him. He's a pathological liar, and he's got a grudge against me. I wouldn't provide him with drugs—"

"Wouldn't you? I thought that's what you were doing, and I've been wondering why. I've also been wondering what happened in your office three years ago."

"When?" He was hedging for time, time to build a story with escape hatches, underground passages, somewhere, anywhere to hide.

"You know when. How did Alicia Hallman die?"

He took a deep breath. "This will come as a surprise to you. Alicia died by accident. If anyone was culpable, it was her son Jerry who was. He'd made a special night appointment for her, and drove her to my office himself. She was terribly upset about something, and she wanted drugs to calm her nerves. I wouldn't prescribe any for her. She pulled a gun out of her purse and tried to shoot me with it. Jerry heard the shot. He rushed in from the waiting-room and grappled with her. She fell and struck her head on the radiator. She was mortally hurt. Jerry begged me to keep it quiet, to protect him and his mother's name and save the family from scandal. I did what I could to shield them. They were my friends as well as my patients."

He lowered his head, the serviceable martyr.

"It's a pretty good story. Are you sure it wasn't rehearsed?"

He looked up sharply. His eyes met mine for an instant. There were red fiery points in their centers. They veered away past me to the window and I glanced over my shoulder. The window framed only the half-lit sky above the city.

"Is that the story you told Carl this morning?"

"It is, as a matter of fact. Carl wanted the truth. I felt I had no right to keep it from him. It had been a load on my conscience for three years."

"I know how conscientious you are, Doctor. You got your hooks into a sick man, told him a lying story about his mother's death, gave him a gun and sicked him on his brother and turned him loose."

"It wasn't like that. He asked to see the gun. It was evidence of the truth. I suppose I'd kept it with that in mind. I brought it out of the safe and showed it to him."

"You kept it with murder in mind. You had it loaded, ready for him, didn't you?"

"That simply isn't so. Even if it were, you could never prove it. Never. He grabbed the gun and ran. I was helpless to stop him."

"Why did you lie to him about his mother's death?"

"It wasn't a lie."

"Don't contradict me, brother." I wagged the gun to remind him of it. "It wasn't Jerry who drove his mother into town. It was Sam Yogan. It wasn't Jerry who beat her to death. He was in Berkeley with his father. You wouldn't stick your neck out for Jerry, anyway. I can only think of two people you'd take that risk for—yourself, or Zinnie. Was Zinnie in your office with Alicia?"

He looked at me with flaring eyes, as if his brains were burning in his skull. "Go on. This is very interesting."

"Tom Rica saw a woman come out of there dripping blood. Was Zinnie wounded by Alicia's shot?"

"It's your story," he said.

"All right. I think it was Zinnie. She panicked and ran. You stayed behind and disposed of her mother-in-law's body. Your only motive was self-protection, but Zinnie wouldn't think of that, with the fear and guilt she had on her mind. She wouldn't stop to think that when you pushed that body into the ocean, you were converting justifiable manslaughter into murder—making a murderer out of your true love. No doubt she was grateful to you.

"Of course she wasn't your true love at the time. She wasn't rich enough yet. You wouldn't want her, or any woman, without money. Sooner or later, though, when the Senator died, Zinnie and her husband were due to come into a lot of money. But the years dragged on, and the old man's heart kept beating, and you got impatient, tired of sweating it out, living modestly on the profits from pills while other people had millions.

"The Senator needed a little help, a little send-off. You were his doctor, and you could easily have done it for him yourself, but that's not the way you operate. Better to let somebody else take the risks. Not too many risks, of course—Zinnie was going to be worth money to you. You helped her to set the psychological stage, so that Carl would be the obvious suspect. Shifting the blame onto Carl served a double purpose. It choked off any real investigation, and it got Carl and Mildred out of the picture. You wanted the Hallman money all to yourself.

"Once the Senator was gone, there was only one hurdle left between you and the money. Zinnie wanted to take it the easy way in a divorce settlement, but her child got in the way of a divorce. I imagine you did, too. You had one death to go, for the whole five million less taxes and a wife who would have to take orders the rest of her life. That death occurred today, and you've practically admitted that you set it up."

"I admitted nothing. I gave you practical proof that Carl Hallman killed his brother. The chances are he killed Zinnie, too. He could have made it across town in a stolen car."

"How long ago was Zinnie killed?"

"I'd say about four hours."

"You're a liar. Her body was warm when I found it, less than an hour ago."

"You must have been mistaken. You may not think much of me, but I am a qualified doctor. I left her before eight, and she must have died soon after. It's midnight now."

"What have you been doing since then?"

Grantland hesitated. "I couldn't move for a long time after I found her. I simply lay on the bed beside her."

"You say you found her in bed?"

"I did find her in bed."

"How did the blood get in the hall?"

"When I was carrying her out." He shuddered. "Can't you see that I'm telling you the truth? Carl must have come in and found her asleep. Perhaps he was looking for me. After all, I'm the doctor who committed him. Perhaps he killed her to get back at me. I left the door unlocked, like an idiot."

"You wouldn't have been setting her up for him? Or would you?"

"What do you think I am?"

It was a hard question. Grantland was staring down at Zinnie's clothes, his face distorted by magnetic lines of grief. I'd known murderers who killed their lovers and grieved for them. Most of them were half-hearted broken-minded men. They killed and cried and tore their prison blankets and twisted their blankets into nooses. I doubted that Grantland fitted the pattern, but it was possible.

"I think you're basically a fool," I said, "like any other man who tries to beat the ordinary human averages. I think you're a dangerous fool, because you're frightened. You proved that when you tried to silence Rica. Did you try to silence Zinnie, too, with a knife?"

"I refuse to answer such questions."

He rose jerkily and moved to the window. I stayed close to him, with the gun between us. For a moment we stood looking down the long slope of the city. Its after-midnight lights were scattered on the hillsides, like the last sparks of a firefall.

"I really loved Zinnie. I wouldn't harm her," he said.

"I admit it doesn't seem likely. You wouldn't kill the

golden goose just when she was going to lay for you. Six months from now, or a year, when she'd had time to marry you and write a will in your favor, you might have started thinking of new angles."

He turned on me fiercely. "I don't have to listen to any more of this."

"That's right. You don't. I'm as sick of it as you are. Let's go, Grantland."

"I'm not going anywhere."

"Then we'll tell them to come and get you. It will be rough while it lasts, but it won't last long. You'll be signing a statement by morning."

Grantland hung back. I prodded him along the hallway to the telephone.

"You do the telephoning, Doctor."

He balked again. "Listen. There doesn't have to be any telephoning. Even if your hypothesis were correct, which it isn't, there's no real evidence against me. My hands are clean."

His eyes were still burning with fierce and unquenched light. I thought it was a light that burned from darkness, a blind arrogance masking fear and despair. Behind his several shifting masks, I caught a glimpse of the unknown dispossessed, the hungry operator who sat in Grantland's central darkness and manipulated the shadow play of his life. I struck at the shape in the darkness.

"Your hands are dirty. You don't keep your hands clean by betraying your patients and inciting them to murder. You're a dirty doctor, dirtier than any of your victims. Your hands would be cleaner if you'd taken that gun and used it on Hallman yourself. But you haven't the guts to live your own life. You want other people to do it for you, do your living, do your killing, do your dying."

He twisted and turned. His face changed like smoke and set in a new smiling mask. "You're a smart man. That hypothesis of yours, about Alicia's death—it wasn't the way it happened, but you hit fairly close in a couple of places."

"Straighten me out."

"If I do, will you let me go? All I need is a few hours to get to Mexico. I haven't committed any extraditable offense, and I have a couple of thousand—"

"Save it. You'll need it for lawyers. This is it, Grantland." I gestured with the gun in my hand. "Pick up the telephone and call the police."

His shoulders slumped. He lifted the receiver and started to dial. I ought to have distrusted his hangdog look.

He kicked sideways and upset the gasoline can. Its contents spouted across the carpet, across my feet.

"I wouldn't use that gun," he said. "You'd be setting off a bomb."

I struck at his head with the automatic. He was a millisecond ahead of me. He swung the base of the telephone by its cord and brought it down like a sledge on top of my head.

I got the message. Over and out.

chapter 31

I CAME to crawling across the floor of a room I'd never seen. It was a long, dim room which smelled like a gas station. I was crawling toward a window at the far end, as fast as my cold and sluggish legs would push me along.

Behind me, a clipped voice was saying that Carl Hallman was still at large, and was wanted for questioning in a second murder. I looked back over my shoulder. Time and space came together, threaded by the voice from Grantland's radio. I could see the doorway into the lighted hall from which my instincts had dragged me.

There was a puff of noise beyond the doorway, a puff of color. Flames entered the room like dancers, orange-colored and whirring. I got my feet under me and my hands on a chair, carried it to the window and smashed the glass out of the frame.

Air poured in over me. The dancing flames behind me began to sing. They postured and beckoned when I looked at them, and reached for my cold wet legs, offering to warm them. My dull brain put several facts together, like a boy playing with blocks on the burning deck, and realized that my legs were gasoline-soaked.

I went over the jagged sill, fell further than I expected to, struck the earth full length and lay whooping for breath. The fire bit into my legs like a rabid fox.

I was still going on instinct. All instinct said was, Run. The fire ran with me, snapping. The providence that suffers fools and cushions drunks and tempers the wind to shorn lambs and softening hardheads rescued me from the final barbecue. I ran blind into the rim of a goldfish pond and fell down in the water. My legs Suzette sizzled and went out.

I reclined in the shallow, smelly blessed water and looked back at Grantland's house. Flames blossomed in the window I had broken and grew up to the eaves like quick yellow hollyhocks. Orange and yellow lights appeared behind other windows. Tendrils of smoke thrust delicately through the shake roof.

In no time at all, the house was a box of brilliant jumping lights. Breaking windows tinkled distinctly. Trellised vines of flame climbed along the walls. Little flame salamanders ran up the roof, leaving bright zigzag trails.

Above the central furnace roar, I heard a car engine start. Skidding in the slime at the bottom of the pool, I got to my feet and ran toward the house. The sirens were whining in the city again. It was a night of sirens.

Radiating heat kept me at a distance from the house. I waded through flowerbeds and climbed over a masonry wall. I was in time to see Grantland gun his Jaguar out of the driveway, its twin exhausts tracing parallel curves on the air.

I ran to my car. Below, the Jaguar was dropping down the hill like a bird. I could see its lights on the curves, and further down the red shrieking lights of a fire truck. Grantland had to stop to let it pass, or I'd have lost him for good.

He crossed to a boulevard running parallel with the main street, and followed it straight through town. I thought he was on his way to the highway and Mexico, until he turned left on Elmwood, and again left. When I took the second turn, into Grant Street, the Jaguar was halfway up the block with one door hanging open. Grantland was on the front porch of Mrs. Gley's house.

The rest of it happened in ten or twelve seconds, but each of the seconds was divided into marijuana fractions. Grantland shot out the lock of the door. It took three shots to do it. He pushed through into the hallway. By that time I was braking in front of the house, and could see the whole length of the hallway to the stairs. Carl Hallman came down them.

Grantland fired twice. The bullets slowed Carl to a walk. He came on staggering, as if the knife in his lifted hand was holding him up. Grantland fired again. Carl stopped in his tracks, his arms hanging loose, came on in a spraddling shuffle.

I started to run up the walk. Now Mildred was at the

foot of the stairs, clinging to the newel post. Her mouth was open, and she was screaming something. The scream was punctuated by Grantland's final shot.

Carl fell in two movements, to his knees, then forehead down on the floor. Grantland aimed across him. The gun clicked twice in his hand. It held only seven shells. Mildred shuddered under imaginary bullets.

Carl rose from the floor with a Lazarus grin, bright badges of blood on his chest. His knife was lost. He looked blind. Bare-handed he threw himself at Grantland, fell short, lay prone and still in final despair.

My feet were loud on the veranda boards. I got my hands on Grantland before he could turn, circled his neck with my arm and bent him over backwards. He was slippery and strong. He bucked and twisted and broke my hold with the hammering butt of the gun.

Grantland moved away crabwise along the wall. His face was bare as bone, a wet yellow skull from which the flesh had been dissolved away. His eyes were dark and empty like the eye of the empty gun that he was still clutching.

A door opened behind me. The hallway reverberated with the roar of another gun. A bullet creased the plaster close above Grantland's head and sprinkled it with dust. It was Ostervelt, in the half-shadow under the stairs:

"Out of the way, Archer. You, Doctor, stand still, and drop it. I'll shoot to kill you this time."

Perhaps in his central darkness Grantland yearned for death. He threw the useless gun at Ostervelt, jumped across Carl's body, took off from the veranda and seemed to run in air.

Ostervelt moved to the doorway and sent three bullets after him in rapid fire, faster than any man runs. They must have been very heavy. Grantland was pushed and hustled along by their blows, until his legs were no longer under him. I think he was dead before he struck the road.

"He oughtn't to have ran," Ostervelt said. "I'm a sharpshooter. I still don't like to kill a man. It's too damn easy to wipe one out and too damn hard to grow one." He looked down at his Colt .45 with a kind of shamed awe, and replaced it in its holster.

I liked the sheriff better for saying that, though I didn't let it run away with me. He was looking out toward the street where Grantland's body lay. People from the other houses had already begun to converge on him. Carmichael appeared from somewhere and kept them off.

Ostervelt turned to me. "How in hell did you get here? You look like you swam through a swamp."

"I followed Grantland from his house. He just got finished setting fire to it."

"Was he off his rocker, too?" Ostervelt sounded ready to believe anything.

"Maybe he was in a way. His girlfriend was murdered."

"I know that. What's the rest of the story? Hallman knocked off his girl, so Grantland knocked Hallman off?"

"Something like that."

"You got another theory?"

"I'm working on one. How long have you been here?"

"Couple of hours, off and on."

"In the house?"

"Out back, mostly. I came in through the kitchen when I heard the gunfire. I just relieved Carmichael at the back. He's been keeping guard on the house for more than four hours. According to him nobody came in or went out."

"Does that mean Hallman's been in the house all this time?"

"It sure looks like it. Why?"

"Zinnie's body was warm when I found her."

"What time was that?"

"Shortly before eleven. It's a cold night for September. If she was killed before eight, you'd expect her to lose some heat."

"That's pretty thin reasoning. Anyway, she's refrigerated now. Why in hell didn't you report what you found when you found it?"

I didn't answer him. It was no time for argument. To myself, I had to admit that I was still committed to Carl Hallman. Mental case or not, I couldn't imagine a man of his courage shooting his brother in the back or cutting a defenseless woman.

Carl was still alive. His breathing was audible. Mildred was kneeling beside him in a white slip. She'd turned his head to one side and supported it on one of his limp arms. His breath bubbled and sighed.

"Better not move him any more. I'll radio for an ambulance." Ostervelt went out.

Mildred didn't seem to have heard him. I had to speak twice before she paid any attention. She looked up through the veil of hair that had fallen over her face:

"Don't look at me."

She pushed her hair back and covered the upper parts of her breasts with her hands. Her arms and shoulders were rough with gooseflesh.

"How long has Carl been here in the house?"

"I don't know. Hours. He's been asleep in my room."

"You knew he was here?"

"Of course. I've been with him." She touched his shoulder, very lightly, like a child fingering a forbidden object. "He came to the house when you and Miss Parish were here. While I was changing my clothes. He threw a stick at my window and came up the back stairs. That's why I had to get rid of you."

"You should have taken us into your confidence."

"Not *her.* That Parish woman hates me. She's been trying to take Carl away from me."

"Nonsense," though I suspected it wasn't entirely nonsense. "You should have told us. You might have saved his life."

"He isn't going to die. They won't let him die."

She hid her face against his inert shoulder. Her mother was watching us from the curtained doorway below the stairs. Mrs. Gley looked like the wreck of dreams. She turned away, and disappeared into the back recesses of the house.

I went outside, looking for Carmichael. The street was filling up with people now. Rifles glinted among them, but there was no real menace in the crowd. Carmichael was having no trouble keeping them away from the house.

I talked to him for a minute. He confirmed the fact that he had been watching the house from various positions since eight o'clock. He couldn't be absolutely sure, but he was reasonably sure, that no one had entered or left it in that time. Our conversation was broken up by the ambulance's arrival.

I watched two orderlies roll Carl Hallman into a wire basket. He had a leg wound, at least one chest wound, and one wound in the abdomen. That was bad, but not so finally bad as it would have been in the days before antibiotics. Carl was a durable boy; he was still breathing when they carried him out.

I looked around for the knife that had dropped from his hand. It wasn't there any longer. Perhaps the sheriff had picked it up. From what I had seen of it at a distance, it was a medium-sized kitchen knife, the kind that women use for paring or chopping. It could also have been used for stabbing Zinnie, though I still didn't see how.

chapter 32

I FOUND Mrs. Gley in the dim, old mildew-smelling kitchen. She was barricaded behind an enamel-topped table under a hanging bulb, making a last stand against sobriety. I smelled vanilla extract when I approached her. She clutched a small brown bottle to her breast, like an only child which I was threatening to kidnap.

"Vanilla will make you sick."

"It never has yet. Do you expect a woman to face these tragedies without a drink?"

"As a matter of fact, I could use a drink myself."

"There isn't enough for me!" She remembered her manners then: "I'm sorry, I ran out of liquor way back when. You *look* as if you could use a drink."

"Forget it." I noticed a bowl of apples on the worn woodstone sink behind her. "Mind if I peel myself an apple?"

"Please do," she said very politely. "I'll get you my paring knife."

She got up and rummaged in a drawer beside the sink. "Dunno what happened to my paring knife," she muttered, and turned around with a butcher knife in her hand. "Will this do?"

"I'll just eat it in the skin."

"They say you get more vitamins."

She resumed her seat at the table. I sat across from her on a straight-backed chair, and bit into my apple. "Has Carl been in the kitchen tonight?"

"I guess he must have been. He always used to come through here and up the back stairs." She pointed towards a half-open door in the corner of the room. Behind it, bare wooden risers mounted steeply.

"Has he come in this way before?"

"I hope to tell you he has. That boy has been preying on my little girl for more years than I care to count. He cast a spell on her with his looks and his talk. I'm glad he's finally got what's coming to him. Why, when she was a little slip of a thing in high school, he used to sneak in through my kitchen and up to her room."

"How do you know?"

"I've got eyes in my head, haven't I? I was keeping boarders then, and I was ashamed they'd find out about the carryings-on in her room. I tried to reason with her time and again, but she was under his spell. What could I do with my girl going wrong and no man to back me up in it? When I locked her up, she ran away, and I had to get the sheriff to bring her back. Finally she ran away for good, went off to Berkeley and left me all alone. Her own mother."

Her own mother set the brown bottle to her mouth and swallowed a slug of vanilla extract. She thrust her haggard face toward me across the table:

"But she learned her lesson, let me tell you. When a girl gets into trouble, she finds out that she can't do without her mother. I'd like to know where she would have been after she lost her baby, without me to look after her. I nursed her like a saint."

"Was this since her marriage?"

"It was not. He got her into trouble, and he wasn't man enough to stay around and help her out of it. He couldn't stand up to his family and face his responsibility. My girl wasn't good enough for him and his mucky-muck folks. So look what *he* turned out to be."

I took another bite of my apple. It tasted like ashes. I got up and dropped the apple into the garbage container in the sink. Mrs. Gley depressed me. Her mind veered fuzzily, like a moth distracted by shifting lights, across the fibrous surface of the past, never quite making contact with its meaning.

Voices floated back from the front of the house, too far away for me to make out the words. I went into the corridor, which darkened as I shut the door behind me. I stayed in the shadow.

Mildred was talking to Ostervelt and two middle-aged men in business suits. They had the indescribable unmistakable look of harness bulls who had made it into plain clothes but would always feel a little uncomfortable in them. One of them was saying:

"I can't figure out what this doctor had against him. Do you have any ideas on the subject, ma'am?"

"I'm afraid not." I couldn't see Mildred's face, but she had changed to the clothes in which she'd met Rose Parish.

"Did Carl kill his sister-in-law tonight?" Ostervelt said.

"He couldn't have. Carl came directly here from the beach. He was here with me all evening. I know I did wrong in hiding him. I'm willing to take the consequences."

"It ain't legal," the second detective said, "but I hope my wife would do the same for me. Did he mention the shooting of his brother Jerry?"

"No. We've been over that. I didn't even bring the subject up. He was dog-tired when he dragged himself in. He must have run all the way from Pelican Beach. I gave him something to eat and drink, and he went right off to sleep. Frankly, gentlemen, I'm tired, too. Can't the rest of this wait till morning?"

The detectives and the sheriff looked at each other and came to a silent agreement. "Yeah, we'll let it ride for now," the first detective said. "Under the circumstances.

Thanks for your co-operation, Mrs. Hallman. You have our sympathy."

Ostervelt lingered behind after they left to offer Mildred his own brand of sympathy. It took the form of a heavy pass. One of his hands held her waist. The other stroked her body from breast to thigh. She stood and endured it.

Anger stung my eyes and made me clench my fists. I hadn't been so mad since the day I took the strap away from my father. But something held me still and quiet. I'd been wearing my anger like blinders, letting it be exploited, and exploiting it for my own unacknowledged purposes. I acknowledged now that my anger against the sheriff was the expression of a deeper anger against myself. In plain terms, he was doing what I had wanted to be doing.

"Don't be so standoffish," he was saying. "You were nice to Dr. Grantland; why can't you be nice to me?"

"I don't know what you're talking about."

"Sure you do. You're not as hard to get as you pretend to be. So why play dumb with Uncle Ostie? My yen for you goes back a long ways, kid. Ever since you were a filly in high school giving your old lady a hard time. Remember?"

Her body stiffened in his hands. "How could I forget?"

Her voice was thin and sharp, but his aging lust converted it into music. He took what she said for romantic encouragement.

"I haven't forgotten, either, baby," he said, huskily. "And things are different now, now that I'm not married any more. I can make you an offer on the up-and-up."

"*I'm* still married."

"Maybe, if he lives. Even if he does live, you can get it annulled. Carl's going to be locked up for the rest of his life. I got him off easy the first time. This time he goes to the Hospital for the Criminally Insane."

"No!"

"Yes. You been doing your best to cover for him, but you know as well as I do he knocked off his brother and sister-in-law. It's time for you to cut your losses, kid, think of your own future."

"I have no future."

"I'm here to tell you you have. I can be a lot of help to you. One hand washes the other. There's no legal proof he killed his father, without me there never will be. It's a closed case. That means you can get your share of the inheritance. Your life is just beginning, baby, and I'm a part of it, built right into it."

His hands busied themselves with her. She stood quiescent, keeping her face away from his. "You always wanted me, didn't you?"

There was despair in her voice, but he heard only the words. "More than ever now. There's plenty of shots in the old locker. I'm planning to retire next year, after we settle the case and the estate. You and me, we can go anywhere we like, do anything we want."

"Is this why you shot Grantland?"

"One of the reasons. He had it coming, anyway. I'm pretty sure he masterminded Jerry's murder, if that's any comfort to you—talked Carl into doing it. But it makes a better case without Grantland in it. This way there's no danger that the Senator's death will have to be dragged in. Or the thing between you and Grantland."

Mildred lifted her face. "That was years ago, before my marriage. How did you know about it?"

"Zinnie told me this afternoon. He told Zinnie."

"He always was a rat. I'm glad you shot him."

"Sure you are. Uncle Ostie knows best."

She let him have her mouth. He seemed to devour it. She hung limp in his arms until he released her.

"I know you're tired tonight, honey. We'll leave it lay

for now. Just don't do any talking, except to me. Remember we got a couple of million bucks at stake. Are you with me?"

"You know I am, Ostie." Her voice was dead.

He lifted his hand to her and went out. She wedged a newspaper between the splintered door and the doorframe. Coming back toward the stairs, her movements were awkward and mechanical, as though her body was a walking doll run by remote control. Her eyes were like blue china, without sight, and as her heels tapped up the stairs I thought of a blind person in a ruined house tapping up a staircase that ended in nothing.

In the kitchen, Mrs. Gley was subsiding lower and lower on her bones. Her chin was propped on her arms now. The brown bottle lay empty at her elbow.

"I was thinking you deserted me," she said with elocutionary carefulness. "Everybody else has."

The blind footsteps tapped across the ceiling. Mrs. Gley cocked her head like a molting red parrot. "Izzat Mildred?"

"Yes."

"She ought to go to bed. Keep up her strength. She's never been the same since she lost that child of grief."

"How long ago did she lose it?"

"Three years, more or less."

"Did she have a doctor to look after her?"

"Sure she did. It was this same Dr. Grantland, poor fellow. It's a shame what had to happen to him. He treated her real nice, never even sent her a bill. That was before she got married, of course. Long before. I told her at the time, here was her chance to break off with that Carl and make a decent connection. A rising young doctor, and all. But she never listened to me. It had to be Carl Hallman or nothing. So now it's nothing. They're both gone."

"Carl isn't dead yet."

"He might as well be. I might as well be, too. My life is

nothing but disappointment and trouble. I brought my girl up to associate with nice people, marry a fine young man. But no, she had to have him. She had to marry into trouble and sickness and death." Her drunken self-pity rose in her throat like vomit. "She did it to spite me, that's what she did. She's trying to kill me with all this trouble that she brought into my house. I used to keep a nice house, but Mildred broke my spirit. She never gave me the love that a daughter owes her mother. Mooning all the time over her no-good father—you'd think *she* was the one that married him and lost him."

Her anger wouldn't come in spite of the invocation. She looked in fear at the ceiling, blinking against the light from the naked bulb. The fear in her drained parrot's eyes refused to dissolve. It deepened into terror.

"I'm not a good mother, either," she said. "I never have been any good to her. I've been a living drag on her all these years, and may God forgive me."

She slumped forward across the table, as if the entire weight of the night had fallen on her. Her harsh red hair spilled on the white tabletop. I stood and looked at her without seeing her. A pit or tunnel had opened in my mind, three years deep or long. Under white light at the bottom of it, fresh and vivid as a hallucination, I could see the red spillage where life had died and murder had been born.

I was in a stretched state of nerves where hidden things are coming clear and ordinary things are hidden. I thought of the electric blanket on the floor of Grantland's bedroom. I didn't hear Mildred's quiet feet till she was half-way down the back stairs. I met her at the foot of them.

Her whole body jerked when she saw me. She brought it under control, and tried to smile:

"I didn't know you were still here."

"I've been talking to your mother. She seems to have passed out again."

"Poor mother. Poor everybody." She shut her eyes against the sight of the kitchen and its raddled occupant. She brushed her blue-veined eyelids with the fingertips of one hand. Her other hand was hidden in the folds of her skirt. "I suppose I should put her to bed."

"I have to talk to you first."

"What on earth about? It's terribly late."

"About poor everybody. How did Grantland know that Carl was here?"

"He didn't. He couldn't have."

"I think you're telling the truth for once. He didn't know Carl was here. He came here to kill you, but Carl was in his way. By the time he got to you, the gun was empty."

She stood silent.

"Why did Grantland want to kill you, Mildred?"

She moistened her dry lips with the tip of her tongue. "I don't know."

"I think I do. The reasons he had wouldn't drive an ordinary man to murder. But Grantland was frightened as well as angry. Desperate. He had to silence you, and he wanted to get back at you. Zinnie meant more to him than money."

"What's Zinnie got to do with me?"

"You stabbed her to death with your mother's paring knife. I didn't see at first how it was possible. Zinnie's body was warm when I found her. You were here under police surveillance. The timing didn't fit, until I realized that her body was kept warm under an electric blanket in Grantland's bed. You killed her before you drove to Pelican Beach. You heard over Grantland's radio that Carl was seen there. Isn't that true?"

"Why would I do a thing like that?" she whispered.

The question wasn't entirely rhetorical. Mildred looked as if she earnestly desired an answer. Like an independent entity, her hidden fist jumped up from the folds of her skirt to supply an answer. A pointed blade projected downward from it. She drove it against her breast.

Even her final intention was divided. The knife turned in her hand, and only tore her blouse. I had it away from her before she could do more damage.

"Give it back to me. Please."

"I can't do that." I was looking at the knife. Its blade was etched with dry brown stains.

"Then kill me. Quickly. I have to die anyway. I've known it now for years."

"You have to live. They don't gas women any more."

"Not even women like me? I couldn't bear to live. Please kill me. I know you hate me."

She tore her blouse gaping and offered her breast to me in desperate seduction. It was like a virgin's, unsunned, the color of pearl.

"I'm sorry for you, Mildred."

My voice sounded strange; it had broken through into a tone that was new to me, deep as the sorrow I felt. It had nothing to do with sex, or with the possessive pity that changed to sex when the wind blew from the south. She was a human being with more grief on her young mind than it was able to bear.

chapter 33

MRS. GLEY groaned in her sleep. Mildred ran up the stairs away from both of us. I went up after her, across a drab brown hallway, into a room where she was struggling to raise the window.

It wasn't a woman's room, or anybody's room. It was more like an unused guestroom where unwanted things were kept: old books and pictures, an old iron double bed, a decaying rug. I felt a strange proprietary embarrassment, like a pawnbroker who's lent money on somebody else's possessions, sight unseen.

The window resisted her efforts. I saw her watching me in its dark mirror. Her own reflected face was like a ghost's peering from outer darkness.

"Go away and leave me alone."

"A lot of people have. Maybe that's the trouble. Come away from the window, eh?"

She moved back into the room and stood by the bed. There was a soiled depression in the cheap chenille spread where I guessed Carl had been lying. She sat on the edge of the iron bed.

"I don't want any of your phony sympathy. People always want to be paid for it. What do you want from me? Sex? Money? Or just to see me suffer?"

I didn't know how to answer her.

"Or do you simply want to hear me say it? Listen then, I'm a murderer. I murdered four people."

She sat and looked at the faded flowers in the wallpaper. I thought that it was a place where dreams could grow rank without much competition from the actual.

"What did you want, Mildred?"

She put a name to one of the dreams. "Money. That was what set him off from everyone—the thing that made him so handsome to me, so—shining."

"Do you mean Carl?"

"Yes. Carl." Her hand moved behind her to the depression in the spread. She leaned on it. "Even tonight, when he was lying here, all dirty and stinking, I felt so happy with him. So rich. Mother used to say I talked like a whore, but I was never a whore. I never took money from him. I gave myself to him because he needed me. The books said he had to have sex. So I used to let him come up here to the room."

"What books are you talking about?"

"The books he used to read. We read them together. Carl was afraid of going homosexual. That's why I used to pretend to be excited with him. I never really was, though, with him or any man."

"How many men were there?"

"Only three," she said, "and one of them only once."

"Ostervelt?"

She made an ugly face. "I don't want to talk about him. It was different with Carl. I'd be glad for him, but then the gladness would split off from my body. I'd be in two parts, a hot part and a cold part, and the cold part would rise up like a spirit. Then I'd imagine that I was in bed with a golden man. He was putting gold in my purse, and I'd invest it and make a profit and reinvest. Then I'd feel rich and real, and the spirit would stop watching me. It was just a game I played with myself. I never told Carl about it; Carl never really knew me. Nobody ever knew me."

She spoke with the desperate pride of loneliness and lostness. Then hurried on, as though some final disaster was about to fall, and I was her one chance to be known:

"I thought if we could get married, and I was Mrs. Carl Hallman, then I'd feel rich and solid all the time. When he went away to the university I followed him. No other girl was going to get him from me. I went to business college and found a job in Oakland. I rented an apartment of my own where he could visit me. I used to make supper for him, and help him with his studies. It was almost like being married.

"Carl wanted to make it legal, too, but his parents couldn't see it, especially his mother. She couldn't see *me*. It made me mad, the way she talked about me to Carl. You'd think I was human garbage. That was when I decided to stop taking precautions.

"It took me over a year to get our baby started. I wasn't in very good health. I don't remember very much about that time. I know I went on working in the office. They even gave me a raise. But it was the nights I lived for, not so much the times with Carl—the times after he left when I would lie awake and think about the child I was going to have. I knew that he would have to be a boy. We'd call him Carl, and bring him up just right. I'd do everything for him myself, dress him and feed him his vitamins and keep him away from bad influences, such as his grandmother. Both his grandmothers.

"After Zinnie had Martha, I thought about him all the time and I became pregnant at last. I waited two months to be sure, and then I told Carl. He was frightened, he couldn't hide it. He didn't want our baby. Mainly, he was afraid of what his mother would do. She was far gone by that time, ready to do anything to have her way. When Carl first told her about me, long before, she said she'd rather kill herself than let him marry me.

"She still had him hypnotized. I have a nasty tongue, and I told him so. I told him that he was the daring young man on the umbilical cord, but it was a hangman's noose. We had a battle. He smashed my new set of dishes in the sink. I was afraid he was going to smash me, too. Perhaps that's why he ran away. I didn't see him for days, or hear from him.

"His landlady said he'd gone home. I waited as long as I could stand it before I phoned the ranch. His mother said he hadn't been there. I thought she was lying to me, trying to get rid of me. So I told her I was pregnant, and Carl would have to marry me. She called me a liar, and other things, and then she hung up on me.

"That was a little after seven o'clock on a Friday night. I'd waited for the night rates before I phoned. I sat and watched night come on. She wouldn't let Carl come back to me, ever. I could see part of the Bay from my window, and the long ramp where the cars climbed towards the Bridge, the mud flats under it, and the water like blue misery. I thought that the place for me was in the water. And I'd have done it, too. She shouldn't have stopped me."

I had been standing over her all this time. She looked up and pushed me away with her hands, not touching me. Her movements were slow and gingerly, as if any sudden gesture might upset a delicate balance, in the room or in her, and let the whole thing collapse.

I placed a straight chair by the bed and straddled it, resting my arms on the back. It gave me a queer bedside feeling, like a quack doctor, without a bedside manner:

"Who stopped you, Mildred?"

"Carl's mother did. She should have let me kill myself and be done with it. It doesn't lessen my guilt, I know that, but Alicia brought what happened on herself. She phoned me back while I was sitting there, and told me that she was sorry for what she'd said. Could I forgive her? She'd thought the whole thing over and wanted to talk to me, help me, see that I was looked after. I believed that she'd come to her senses, that my baby would bring us all together and we'd be a happy family.

"She made an appointment for me to meet her on the Purissima wharf next evening. She said she wanted to get to know me, just the two of us. I drove down Saturday, and she was waiting in the parking lot when I got there. I'd never met her face to face before. She was a big woman, wearing mink, very tall and impressive. Her eyes shone like a cat, and her voice buzzed. I think she must have been high on some kind of drug. I didn't know it then. I was so pleased that we were coming together. I was proud to have her sitting in my old clunk in a mink coat.

"But she wasn't there to do me any favors. She started out all right, very sympathetic. It was a dirty trick Carl played on me, running out like that. The worst of it was, she had her doubts that he would ever come back. Even if he did, he'd be no bargain as a husband or a father. Carl was hopelessly unstable. She was his mother, and she ought to know. It ran in the family. Her own father had died in a sanitarium, and Carl took after him.

"Even without an ancestral curse hanging over you—that was what she called it—it was a hideous world, a crime to bring children into it. She quoted a poem to me:

'Sleep the long sleep;
The Doomsters heap
Travails and teens around us here . . .'

I don't know who wrote it, but I've never been able to get those lines out of my head.

"She said it was written to an unborn child. Teens meant heartaches and troubles, and that was all any child had to look forward to in this life. The Doomsters saw to that. She talked about those Doomsters of hers as if they really existed. We were sitting looking out over the sea, and I almost thought I could see them walking up out of the black water and looming across the stars. Monsters with human faces.

"Alicia Hallman was a monster herself, and I knew it. Yet everything she said had some truth to it. There was no way to argue except from the way I felt, about my baby. It was hard to keep my feeling warm through all the talk. I didn't have sense enough to leave her, or shut my ears. I even caught myself nodding and agreeing with her, partly. Why go to all the trouble of having a child if he was going to live in grief, cut off from the stars. Or if his daddy was never coming back.

"She almost had me hypnotized with that buzzing voice of hers, like violins out of tune. I went along with her to Dr. Grantland's office. The same part of me that agreed with her knew that I was going to lose my baby there. At the last minute, when I was on the table and it was too late, I tried to stop it. I screamed and fought against him. She came into the room with that gun of hers and told me to lie down and be quiet, or she'd kill me on the spot. Dr. Grantland didn't want to go through with it. She said if he didn't she'd run him out of his practice. He put a needle in me.

"When I came back from the anesthetic, I could see her cat eyes watching me. I had only the one thought, she had killed my baby. I must have picked up a bottle. I remember smashing it over her head. Before that, she must have tried to shoot me. I heard a gun go off, I didn't see it.

"Anyway, I killed her. I don't remember driving home, but I must have. I was still drunk on pentothal; I hardly knew what I was doing. Mother put me to bed and did what she could for me, which wasn't much. I couldn't go to sleep. I couldn't understand why the police didn't come and get me. Next day, Sunday, I went back to the doctor. He frightened me, but I was even more frightened not to go.

"He was gentle with me. I was surprised how gentle. I almost loved him when he told me what he'd done for me, making it look like a suicide. They'd already recovered her body from the sea, and nobody even asked me a question about it. Carl came back on Monday. We went to the funeral together. It was a closed-coffin funeral, and I could nearly believe that the official story of suicide was true, that the rest was just a bad dream.

"Carl thought she'd drowned herself. He took it better than I expected, but it had a strange effect on him. He said he'd been in the desert for almost a week, thinking and praying for guidace. He was coming back from Death Valley when a highway patrolman stopped him and told him his family was looking for him, and why. That was on Sunday, just before sunset.

"Carl said he looked up at the Sierra, and saw an unearthly light behind it in the west toward Purissima. It streamed, like milk, from the heavens, and it made him realize that life was a precious gift which had to be justified. He saw an Indian herding sheep on the hillside, and took it for a sign. He decided then and there to study medicine and devote his life to healing, perhaps on the Indian reservations, or in Africa like Schweitzer.

"I was carried away myself. That glorious light of Carl's seemed like an answer to the darkness I'd been in since Saturday night. I told Carl I'd go along with him if he still wanted me. Carl said that he would need a worthy helpmeet, but we couldn't get married yet. He wasn't twenty-one. It was too soon after his mother's death. His father was opposed to early marriages, anyway, and we mustn't do anything to upset an old man with a heart condition. In the meantime we should live as friends, as brother and sister, to prepare ourselves for the sacrament of marriage.

"Carl was becoming more and more idealistic. He took up theology that fall, on top of his premed courses. My own little spurt of idealism, or whatever you want to call it, didn't last very long. Dr. Grantland came to see me one day that summer. He said that he was a businessman, and he understood that I was a businesswoman. He certainly hoped I was. Because if I played my cards right, with him kibitzing for me, I could be worth a lot of money with very little effort.

"Dr. Grantland had changed, too. He was very smiley and businesslike, but he didn't look like a doctor any more. He didn't talk like one—more like a ventriloquist's dummy moving his lips in time to somebody else's lines. He told me the Senator's heart and arteries were deteriorating, he was due to die before long. When he did, Carl and Jerry would divide the estate between them. If I was married to Carl, I'd be in a position to repay my friends for any help they'd given me.

"He considered us good friends, but it would sort of set the seal on our friendship if we went to bed together. He'd been told that he was very good in bed. I let him. It made no difference to me, one way or the other. I even liked being with him, in a way. He was the only one who knew about me. When I was in Purissima after that, I used to go and visit him in his office. Until I married Carl, I mean. I quit seeing Grantland then. It wouldn't have been right.

"Carl was twenty-one on the fourteenth of March, and we were married in Oakland three days later. He moved into the apartment with me, but he thought we should make up for our earlier sins by living in chastity for another year. Carl was so tense about it that I was afraid to argue with him. He was pale, and bright in the eyes. Sometimes he wouldn't talk for days at a time, and then the floodgates would open and he'd talk all night.

"He'd begun to fail in his studies, but he was full of ideas. We used to discuss reality, appearance and reality. I always thought appearance was the front you put on for people, and reality was how you really felt. Reality was death and blood and the curse. Reality was hell. Carl told me I had it all wrong, that pain and evil were only appearances. Goodness was reality, and he would prove it to me in his life. Now that he'd discovered Christian existentialism, he saw quite clearly that suffering was only a test, a fire that purified. That was the reason we couldn't sleep together. It was for the good of our souls.

"Carl had begun to lose a lot of weight. He got so nervous that spring, he couldn't sit still to work. Sometimes I'd hear him walking in the living-room all night. I thought if I could get him to come to bed with me, it would help him to get some sleep, settle him down. I had some pretty weird ideas of my own. I paraded around in floozie nightgowns, and drenched myself with perfume, and did my best to seduce him. My own husband. One night in May, I served him a candlelight dinner with wine and got him drunk enough.

"It didn't work, not for either of us. The spirit rose up from me and floated over the bed. I looked down and watched Carl using my body. And I hated him. He didn't love *me*. He didn't want to know *me*. I thought that we were both dead, and our corpses were in bed together. Zombies. Our two spirits never met.

"Carl was still in bed when I came home the next night. He hadn't been to his classes, hadn't moved all day. I thought at first he was sick, physically sick, and I called a doctor. Carl told him that the light of heaven had gone out. He had done it himself by putting out the light in his own mind. Now there was nothing in his head but darkness.

"Dr. Levin took me into the next room and told me that Carl was mentally disturbed. He should probably be committed. I telephoned Carl's father, and Dr. Levin talked to him, too. The Senator said that the idea of commitment was absurd. Carl had simply been hitting the books too hard, and what he needed was some good, hard down-to-earth work.

"Carl's father came and took him home the next day. I gave up my apartment and my job, and a few days later I followed them. I should have stayed where I was, but I wanted to be with Carl. I didn't trust his family. And I had a sneaking desire, even under the circumstances, to live on the ranch and be Mrs. Carl Hallman in Purissima. Well, I was, but it was worse than I expected. His family didn't like me. They blamed me for Carl's condition. A *good* wife would have been able to keep him healthy and wealthy and wise.

"The only person there who really liked me was Zinnie's baby. I used to play a game pretending that Martha was *my* baby. That was how I got through those two years. I'd pretend that I was alone with her in the big house. The others had all gone away, or else they'd died, and I was Martha's mother, doing for her all by myself, bringing her up just right, without any nasty influences. We did have good times, too. Sometimes I really believed that the nightmare in the doctor's office hadn't happened at all. Martha was there to prove it, my own baby, going on two.

"But Dr. Grantland was often there to remind me that it had happened. He was looking after Carl and his father, both. The Senator liked him because he didn't charge much or make expensive suggestions, such as hospitals or psychiatric treatment. Carl's father was quite a money-saver. We had margarine on the table instead of butter, and nothing but the culled oranges for our own use. I was even expected to pay board, until my money ran out. I didn't have a new dress for nearly two years. Maybe if I had, I wouldn't have killed him."

Mildred said that quietly, without any change in tone, without apparent feeling. Her face was expressionless.

Only her forefinger moved on her skirted knee, tracing a small pattern: a circle and then a cross inside of the circle; as though she was trying to exorcise bad thoughts.

"I certainly wouldn't have killed him if he'd died when he was supposed to. Dr. Grantland had said a year, but the year went by, then most of another year. I wasn't the only one waiting. Jerry and Zinnie were waiting just as hard. They did their best to stir up trouble between Carl and his father, which wasn't hard to do. Carl was a little better, but still depressed and surly. He wasn't getting along with his father, and the old man kept threatening to change his will.

"One night Jerry baited Carl into a terrible argument about the Japanese people who used to own part of the valley. The Senator jumped into it, of course, as he was supposed to. Carl told him he didn't want any part of the ranch. If he ever did inherit any share of it, he'd give it back to the people who'd been sold up. I never saw the old man so angry. He said Carl was in no danger of inheriting anything. This time he meant it, too. He asked Jerry to make an appointment with his lawyer in the morning.

"I telephoned Dr. Grantland and he came out, ostensibly to see the Senator. Afterwards I talked to him outside. He took a very dim view. It wasn't that he was greedy, but he was thousands of dollars out of pocket. It was the first time he told me about the other man, this Rickey or Rica who'd been blackmailing him ever since Alicia's death. The same man who escaped with Carl last night."

"Grantland had never mentioned him to you?"

"No, he said he'd been trying to protect me. But now he was just about bled white, and something had to be done. He didn't tell me outright that I had to kill the Senator. I didn't have to be told. I didn't even have to think about it. I simply let myself forget who I was, and went through the whole thing like clockwork."

Her forefinger was active on her knee, repeating the symbol of the cross in the circle. She said, as if in answer to a question:

"You'd think I'd been planning it for years, all my life, ever since—"

She broke off, and covered the invisible device on her knee with her whole hand. She rose like a sleepwalker and went to the window. An oak tree in the backyard was outlined like a black paper cutout against the whitening sky.

"Ever since what?" I said to her still back.

"I was just remembering. When my father went away, afterwards, I used to think of funny things when I was in bed before I went to sleep. I wanted to track him down, and find him, and—"

"Kill him?"

"Oh no!" she cried. "I wanted to tell him how much we missed him and bring him back to Mother, so that we could be a happy family again. But if he wouldn't come—"

"What if he wouldn't come?"

"I don't want to talk about it. I don't remember." She struck the window where her reflection had been, not quite hard enough to break it.

chapter 34

DAWN was coming on over the trees, like fluorescent lights in an operating room. Mildred turned away from the white agony of the light. Her outburst of feeling had passed, leaving her face smooth and her voice unshaken. Only her eyes had changed. They were heavy, and the color of ripe plums.

"It wasn't like the first time. This time I felt nothing. It's strange to kill someone and have no feeling about it. I wasn't even afraid while I was waiting for him in his bathroom closet. He always took a warm bath at night to help him sleep. I had an old ball-peen hammer I'd found on Jerry's workbench in the greenhouse. When he was in the bathtub, I slipped out of the closet and hit him on the back of the head with the hammer. I held his face under the water until the bubbles stopped.

"It only took a few seconds. I unlocked the bathroom door and locked it again on the outside and wiped the key and pushed it back under the door. Then I put the hammer where I found it, with Jerry's things. I hoped it would be taken for an accident, but if it wasn't I wanted Jerry to be blamed. It was really his fault, egging Carl on to quarrel with his father.

"But Carl was the one they blamed, as you well know. He seemed to *want* to be blamed. I think for a while he convinced himself that he had actually done it, and everyone else went along with it. The sheriff didn't even investigate."

"Was he protecting you?"

"No. If he was, he didn't know it. Jerry made some kind of a deal with him to save the county money and save the family's face. He didn't want a murder trial in his distinguished family. Neither did I. I didn't try to interfere when Jerry arranged to send Carl to the hospital. I signed the papers without a word.

"Jerry knew what he was doing. He was trained in the law, and he arranged it so that he was Carl's legal guardian. It meant that he controlled everything. I had no rights at all, as far as the family estate was concerned. The day after Carl was committed, Jerry hinted politely that I might as well move out. I believe that Jerry suspected me, but he was a cagey individual. It suited him better to blame it all on Carl, and keep his own cards face down.

"Dr. Grantland turned against me, too. He said he was through with me, after the mess I'd made of things. He said that he was through protecting me. For all he cared, the man he'd been paying off could go to the police and tell them all about me. And I mustn't think that I could get back at him by talking him into trouble. It would be my word against his, and I was as schitzy as hell, and he could prove it. He slapped me and ordered me out of his house. He said if I didn't like it, he'd call the police right then.

"I've spent the last six months waiting for them," she said. "Waiting for the knock on the door. Some nights I'd wish for them to come, *will* them to come, and get it over with. Some nights I wouldn't care one way or the other. Some nights—they were the worst—I'd lie burning up with cold and watch the clock and count its ticks, one by one, all night. The clock would tick like doom, louder and louder, like doomsters knocking on the door and clumping up the stairs.

"I got so I was afraid to go to sleep at night. I haven't slept for the last four nights, since I found out about Carl's friend on the ward. It was this man, Rica, the one who knew all about me. I could imagine him telling Carl. Carl would turn against me. There'd be nobody left in the world who even liked me. When they phoned me yesterday morning that Carl had escaped with him, I knew that this had to be it." She looked at me quite calmly. "You know the rest. You were here."

"I saw it from the outside."

"That's all there was, the outside. There wasn't any inside, at least for me. It was like a ritual which I made up as I went along. Every step I took had a meaning at the time, but I can't remember any of the meanings now."

"Tell me what you did, from the time that you decided to kill Jerry."

"It decided itself," she said. "I had no decision to make, no choice. Dr. Grantland phoned me at the office a little while before you got to town. It was the first I'd heard from him in six months. He said that Carl had got hold of a loaded gun. If Carl shot Jerry with it, it would solve a lot of problems. Money would be available, in case this man Rica tried to make more trouble for us. Also, Grantland would be able to use his influence with Zinnie to head off investigation of the other deaths. I'd even have a chance at my share of the property. If Carl didn't shoot Jerry, the whole thing would blow up in our faces.

"Well, Carl had no intention of shooting anybody. I found that out when I talked to him in the orange grove. The gun he had was his mother's gun, which Dr. Grantland had given him. Carl wanted to ask Jerry some questions about it—about her death. Apparently Grantland told him that Jerry killed her.

"I didn't know for certain that Jerry suspected me, but I was afraid of what he would say to Carl. This was on top of all the other reasons I had to kill him, all the little snubs and sneers I'd had to take from him. I said I'd talk to Jerry instead, and I persuaded Carl to hand over the gun to me. If he was found armed, they might shoot him without asking questions. I told him to stay out of sight, and come here after dark if he could make it. That I would hide him.

"I hid the gun away, inside my girdle—it hurt so much I fainted, there on the lawn. When I was alone, I switched it to my bag. Later, when Jerry was alone, I went into the greenhouse and shot him twice in the back. I wiped the gun and left it there beside him. I had no more use for it."

She sighed, with the deep bone-tiredness that takes

years to come to. Even the engine of her guilt was running down. But there was one more death in her cycle of killings.

And still the questions kept rising behind my teeth, always the questions, with the taste of their answers, salt as sea or tears, bitter as iron or fear, sweet-sour as folding money that has passed through many hands:

"Why did you kill Zinnie? Did you actually believe that you could get away with it, collect the money and live happily ever after?"

"I never thought of the money," she said, "or Zinnie, for that matter. I went there to see Dr. Grantland."

"You took a knife along."

"For him," she said. "I was thinking about him when I took that knife out of the drawer. Zinnie happened to be the one who was there. I killed her, I hardly know why. I felt ashamed for her, lying naked like that in his bed. It was almost like killing myself. Then I heard the radio going in the front room. It said that Carl had been seen at Pelican Beach.

"It seemed like a special message intended for me. I thought that there was hope for us yet, if only I could reach Carl. We could go away together and start a new life, in Africa or on the Indian reservations. It sounds ridiculous now, but that's what I thought on the way down to Pelican Beach. That somehow everything could be made good yet."

"So you walked in front of a truck."

"Yes. Suddenly I saw what I had done. Especially to Carl. It was my fault he was being hunted like a murderer. I was the murderer. I saw what I was, and I wanted to put an end to myself before I killed more people."

"What people are you talking about?"

Averting her face, she stared fixedly at the rumpled pillow at the head of the bed.

"Were you planning to kill Carl? Is that why you sent us away to Mrs. Hutchinson's, when he was already here?"

"No. It was Martha I was thinking about. I didn't want anything to happen to Martha."

"Who would hurt her if you didn't?"

"I was afraid I would," she said miserably. "It was one of the thoughts that came to me, that Martha had to be killed. Otherwise the whole thing made no sense."

"And Carl too? Did he have to be killed?"

"I thought I could do it," she said. "I stood over him with the knife in my hand for a long time while he was sleeping. I could say that I killed him in self-defense, and that he confessed all the murders before he died. I could get the house and the money all to myself, and pay off Dr. Grantland. Nobody else would suspect me.

"But I couldn't go through with it," she said. "I dropped the knife on the floor. I couldn't hurt Carl, or Martha. I wanted them to live. It made the whole thing meaningless, didn't it?"

"You're wrong. The fact that you didn't kill them is the only meaning left."

"What difference does it make? From the night I killed Alicia and my baby, every day I've lived has been a crime against nature. There isn't a person on the face of the earth who wouldn't hate me if they knew about me."

Her face was contorted. I thought she was trying not to cry. Then I thought she was trying to cry.

"I don't hate you, Mildred. On the contrary."

I was an ex-cop, and the words came hard. I had to say them, though, if I didn't want to be stuck for the rest of my life with the old black-and-white picture, the idea that there were just good people and bad people, and everything would be hunky-dory if the good people locked up the bad ones or wiped them out with small personalized nuclear weapons.

It was a very comforting idea, and bracing to the ego. For years I'd been using it to justify my own activities, fighting fire with fire and violence with violence, running on fool's errands while the people died: a slightly earthbound Tarzan in a slightly paranoid jungle. Landscape with figure of a hairless ape.

It was time I traded the picture in on one that included a few of the finer shades. Mildred was as guilty as a girl could be, but she wasn't the only one. An alternating current of guilt ran between her and all of us involved with her. Grantland and Rica, Ostervelt, and me. The redheaded woman who drank time under the table. The father who had deserted the household and died for it symbolically in the Senator's bathtub. Even the Hallman family, the four victims, had been in a sense the victimizers, too. The current of guilt flowed in a closed circuit if you traced it far enough.

Thinking of Alicia Hallman and her open-ended legacy of death, I was almost ready to believe in her doomsters. If they didn't exist in the actual world they rose from the depths of every man's inner sea, gentle as night dreams, with the back-breaking force of tidal waves. Perhaps they existed in the sense that men and women were their own doomsters, the secret authors of their own destruction. You had to be very careful what you dreamed.

The wave of night had passed through Mildred and left her cold and shaking. I held her in my arms for a little while. The light outside the window had turned to morning. The green tree-branches moved in it. Wind blew through the leaves.

chapter 35

I TALKED to Rose Parish at breakfast, in the cafeteria of the local hospital. Mildred was in another part of the same building, under city police guard and under sedation. Rose and I had insisted on these things, and got our way. There would be time enough for further interrogations, statements, prosecution and defense, for all the awesome ritual of the law matching the awesome ritual of her murders.

Carl had survived a two-hour operation, and wasn't out from under the anesthetic. His prognosis was fair. Tom Rica was definitely going to live. He was resting in the men's security ward after a night of walking. I wasn't sure that Rose and the others who had helped to walk him, had done him any great favor.

Rose listened to me in silence, tearing her toast into small pieces and neglecting her eggs. The night had left bruises around her eyes, which somehow improved her looks.

"Poor girl," she said, when I finished. "What will happen to her?"

"It's a psychological question as much as a legal question. You're the psychologist."

"Not much of a one, I'm afraid."

"Don't underestimate yourself. You really called the shots last night. When I was talking to Mildred, I remembered what you said about whole families breaking down together, but putting it off onto the weakest one. The scapegoat. Carl was the one you had in mind. In a way, though, Mildred is another."

"I know. I've watched her, at the hospital, and again last night. I couldn't miss her mask, her coldness, her not-being-there. But I didn't have the courage to admit to myself that she was ill, let alone speak out about it." She bowed her head over her uneaten breakfast, maltreating a fragment of toast between her fingers. "I'm a coward and a fraud."

"I don't understand why you say that."

"I was jealous of her, that's why. I was afraid I was projecting my own wish onto her, that all I wanted was to get her out of the way."

"Because you're in love with Carl?"

"Am I so obvious?"

"Very honest, anyway."

In some incredible reserve of innocence, she found the energy to blush. "I'm a complete fake. The worst of it is, I intend to go right on being one. I don't care if he is my patient, and married to boot. I don't care if he's ill or an invalid or anything else. I don't care if I have to wait ten years for him."

Her voice vibrated through the cafeteria. Its drab utilitarian spaces were filling up with white-coated interns, orderlies, nurses. Several of them turned to look, startled by the rare vibration of passion.

Rose lowered her voice. "You won't misunderstand me. I expect to have to wait for Carl, and in the meantime I'm not forgetting his wife. I'll do everything I can for her."

"Do you think an insanity plea could be made to stick?"

"I doubt it. It depends on how sick she is. I'd guess, from what I've observed and what you tell me, that she's borderline schizophrenic. Probably she's been in-and-out for several years. This crisis may bring her completely out of it. I've seen it happen to patients, and she must have considerable ego strength to have held herself together for so long. But the crisis could push her back into very deep withdrawal. Either way, there's no way out for her. The most we can do is see that she gets decent treatment. Which I intend to do."

"You're a good woman."

She writhed under the compliment. "I wish I were. At least I used to wish it. Since I've been doing hospital work, I've pretty well got over thinking in terms of good and bad. Those categories often do more harm than—well, good. We use them to torment ourselves, and hate ourselves because we can't live up to them. Before we know it, we're turning our hatred against other people, especially the unlucky ones, the weak ones who can't fight back. We think we have to punish somebody for the human mess we're in, so we single out the scapegoats and call them evil. And Christian love and virtue go down the drain." She poked with a spoon at the cold brown dregs of coffee in her cup. "Am I making any sense, or do I just sound soft-headed?"

"Both. You sound soft-headed, and you make sense to me. I've started to think along some of the same lines."

Specifically, I was thinking about Tom Rica: the hopeful boy he had been, and the man he had become, hopeless and old in his twenties. I vaguely remembered a time in between, when hope and despair had been fighting for him, and he'd come to me for help. The rest of it was veiled in an old alcoholic haze, but I knew it was ugly.

"It's going to be a long time," Rose was saying, "before people really know that we're members of one another. I'm afraid they're going to be terribly hard on Mildred. If only there were some mitigation, or if there weren't so many. She killed so many."

"There were mitigating circumstances in the first one—the one that started her off. A judge trying it by himself would probably call it justifiable homicide. In fact, I'm not even sure she did it."

"Really?"

"You heard what Tom Rica said. He blamed that death on Grantland. Did he add anything to that in the course of the night?"

"No. I didn't press him."

"Did he do any talking at all?"

"Some." Rose wouldn't meet my eyes.

"What did he say?"

"It's all rather vague. After all, I wasn't taking notes."

"Listen, Rose. There's no point in trying to cover up for Tom, not at this late date. He's been blackmailing Grantland for years. He broke out of the hospital with the idea of converting it into a big-time operation. Carl probably convinced him that Grantland had something to do with his father's death, as well as his mother's, and that there was a lot of money involved. Tom persuaded Carl to come over the wall with him. His idea was to pile more pressure on Grantland. In case Carl couldn't boil up enough trouble by himself, Tom sent him to me."

"I know."

"Did Tom tell you?"

"If you really want to know, he told me a lot of things. Have you stopped to wonder why he picked on you?"

"We used to know each other. I guess my name stuck in his head."

"More than your name stuck. When he was a boy in high school, you were his hero. And then you stopped being." She reached across the littered table and touched the back of my hand. "I don't mean to hurt you, Archer. Stop me if I am."

"Go ahead. I didn't know I was important to Tom." But I was lying. I knew. You always know. On the firing range, in the gym, he even used to imitate my mistakes.

"He seems to have thought of you as a kind of foster-father. Then your wife divorced you, and there were some things in the newspapers, he didn't say what they were."

"They were the usual. Or a little worse than the usual."

"I am hurting you," she said. "This sounds like an accusation, but it isn't. Tom hasn't forgotten what you did for him before your private trouble interfered. Perhaps it was unconscious on his part, but I believe he sent Carl to you in the hope that you could help him."

"Which one? Tom or Carl?"

"Both of them."

"If he thought that, how wrong he was."

"I disagree. You've done what you can. It's all that's expected of anyone. You helped to save Carl's life. I know you'll do what you can for Tom, too. It's why I wanted you to know what he said, before you talk to him."

Her approval embarrassed me. I knew how far I had fallen short. "I'd like to talk to him now."

The security ward occupied one end of a wing on the second floor. The policeman guarding the steel-sheathed door greeted Rose like an old friend, and let us through. The morning light was filtered through a heavy wire mesh screen over the single window of Tom's cubicle.

He lay like a forked stick under the sheet, his arms inert outside it. Flesh-colored tape bound his hands and wrists. Except where the beard darkened it, his face was much paler than the tape. He bared his teeth in a downward grin:

"I hear you had a rough night, Archer. You were asking for it."

"I hear you had a rougher one."

"Tell me I asked for it. Cheer me up."

"Are you feeling better?" Rose asked him.

He answered with bitter satisfaction: "I'm feeling worse. And I'm going to feel worse yet."

"You've been through the worst already," I said. "Why don't you kick it permanently?"

"It's easy to say."

"You almost had it made when you were with us," Rose said. "If I could arrange a few months in a federal hospital—"

"Save your trouble. I'd go right back on. It's my meat and drink. When I kick it there's nothing left, I know that now."

"How long have you been on heroin?"

"Five or six hundred years." He added, in a different, younger voice: "Right after I left high school. This broad I met in Vegas—" His voice sank out of hearing in his throat. He twitched restlessly, and rolled his head on the pillow, away from Rose and me and memory. "We won't go into it."

Rose moved to the door. "I'll go and see how Carl is."

I said, when the door had closed behind her: "Was it Maude who got you started on horse, Tom?"

"Naw, she's death on the stuff. She was the one that made me go to the hospital. She could have sprung me clean."

"I hear you saying it."

"It's the truth. She got my charge reduced from possession so they'd send me up for treatment."

"How could she do that?"

"She's got a lot of friends. She does them favors, they do her favors."

"Is the sheriff one of her friends?"

He changed the subject. "I was going to tell you about this kid in Vegas. She was just a kid my own age, but she was main-lining already. I met her at this aluminus party where they wanted me to play football for their college. The old boys had a lot of drinks, and we young people had some, and then they wanted me to put on a show with this kid. They kept chunking silver dollars at us when we were doing it. We collected so many silver dollars I had a hard time carrying them up to her room. I was strong in those days, too."

"I remember you were."

"Damn them!" he said in weak fury. "They made a monkey out of me. I let them do it to me, for a couple of hundred lousy silver dollars. I told them what they could do with their football scholarship. I didn't want to go to college anyway. Too much like work."

"What's the matter with work?"

"Only suckers work. And you can pin it in your hat Tom Rica is no sucker. You want to know who finally cured me of suckering for all that uplift crap? You did, and I thank you for it."

"When did all this happen?"

"Don't you kid me, you remember that day I came to your office. I thought if I could talk—but we won't go into that. You wanted no part of me. I wanted no part of you. I knew which side I was on from there on out."

He sat up in bed and bared his arm as if the marks of the needle were battle scars; which I had inflicted on him: "The day you gave me the old rush, I made up my mind I'd rather be an honest junkie than a double-talking hypocrite. When they grabbed me this last time, I was main-lining two-three times a day. And liking it," he said, in lost defiance. "If I had my life to live over, I wouldn't change a thing."

I'd begun to feel restless, and a little nauseated. The alcoholic haze was lifting from the half-forgotten afternoon when Tom had come to my office for help, and gone away without it.

"What did you come to see me about, Tom?"

He was silent for quite a while. "You really want to know?"

"Very much."

"All right, I had a problem. Matter of fact, I had a couple of problems. One of them was the heroin. I wasn't all the way gone on it yet, but I was close to gone. I figured maybe you could tell me what to do about it, where I could get treatment. Well, you told me where to go."

I sat and let it sink in. His eyes never left my face. I said, when I got my voice back:

"What was the other problem you had?"

"They were the same problem, in a way. I was getting the stuff from Grantland, all I wanted. I hear the good doctor got his last night, by the way." He tried to say it casually, but his eyes were wide with the question.

"Grantland's in the basement in a cold drawer."

"He earned it. He killed an old lady, one of his own patients. I told you that last night, didn't I? Or was it just a part of the dream I had?"

"You told me, all right, but it was just part of the dream. A girl named Mildred Hallman killed the old lady. Grantland was only an accessory after the fact."

"If he told you that, he's a liar."

"He wasn't the only one who told me that."

"They're all liars! The old lady was hurt, sure, but she was still alive when Grantland dropped her off the dock. She even tried to—" Tom put his hand over his mouth. His eyes roved round the walls and into the corners like a trapped animal's. He lay back and pulled the sheet up to his chin.

"What did she try to do, Tom? Get away?"

A darkness crossed his eyes like the shadow of a wing. "We won't talk about it."

"I think you want to."

"Not any more. I tried to tell you about her over three years ago. It's too late now. I don't see any good reason to talk myself into more trouble. How would it help *her?* She's dead and gone."

"It could help the girl who thinks she murdered her.

She's in worse trouble than you are. A lot worse. And she's got a lot more guilt. You could take some of it away from her."

"Be a hero, eh? Make the home folks proud of me. The old man always wanted me to be a hero." Tom couldn't sustain his sardonic bitterness. "If I admit I was on the dock, does that make me what you call accessory?"

"It depends on what you did. They're not so likely to press it if you volunteer the information. Did you help Grantland push her in?"

"Hell no, I argued with him when I saw she was still alive. I admit I didn't argue very much. I needed a fix, and he promised me one if I'd help him."

"How did you help him?"

"I helped him carry her out of his office and put her in his car. And I drove the car. He was too jittery to drive for himself. I did argue with him, though."

"Why did he drown her, do you know?"

"He said he couldn't afford to let her live. That if it came out, what happened that night, it would knock him right out of business. I figured if it was that important, I should start a little business of my own."

"Blackmailing Grantland for drugs?"

"You'll never prove it. He's dead. And I'm not talking for the record."

"You're still alive. You'll talk."

"Am I? Will I?"

"You're a better man than you think you are. You think it's the monkey that's killing you. I say you can train the monkey, chain him up and put him in the goddam zoo where he belongs. I say it's that old lady that's been weighing you down."

His thin chest rose and fell with his breathing. He fingered it under the sheet, as if he could feel a palpable weight there.

"Christ," he said. "She floated in the water for a while. Her clothes held her up. She was trying to *swim.* That was the hell of it that I couldn't forget."

"And that's why you came to see me?"

"Yeah, but it all went down the drain with the bath-water. You wouldn't listen. I was scared to go to the law. And I got greedy, let's face it. When I bumped into Carl in the hospital, and he filled me in on the family, I got greedy as hell. He said there was five million bucks there, and Grantland was knocking them off to get his hands on it. I thought here was my big chance for real."

"You were wrong. This is your real chance now. And you're taking it."

"Come again. You lost me somewhere."

But he knew what I meant. He lay and looked up at the ceiling as if there might just possibly be sky beyond it. And stars at night. Like any man with life left in him, he wanted to find a use for himself.

"Okay, Archer. I'm willing to make a statement. What have I got to lose?" He freed his arms from the sheet, grinning derisively, and flapped them like a small boy playing airman. "Bring on the D.A. Just keep Ostervelt out of it if you can, will you? He won't like all I got to say."

"Don't worry about him. He's on his way out."

"I guess it's Maude I'm worried about." His mood swung down with a hype's lability, but not as far down as it had been. "Jesus, I'm a no-good son. When I think of the real chances I had, and the dirty trouble I stirred up for the people that treated me good. I don't want Maude to be burned."

"I think she can look after herself."

"Better than I can, eh? If you see Carl, tell him I'm sorry, will you? He treated me like a brother when I was in convulsions, spouting like a whale from every hole in my head. And I got more holes than most, don't think I don't know it. Pass the word to Archer when you see him?"

"What word?"

"Sorry." It cost him an effort to say it directly.

"Double it, Tom."

"Forget it." He was getting expansive again. "This being Old Home Week, you might as well tell the Parish broad I'm sorry for brushing *her* off. She's a pretty good broad, you know?"

"The best."

"You ever think of getting married again?"

"Not to her. She's got a waiting list."

"Too bad for you."

Tom yawned and closed his eyes. He was asleep in a minute. The guard let me out and told me how to reach the post-operative ward. On the way there, I walked through the day in the past when this story should have begun for me, but didn't.

It was a hot day in late spring, three years and a summer before. The Strip fluttered like tinsel in the heat-waves rising from the pavements. I'd had five or six Gibsons with lunch, and I was feeling sweaty and cynical. My latest attempt to effect a reconciliation with Sue had just failed. By way of compensation, I'd made a date to go to the beach with a younger blonde who had some fairly expensive connections. If she liked me well enough, she could get me a guest membership in a good beach club.

When Tom walked in, my first and final thought was to get him out. I didn't want the blonde to find him in my office, with his special haircut and his Main Street jacket, his blank smile and his sniff and the liquid pain in the holes he was using for eyes. I gave him a cheap word or two, and the walking handshake that terminates at the door.

There was more to it than that. There always is. Tom had failed me before, when he dropped out of the boys' club I was interested in. He hadn't wanted to be helped the way I wanted to help him, the way that helped me. My vanity hadn't forgiven him, for stealing his first car.

There was more to it than that. I'd been a street boy in my time, gang-fighter, thief, poolroom lawyer. It was a fact I didn't like to remember. It didn't fit in with the slick polaroid picture I had of myself as the rising young man of mystery who frequented beach clubs in the company of starlets. Who groped for a fallen brightness in private white sand, private white bodies, expensive peroxide hair.

When Tom stood in my office with the lost look on him, the years blew away like torn pieces of newspaper. I saw myself when I was a frightened junior-grade hood in Long Beach, kicking the world in the shins because it wouldn't dance for me. I brushed him off.

It isn't possible to brush people off, let alone yourself. They wait for you in time, which is also a closed circuit. Years later on a mental-hospital ward, Tom had a big colored dream and cast me for a part in it, which I was still playing out. I felt like a dog in his vomit.

I stopped and leaned on a white wall and lit a cigarette. When you looked at the whole picture, there was a certain beauty in it, or justice. But I didn't care to look at it for long. The circuit of guilty time was too much like a snake with its tail in its mouth, consuming itself. If you looked too long, there'd be nothing left of it, or you. We were all guilty. We had to learn to live with it.

Rose met me with a smile at the door of Carl's private room. She held up her right hand and brought the thumb and forefinger together in a closed circle. I smiled and nodded in response to her good news, but it took a while to penetrate to my inner ear. Where the ash-blond ghosts were twittering, and the hype dream beat with persistent violence, like colored music, trying to drown them out.

It was time I traded that in, too, on a new dream of my own. Rose Parish had hers. Her face was alive with it, her body leaned softly on it. But whatever came of her dream for better or worse belonged to her and Carl. I had no part in it, and wanted none. No Visitors, the sign on the door said.

For once in my life I had nothing and wanted nothing. Then the thought of Sue fell through me like a feather in a vacuum. My mind picked it up and ran with it and took flight. I wondered where she was, what she was doing, whether she'd aged much as she lay in ambush in time, or changed the color of her bright head.

Printed in the United States
by Baker & Taylor Publisher Services